OUTLAWS ALL

A Western Trio

MAX BRAND™

SAGEBRUSH
Large Print Westerns

First published in Great Britain by ISIS Publishing Ltd.
First published in the United States by Five Star

Published in Large Print 2013 by ISIS Publishing Ltd.,
7 Centremead, Osney Mead, Oxford OX2 0ES
by arrangement with
Golden West Literary Agency

British Library Cataloguing in Publication Data
Brand, Max, 1892–1944.
    Outlaws all.
    1. Western stories.
    2. Large type books.
    I. Title II. Brand, Max, 1892–1944. Alec the Great.
    III. Brand, Max, 1892–1944. Riding into peril.
    813.5'2–dc23

ISBN 978–0–7531–9128–6 (pb)

Printed and bound in Great Britain by
T. J. International Ltd., Padstow, Cornwall

OUTLAWS ALL

Table of Contents

Alec The Great

A

PROLOGUE

TO

Sixteen in Nome

"Sixteen is a bad age for a boy," Joe May reflects in *Sixteen in Nome*, a Five Star Western by Max Brand. "It is too full of growing and not full enough of strength." *Sixteen in Nome* isn't only the story of Joe May's coming of age in Alaska during the gold rush days of the 1890s. It is also the story of the clash of two titans for possession of a most extraordinary and powerful dog known as Alec the Great. The story that follows narrates the events that occurred before Joe May encountered Hugh Massey and Arnie Calmont. It first appeared under the title "Two Masters" in Street & Smith's *Western Story Magazine* in the issue dated April 5, 1930 and appears here in book form for the first time.

CHAPTER
ONE

Men and Dogs

Both Massey and Calmont were old-timers and old friends. They were old-timers because they had come over the Chilkoot together. They had gone to Circle City. They had campaigned along the Klondike. They had worked for gold on the Nome beach. When they went out to spend a year prospecting near the edge of the Arctic Circle close to Kotzebue Sound, no one in Alaska would have guessed that they could be turned into bitter enemies. By mysterious agencies this was brought about, until they hated one another with a devotion that surpassed their old friendship. Men say that no two in all the world ever detested each other with a more profound loathing than did these two. This is a chronicle of that hatred, of how it commenced, and the beginning of all that flowed from it.

They were opposite enough in appearance and in character to make hostility seem a natural thing. Calmont looked like a wolf. He had the slant bright eyes, the face rather small and sharp in front but widening to massive jaws. There was so much muscle in his face that usually it appeared as though he were holding something in his mouth. His hair was black, his skin swarthy. He was about five feet ten, and he stripped to a hundred and ninety pounds, though he didn't look it.

Massey was an inch or two taller, and fifteen or twenty pounds lighter. He was a good-looking boy, but his neck seemed a little too thin for the support of his head. He had a boy's way of always smiling, too, so that people rarely took him seriously at the first meeting. His shoulders were not very large or his hips very small, and his arm muscles were as soft as the flesh of a cat. But they had the flexible strength of a cat as well as its softness. If hard muscles mean strength, they also mean slowness. Massey was fast as a flash, and it is well to remember that the strength of a blow is weight plus speed. The god of battle presided over the life of young Massey and claimed him as his own.

He met Arnold Calmont in Skagway, where he saw half a dozen toughs jump that man with the face of a wolf. Calmont knocked one of them senseless and kept the others off for a moment until they began to draw knives. Then Massey went to the rescue.

When they had kicked and thrown the gang through the door of the saloon, Calmont said: "What made you horn in?"

"Oh, I was lonely," said Massey, rubbing a puffed and crimson eye.

From that moment they were friends.

They had been of help to one another in a hundred ways. In snow blindness, "leg craziness," starvation, among the swift dangers of the Yukon, and the thieves and gunmen of the mines, they had been true to one another. Each owed the other his life a dozen times over.

They were so inseparable that when one was seen, the other was looked for. Calmont was in his early thirties, and Massey was twenty-four, so that in addition to their different temperaments, their ages were a gulf; yet wherever one went the other followed.

Calmont loved poker, and Massey detested it. While Calmont sat up all night with his party, Massey was sure to be nodding over a thumb-worn magazine in a corner by the stove. But his sleep was only the sleep of a wild cat, as two or three would-be practical jesters had discovered to their cost.

Massey enjoyed a whirl in a dance hall. He danced with enthusiasm and abandon, while Calmont sat sneering in a corner, refusing to drink, refusing almost to talk, so bent was he upon the performance of his friend. If Massey took a bit too much to whiskey and noise, a stern hand would fall upon his shoulder and a stern voice would order him home. That command he never refused.

They obeyed one another implicitly, a marvelous thing to see, each admitting the other's superiority in certain matters. On the water, Massey was the skipper, and Calmont the man before the mast, slaving. Over the snow, Calmont broke trail like a giant, while Massey performed the easier task of handling the dogs because he had a peculiar talent in dealing with animals. In the woods, Calmont was the commander. He had the natural genius of a wild Indian, with an Indian's ear and silent footing. He could find moose.

Fish came almost of their own volition to his hook or his salmon spear. His rifle would bring down almost anything that his eye could see. So, when they hunted or trailed in the summer woods, Calmont issued orders, and Massey slavishly obeyed them.

At building a log hut, at putting up a snow or soil igloo, Calmont was again the master, or at skinning a bear or a seal, and also in mining, whether on the Klondike Creek or the Nome beach. In the fighting of their battles also, he was the chief director, barking out instructions like a company commander when they fell into a fist fight against odds — as they continually were doing. Massey, shaken with blows and with joyous laughter like a drunkard, would spring in to execute the orders of his older comrade. Their battle tactics were famous but, if the brain of Calmont was feared, the snaky quickness of Massey's hand, once seen, never was forgotten.

When they came into a civilized community, Massey at once assumed direction of everything. He sold, bought, traded. He supplied dogs, food, sled sheets, and all that was required for the march, thus removing from the sullen temper of his friend the annoying friction with other men, for Calmont by nature loved solitude. It was Massey who always made contracts, drove bargains, patched up quarrels started by Calmont, or helped him to finish a fight.

They had done all manner of things. They had hauled freight with two teams and four sleds. They had worked in the woods and rafted the big timbers down to Circle City. They had dragged along Klondike Creek and among the beach diggings of Nome. They had speared salmon and dried them to sell for winter provisions, simmering twenty-pounders down to a seventh of that weight.

Out of their campaigning, they had gained heaped adventures enough to fill a library of books, very little money — and that quickly squandered — and, above all, that friendship which had become famous throughout the cold, white land.

Then they trekked out of Nome with one team of six dogs, two sleds, and went to prospect on the circle. They had heard of the great frozen tundra, the few trees, the silence. The tales of gold prospects were enough to tempt them. So they went out on the snow and, when it left them with bad sledding, they were on the Onmachuk Creek. There they found a hot spring that ran lukewarm waters and gave off a constant mist, but heat is a priceless thing in that region, and by the hot spring they settled down.

They lived chiefly on ptarmigan, at first. The ducks and geese came in later, but thin and worn from their long flight so that they were hardly to be regarded even as dog food. Later, when the young hatched, they could kill the small ones with clubs before they were able to fly. The Onmachuk is a salmon stream, and this they found out as the summer progressed. One morning they found the pools black with backs of closely packed fish, but to get them out for food was not an easy task.

A fifteen-pound salmon has the strength of a small tiger and the same activity. They tried clubbing them, but it was very hard and slow work, each big fellow needing perhaps half a dozen blows before it gave up the battle for life. But then they made a pair of fishing spears out of a couple of steel sled-runners. These were clumsy tools but efficient enough in such crowded waters. They got out three or four hundred selected fish every day, split them open, cleaned out the backbone, and dried the halves on willow frames. They put up enough in their salmon cache to take them comfortably, man and dog, through the longest winter and leave plenty over besides for sale to hungry and ill-provided prospectors of whom a number were drifting about the region. They worked hard at laying up provisions and prospecting, but they found no gold — hardly a trace of it.

At the end of that summer a half-bred Malemute bitch named Chubby — as strong as a bear and as fierce as a tiger — had six puppies in a litter. That was an event which seemed of no importance then, but it led to all the trouble that followed in due time.

With the first coming of winter, when the mist around the hot spring began to turn to hoar frost of a night, the water fowl went south and so did the wandering prospectors. But Massey and Calmont were of sterner stuff. They intended to look over this ground carefully and were determined to wait out the winter, no matter what were the storms and the blizzards of which they had heard so much. That pair of adventurers was so tough that they felt they could live wherever moss grew. And this was a tundra!

First of all, therefore, they made their house. It was of sod, cut in thick lumps, and watered and tamped to make it more solid on the outside. The inside sods were left softer because in their natural form they served as better insulators against the cold. The size of the room was about fourteen by fourteen. The walls were nearly five feet thick.

For a door they made a thick willow frame that they covered with the skins of rabbits, first of all, and on top they fastened the skins of birds, so that the door would not admit cold and yet remain light for opening and closing. There were hinges of willow also. This masterful work was entirely the contribution of Calmont, out of the depths of his Indian lore and his own invention. He was as proud of it as he was of Chubby's litter — for she was his dog.

Massey contributed a second luxury to the igloo. He had a seal bladder which he had got by barter from a group of traveling Eskimos. It was translucent, if not transparent, and this he fitted into the center of the roof, a vast comfort for the winter to come. The house was built up rapidly, for the chill was growing greater every night, but they still had not finished a few details when the winter struck them

It did not come gradually. Having made a few stealthy approaching steps in the preceding days, it now leaped on them in mature strength. Late one afternoon, a blizzard screeched over the tundra, whipped the willows almost level with the ground, and turned everything white and dim in a moment.

The six dogs were more than half wild, and it was considered safe to leave them out. For Chubby and the pups, Massey put in a plea, which Calmont denied with a surly growl. He would not have the cabin turned into a kennel, he said, and, since neither of these two men was willing to bring an argument to a serious point, Massey said no more.

In the morning, five of the six puppies were frozen to death, and the tragedy of the winter began.

CHAPTER
TWO

One white puppy

Neither Chubby nor the five dead puppies, however, was the actual source of the trouble. It was the sole survivor of the litter who counted. He was by far the strongest of the lot, and that difference of strength was what had preserved him when the rest were frozen at their mother's side. And, like many exceptional animals, he differed from the rest in several aspects.

His father was the wolfish leader, belonging also to Calmont and called by him Forty Mile, or Forty for short. Forty was more timber wolf than Husky, and his coat was a dirty yellow, except for the darker fur along his back. Chubby was more dog by far in looks, with a dark coat liberally splashed with white. Especially, she had a broad, snowy vest.

The sole survivor had a color scheme that was all his own. He was a pure fluff of snow except that his muzzle, his ears, and the tip of his tail were dark — almost black. It was something like the marking of a Siamese cat. He had short, pointed ears, like a wolf, and a wolf's wisely wrinkled forehead, but his head did not come to a point at the lips. His eyes were the round, open, confiding eyes of a dog.

When Massey and his partner found the dead puppies, they buried them without a word. Then, without speaking further, Calmont took up the white puppy and carried him into the house. This was a silent admission that he had been wrong. It was more eloquent than words, and there was no meanness in young Massey to make him say: "I told you so."

The white youngster had the run of the place. He was taken out now and then to harden him and to let his mother feed him. He got so that he would flounder through the snow at a furious rate, tumbling and falling, and galloping like a clumsy little seal behind Calmont, his master.

This devotion of the puppy touched the wolfish man. When he lay down in his bunk — there were two, on opposite sides of the room — he used to pick up the puppy by the back of the neck and drop him under the covers. Sometimes he would be seen stroking the back of the little one, a thing which Massey looked on with wonder and almost with awe, because Calmont was not fond of dogs.

They were very busy during the first of the bitter weather in completing their preparations for the full strength of the winter. They knew now that what had been said about circle winters was not a joke, and that they were in for a tough season. So they went off to the willows about the spring, where they grew more than an inch and a half in diameter, and cut down and carried to the igloo a double supply. They took heed of the dogs also, which suffered in spite of their fur robes because of the suddenness with which the long, white night had begun.

They were now equipped with plenty of fuel for the little traveling stove. They had ample provisions for themselves and their dogs. Though the diet was monotonous, they had learned how to endure privation and starvation for so long that this was almost a place of luxury.

Their one problem was amusement. For this they had three magazines and one newspaper, all carefully carted in from the great outer world. This treasure trove had not been broached before. Carefully they had left it for the beginning of the long night. But now they began to read.

They did not read gluttonously. Like marooned sailors in a small boat with a small supply of water, they rationed themselves to a short time each day hungrily swallowing, as it were, a mouthful of print and then putting the magazine away. However, even with this sensible regime, they had read the three magazines and the paper through inside of a fortnight. Within a month they knew the stories with great familiarity. In six weeks they knew the narratives, the articles, even the small print of the advertisements by heart. Before they turned a page, they knew what would meet their eyes on the next. Even so, the magazines remained a resource. The eye can travel with some sort of a dull interest over even the most well-known trail, but the sport was thin and the pain was often great. It put an ache behind the eyes to jog through the often-repeated adventures.

Besides the magazine, they had cards. Calmont was a passionate gambler. Massey preferred to play for fun. For this reason they liked different games. Massey could sit for hours over cribbage, but ten minutes of seven-up or of poker revolted him. Calmont could play poker for a week on end, but cribbage made him groan almost at once.

They devised various ways of making the games more interesting. They kept a record of the various hands. They tried to work out a theory of how much a pair of sevens is worth in two-handed poker, and how much one may bet on any sort of three of a kind. They considered wise minimums of high and low in "shooting the moon" at seven-up. They worked out that three is average pegging in a cribbage board.

Vast columns of statistics proved and illustrated these valuable conclusions, at which neither of the men ever smiled. It does not do to be light minded regarding one's relaxations when there are at least six months of silence before one.

Over and over again, partners, old and seasoned companions, have gone on into the wilderness and, after a few months of silence, have come back loathing the sight of one another. The sight of a stranger, no matter who — Chinaman or Indian — and no matter if it were for only five minutes would be enough to break the strain of that long, inescapable companionship. Otherwise, the friction grows incredibly great.

A man might grow to hate another because he had a crooked nose, or a habit of wrinkling his forehead. A man might learn to hate his dearest friend because the other stuttered. It is possible for tried and proved companions to fall out over the way a tin of salmon is opened, or a dog harness put on. The way a man laces his shoes may become enough to make another curse him. Snoring at night, or singing by day, may be the signal for a fatal struggle. It has become a proverb that it is dangerous for two lonely men to live together through a season too long and confining.

These two had no doubts of one another. They had gone through almost as long a spell before, and they understood the peculiarities, one of another, with an almost perfect intimacy. Yet they treated themselves, one another, and their modes of amusement with the greatest consideration.

In spite, however, of anything they could do, at the end of six weeks, at the very moment when the magazines became almost intolerable torments, they both became so disgusted with cards that one day Calmont opened the stove and poised the two packs above the blaze. Massey nodded without a word, and one hundred and four greasy keys to destiny were deliberately dropped into the flames. Afterward, they rubbed their hands over the heat and grinned at one another, feeling that a weight had been taken from about their necks.

There remained, at the end of a month and a half, one final resource for mutual amusement, and that was to tell stories. This, also, was a thing to be done with deliberation, and scientific care. Stories were divided into three classes. These were tragic, sad, and funny narratives. They were divided into three epochs, brews, or vintages. These were the new, twice-told, and thrice-told tales.

The rule was that a thrice-told tale was not to be repeated unless it was asked for. To offer a threadbare yarn was an insult and an irritation to one's partner who, for the sake of both, had to pretend interest, astonishment, mirth, sorrow, as fitted the occasion. Only after the point had been reached, a certain blankness of the eye usually revealed to the narrator that he had committed this trebly-banned crime.

For two weeks their supply of stories endured. Then one morning Massey said: "Tell me about that fellow Block, that came out to Montana and went into the sheep business, Calmont. That's a good yarn."

Calmont filled his pipe — the tobacco was one fifth the real leaf and four fifths moss and bark, deftly blended — and after a moment of thought he said: "I guess I can't think of no new lies about old Block."

After that, neither of them ever asked for a story or offered to tell one. The springs of imagination had run dry. Only, now and then, they would delightfully torment one another by speaking of roast turkey, ice cream, liver and bacon, baked sausages, or a good roast of venison. Then, with watering mouth, the listener would curse, and exaggerate his annoyance, and each would grin at the other.

Every day they took their exercise. In the morning they wrestled, a sport at which the slower and stronger muscles of Calmont gave him an advantage, though even in wrestling the uncanny handcraft and the speed of Massey sometimes upset the other. These bouts would be prolonged for an hour until their muscles were bruised, and young Massey had the wind knocked out of him. In the afternoon they swathed their hands and smote one another like giants.

There was a difference between the wrestling and the boxing, however. In wrestling, Calmont put forth every ounce of his strength, exerted every trick of his craft. Even so he could feel the science of the boy creep in upon him like a tide that one day would rise over his head. This disturbed Calmont, because he was a proud and a jealous man. In boxing, on the other hand, Massey had to be very careful. He was so much swifter and more accurate in foot, hand, and eye, that he could strike Calmont almost at will, and hard blows, especially to the head, are not things to be received with any patience. Therefore, Massey used to sham even beyond the knowledge of the other man.

Calmont was learning that most intricate of punches — most beautiful, also, when it lands — the right cross. He was learning to step in, to drop on his heels as he jerked the punch home. But he could not master the intricacies of the blow. He never would have landed on the agile Massey had not the latter purposely allowed himself to be hit.

So they lived with a reality, which was that Massey was becoming an excellent wrestler, and with a deception, which was that Calmont was becoming a proficient boxer. However, boxing and wrestling could punctuate the day, not entirely consume it.

The magazines, the card games, the stories were all used up at the end of two months. Aside from the exercise morning and afternoon, there remained only one thing to occupy them. That was the white puppy.

CHAPTER
THREE

In Training

They called him Alexander the Great because in that little world of the cabin there were no more provinces or nations for him to conquer. He had broken into the sugar can. He had been in the flour sack. He had chewed his master's hat and, much more serious, one of Massey's boots. He had tried to digest a blanket. He had tasted tea leaves. He had attempted to chew a piece of iron off the little stove. Greatest conquest of all, like his namesake's distant expedition to India, this Alexander the Great had penetrated to the salmon cache and eaten himself into a howling cramp in the stomach.

He was sick for a week, and Calmont joyously and tenderly and carefully nursed him, held him in his arms like a baby, crooned over him, petted him, made up mysterious potions for him, lulled him at night, amused him in the day. Massey ached to help in this delightful occupation, but Alec was not his, and therefore he tried to turn his back mentally upon the enticing picture.

However, Alexander refused to remain sick long enough. He was soon up again, and by tacit consent, when he was roaming about the floor, he could be noticed or entertained or disciplined by either of the men. If he climbed upon the bunk of Massey, then for the moment Calmont was bound not to call the puppy, attract his attention by antics, tempt him with any bribe, or in any manner attempt to take him from his visit. Similarly, so long as Alexander the Great was with his proper master, Massey dared not so much as snap his fingers or notice the dog in any way. There were also strictly neutral moments when both men sat on their bunks or lounged and watched with a quiet delight the antics of young Alec.

Three months went by. Half of the long winter had worn away. They lived warm. They were growing fat. They endured the monotony of diet and calmly faced the monotony of diversions. For they had with them a third creature, almost more companionable than any man or woman could have been.

"This here dog," said Calmont one morning, "he oughta be educated."

Massey sipped his tea and considered. When one disagrees with one's partner, after three months of solitary confinement, the disagreement must be tenderly expressed.

"Think he ought to go to school?" he said tentatively.

"Yeah. Sure he should. *Pronto!*"

"Three months?" said Massey suggestively.

"He ain't a boy. He don't have to be six years old before he gets his misery started five times a week," declared Calmont confidently.

"Yes, you could teach him something. He knows a good deal already, but a puppy like that needs more persuasion than whipping, I'd say."

20

"Whipping?" said Calmont, reddening. "I'd like to see any man put a whip on that dog of mine! Alec, come here!"

The puppy, sleeping upon his own bed in front of the stove, unfurled the paws which covered his nose. He opened his eyes, closed them again, restored the shelter to his nose.

"Come here, Alec, old son," repeated Calmont gently but with a frown.

Alec did not stir. He slept.

"Alec!" thundered the master.

The stomach of the puppy twitched, as though he had a renewal of the colic pains, but otherwise he gave no sign that he had ears.

"You see for yourself," said Calmont bitterly. "Look at what he's comin' to . . . a dog without no sense!"

"He's only three months," said Massey again and thereby erred.

"You said that before!" snapped Calmont.

Massey made no answer. He merely looked from the dog to the master and from the master to the dog. When delicate moments came in which tact was necessary, it was generally shown by Massey. His better education, his gentler nature, equipped him for the rôle of peacemaker. As for his temper of fire which loved battle, he never used it on his well-proven friend.

"He's gotta be taught something," said Calmont. "Gentle but firm, that's my idea. Whatcha say, Massey? You gotta head for dogs."

He made this admission grudgingly. But the genius of Massey with animals of all kinds was widely known, and Calmont could afford some concessions to an established reputation even where it touched upon Alexander the Great.

"I'd say," said Massey, "that I'd rather let him chew up both my boots than start him in before he's six months. That's the time to start a dog's education, old fellow."

Even the gentleness of this speech did not touch the convinced mind of Calmont. He went to the stove and, picking up the puppy, carried him back to the bunk. Alec shivered with the cold and tried to crawl inside the flap of his master's coat.

"Look it!" said Calmont. He was immensely pleased. "He's gonna know men," he said with conviction. "He's gonna know his master anyway, damn him!"

He liked to curse the creatures he cared for, Massey above all.

"You tell me the main idea about training," said Calmont. "Then I'm gonna teach this pup."

"Patience," said Massey. "That's the main idea."

"Yeah," nodded Calmont, "I'll be patient, all right. I disremember which teacher I had that used to fly off the handle when she got me into percentages. A moldy, unpleasant subject, is percentages. It pretty near ruined me and, instead of explaining, she used to get hot and blow up. She got so hot you could hear her hiss. Her talk sounded like the blowing off of steam. Damn a hot-headed woman, Hugh."

Massey nodded.

"I'll be patient, Hugh. I'll tell you what, young son. I'm gonna teach this dog a trick before you can teach him one."

22

"You'll have to bet on that," said Massey. "He's your dog, Arnie."

"Yeah, he's my dog. You're damn' right he's my dog. I'll bet you twenty that I teach him a trick first. I'll teach him to speak. You teach him to sit down."

"You teach him to come when he's called," suggested Massey. "That's an easier trick, and I think a lot more useful."

"I'll stick to my job," said the other. "You'll teach him to come when he's called! I'm gonna start right now. You can have this afternoon."

He started laboriously. He got bits of fish, which the puppy loved, but Alexander, though willing to eat, was not willing to perform. For three hours Calmont persisted. His forehead was swollen with veins of anger. His voice grew hoarse. He trembled. But he neither shouted nor cursed. Massey was amazed at this self-control in the wild man.

About noon, Calmont gave up and sank back in his bunk. He was deeply hurt.

"That's a dog with a fine lotta character," he observed, "but I reckon that he ain't too strong in the brain. Now you start in."

"I'll let him rest a while," said Massey as Alec the Great wearily crawled back to his place before the stove.

It was not until the middle of the afternoon that Massey began to teach Alec. Then he tied a rag about the puppy's neck as a collar. To the collar he hitched a fifteen-foot length of string, and let Alec play with it. When the little one had forgotten the new encumbrance,

Massey called the puppy by name and twitched on the string. That drew Alec's attention. The fluttering of a bright knife blade took him the rest of the way across the floor to the side of Massey's bunk, where he was duly petted and allowed to roam away again.

This performance Calmont observed with a sort of dark disdain.

"It'll take you a year and a day!" he said.

Massey smiled and shrugged his shoulders. "He's only a kid," he answered.

He had trained them, big and small. He had worked Newfoundlands in a team behind thoroughbred wolves and Huskies. He knew dogs to the tips of his fingers. So he went easily with Alexander the Great.

Twenty times that afternoon he called the puppy and, by the time the day had ended, Alec could be drawn gently forward on the string without struggling or throwing himself back. He knew that the string was not an enemy, that it did not hurt, but that it gently, firmly persuaded him forward to a pleasant goal — the caressing hand of Massey. When he heard his name, he would stand up now, and he prepared for the pull on the lead line.

"You gotta string hitched onto his neck," said Calmont. "I got no string tied to his vocal chords, though."

"I offered you your choice of tricks," said Massey. "It's not my fault, what you chose. But I'll gladly switch with you now. You've seen how to go about teaching him to come when he's called."

Calmont hesitated, bit his lip. Then he suddenly nodded. It was not the money of which he was thinking. It was of the dog. Just as mathematics had been his bane in school and called up dark, swirling clouds into his mind, so now the thought of resuming that education of the puppy made his brain reel.

It was like leaning against a cliff or trying to lift a mountain, to speak to the bright-eyed little thing and see it cant its head in study and bewilderment. He was afraid, too, of the temper which had risen in him.

There was no more education of Alec the Great that night. It was resumed after the next meal — that is to say the next morning. Then, tying the string to the collar, Calmont started.

"Alec!" he called sharply.

Alexander the Great rolled to his feet and faced toward Massey.

Calmont cursed.

"Here, puppy . . . here, Alec!" he called in tones which he intended to be inviting.

Alec started straight across the floor toward Massey. He was stopped by a violent jerk upon the string. At this, bewildered, he turned his head toward Calmont, wobbled his tail violently, and started once more toward Massey.

Here a strong jerk almost floored him. He turned about, but it was only to brace all four feet against the floor. Calmont, his teeth set, drew on the line. Alec, infuriated, started snarling. Strongly as he braced his big feet — for he was a hulking thing now — the string dragged him forward. He caught it in his teeth.

"Come here, you fool!" snarled Calmont.

He gave an extra hard pull but, under the strain and the fretting teeth of the young Husky, the string snapped apart, and Alec the Great tumbled over on his back. He regained his feet, and scampered as hard as he could straight for Massey!

CHAPTER
FOUR

The Test

Massey did not encourage the advance of the dog. He merely allowed the latter to lick the hand which, already, was hanging down toward the ground as he lay in his bunk. The fury of poor Calmont passed all bounds. His strange oaths rippled and growled through the igloo. Yet, just as he was enraged, so Alexander the Great seemed delighted. He bounded clumsily and pawed the hand of Massey. He reared on his hind legs and licked the face of the man who was not his master. Calmont, leaping from his bunk, threw on a coat and rushed out of the shack.

There followed several hours of fury from the wind which made even the thick, squat walls of the soil house tremble. Then Calmont returned. He came back not in a rage outwardly but calm as a statue of stone. He resumed his efforts to teach the young dog. But a dog, like a child, learns fear more quickly and more thoroughly than it learns any other lesson. When a new string was fastened to his neck, he sat down and faced Massey and, without waiting for the lesson to commence, began to howl dismally.

Calmont, wisely enough, took off the collar at once and the string and gave up for the day. Massey resumed where his companion had fallen. To teach a dog to speak is sometimes the simplest thing in the world and sometimes the most difficult. If a dog happens to chance on noise in order to make a request for food, he is apt to learn in a lesson. Otherwise, it may take a month to teach him. Massey had luck, and at the very beginning Alec the Great happened to yip sharply and therefore received at once the waiting shred of smoked salmon.

After that, the main difficulty was to control the floodgates of sound which had been opened. Alec not only had obtained the key to a mystery, but he felt that he must continually be using it. He made the little shack ring and re-ring with his clamors, until at the lifted hand of Massey he deafened all ears.

Still, Massey did not consider the game won. He had made great advances, but the lesson was as yet hardly started. Or perhaps it was that he wished to give his partner a better chance to win the bet. At any rate, he waited until the next morning when Calmont started again methodically to teach Alexander the Great to come to his name.

Alec promptly developed a wild hysteria which grew in violence. He broke a second and a third string and took refuge under the bunk of Massey, where he howled and cried when Calmont came after him. His emotion was so great that Calmont took him upon his bunk and quieted him throughout the rest of the morning.

That afternoon, Massey said quietly: "I'll collect twenty dollars from you now, Calmont."

"Speak, Alec!" he said and raised his hand.

Alec lifted an answering howl that brought Chubby, whining, to sniff under the lower edge of the floor. Calmont without a word opened his money belt — it was already very light — and paid down the required twenty dollars. Massey, at least, was wise enough not to gloat; but Calmont went on in the face of destiny.

"I'll bet you another twenty dollars," he said, "that inside of a week I make him come when I call him."

"Inside of a week," said Massey, his eye gleaming a little, "I'll teach him to sit down, lie down, and go to his corner."

Calmont drew out a double eagle and threw it down upon the floor.

"Money talks better than words," he said.

Promptly Massey threw down the coin he just had won and with such accuracy that it clinked upon Calmont's money. There in the dust lay the bet, while the two resumed their efforts.

Now that this training had settled into a serious contest, it was agreed that a single response would not be enough, but that the puppy should have to obey three times in a row. With this understanding they set to work grimly, tensely, as men who had no other means of occupying their time.

It began to be more than a contest about Alexander the Great. It was a test of moral supremacy and mental control. Calmont, learning through failure, began to employ the same shreds of smoked salmon which

Massey used, but the response of the puppy was very slow. No matter what Calmont did, no matter what he held in his hand, the gaze of that wise young Malemute was directed toward the face of his master, to see if there might not be in the human eyes something to fear.

Calmont had the mornings as he tempted, coaxed, persuaded, begged, and rewarded the puppy. Massey had the afternoons.

Sitting down and lying down were made a continuous performance. Young Alec, receiving the command, was then pressed strongly but gently down over the hind quarters, until he squatted. Then he got his first thin shred of salmon. After that, the pressure was transferred to his forequarters, and he was forced to lie down.

Between the patience, the magic touch of Massey, and Alec's appetite, which raged like a ceaseless fire, there soon came a time when he dropped instantly upon quivering haunches at the word of command with saliva dripping from his mouth. He would lie down also in the same manner, dropping almost as though shot, while with fiery eyes of hunger he followed the movements of the man and watched that hand from which reward descended. This having been achieved, the next thing was to force him to obey the command and to keep down without any reward whatever, and this was very difficult. However, Massey had a peculiar talent for making the thing appear to be a game, and the absence of a reward seemed to appear to the puppy a postponed rather than an abolished payment.

The same spirit of the game was brought into the far more difficult task of making Alec go to a corner. All who have taught a dog know how infinitely more difficult it is to force an animal to go than it is to make him come to the voice and the hand of his master. But Massey persisted in the following manner. First of all, he gave Alec a whiff of a bit of rag or a chip thoroughly rubbed with fat or with fish grease, until the puppy was furious with it. Then he bandaged the eyes of the puppy, hid the chip in a corner, and, taking off the bandage, pointed in the right direction and ordered Alexander the Great to his corner.

When he had found the treasure, to which his keen nose took him almost at once, he was ordered to lie down, which he most willingly did — to chew his find to smithereens! Upon the fifth day of these particular lessons, the instant he heard the command and saw the extended arm of Massey, he rushed in the required direction. Then, at the dropping of the hand, he crouched to the ground.

On the sixth day Massey said: "I'm ready for you, Calmont."

He was suddenly aware that it was at least two days since he had spoken to his comrade!

"The week ain't up till tomorrow," said Calmont.

This was all, but he said it with such meaning that Massey knew what was in his partner's mind. Suddenly he wished that the puppy never had survived the frost which had killed its brothers and sisters. But being young and stubborn, he would not give way. He persisted in this game which was to lead to such deadly trouble.

Massey told himself that though it was true that he had far more experience than his friend in the training of dogs, yet he was giving himself a double and a treble burden to carry. To teach a dog to lie down, sit down, and go to his corner — all in one week — and all against the mere ability to make him come when called! That was very hard indeed. Besides, there were forty golden dollars on the floor untouched where they had lain all those seven days, waiting for the winner of the bet.

The next morning Massey expected Calmont to give the word for the test to begin. Instead Calmont practiced until he had Alec coming to him half a dozen times in a row. All of these approaches seemed definitely reluctant and made with an uneasy spirit, but before the middle of the day Calmont growled that he was ready.

"Go on and lemme see you make him do the three things, three times each." He had more than a challenge in his voice. There was a surly bitterness as well.

So three times, at the voice of Massey, the puppy squatted. Three times he dropped to the ground as though shot. Three times he scampered into corners and crouched there when the pointing hand of his trainer fell. Three times he was beckoned in and rewarded, not with fish, but with a pat on the head.

He had no bitterness for these casual rewards. As stated already he felt that they were merely happiness postponed, and that virtue could not go unnoticed by his god — that is to say by Massey, all wise, all powerful.

Most triumphantly Massey had performed his part of the work, and Calmont growled: "It looks like you hate to lose money, Hugh. You make yourself pretty sure when it comes to winnin' a bet!"

Then he essayed his own turn. Twice the puppy came to him. The third time he hesitated. This pause made the perspiration spring out upon the forehead of his master. It was not that he feared for the money. It was the moral humiliation — to have another man defeat him with his own dog. To be beaten in the only contest which they could now wage — except hand to hand. Instead of putting persuasion into his voice, he roared out his command. That roar was too much for Alec the Great. He remembered another occasion when he had heard that roar and, whirling about, he fled for Massey as fast as he could scamper. He heard the command again and, squeezing under the bunk, he growled defiance.

Calmont, panting hard, snatched up the two coins from the floor and hurled them in silence upon the other bunk.

"It's yours," he said. "The dog's a damned fool! Besides, the only lingo that I can talk is a white man's lingo. I ain't a dog, to talk dog talk!"

Massey, sitting quietly on his bunk, kept his eyes fixed upon the face of his friend and made no answer. He would not have taken a tithe as much as this from another human being, but to him Calmont had certain sacred rights of friendship such as even the hardest man will grant to an old and proven bunkie. He merely stared at Calmont as though seeing in him an undiscovered country. Not a word came from his lips.

Calmont saw that he had done wrong. The knowledge did not make him repentant. He lacked the words to apologize, for apologies were not his talent. Even to Massey he could not say that he was wrong and that he was sorry.

But the knowledge that he was in error embittered him more and more. Furious words stormed up in his throat and were choked back. Anger was multiplied by grief instead of being subdued by it. He grew sullen and hard, and this was the beginning of the end.

He merely snarled out: "The dog's a damned fool. You can train the rest of him!"

CHAPTER
FIVE

Chained

Afterward Calmont had leisure to repent of the permission which he had given, for Massey seized upon it as his right without another word. Thereafter he trained the puppy without interference. Calmont could sit back as an audience, nursing a mad, blind bitterness in his heart while he watched the school days and the school work of Alec.

"Fool," he had called the young dog, and he had personal reasons for the epithet.

Massey seemed determined by constant application to make Calmont burst out into praise of the scholar he had denounced. He began with calling the dog. That was learned in the course of half an hour. How simple to an animal already taught to go!

This was only the start, and marvels were to be achieved thereafter. Walking back and forth through the shack, swinging a light willow stick, he taught Alec the Great to heel perfectly. He was taught not only to lie down but to roll over, to sit up — a trick which made Calmont's lip curl and which Massey himself disdained to force the dog to perform often. It was simply an item in the long list of accomplishments mastered. But it was beneath the real dignity and the size of Alec. He was fairly bursting his skin, he grew so rapidly. He was not altogether a beautiful creature at this time. He seemed grotesquely overbig in head, foot, and leg. He possessed enormous bone, and his feet were a promise of the size to which he would grow. He was clumsy, as a matter of course, but Massey with indefatigable patience worked to reduce that clumsiness.

He constructed a ladder, which he induced Alec the Great to climb, though it was a long and bitter effort to do so. Yet, finally, the big, trembling paws learned the way up, though after many a fall and many a howl of fear. There was this advantage from the first in the course of his instruction that when things went wrong, instead of fleeing from this teacher who never punished him, he ran to him for sympathy, protection, petting.

The ladder, once mastered, suggested another device for giving the clumsy young monster a proper sense of balance. For this purpose Massey erected several hurdles and placed upon them, lashed firmly side by side, three willows. It made a narrow bridge to which the ladder led, and Alec crouched whimpering upon it, though as a matter of fact the distance to the floor was too slight to make a serious hurt possible. Finally, he learned to go across the bridge, raising and putting down his big feet with a studious caution and leaping off into the strong arms of Massey at the end of the trip. That was his reward. He was thrown high up into the air, caught as he hurtled down again, tumbled, rolled, and wooled about until he was gasping with delight and with fatigue.

Then he would begin again. Finally a morning came when Massey was awakened to find big young Alec standing at the end of the bridge, whining to be received when he sprang at the other end. So the bridge was made more difficult.

The three willows were narrowed to two, a narrowness which increased the difficulty of walking along them at least threefold. Yet, Alec accomplished the journey after a good many tumbles into the arms of Massey who walked cautiously beside him. He could eventually walk, trot, fairly run along the narrow scaffolding.

Then came the supreme test. One of the two willows was removed. There now remained only a single stick an inch in diameter, sagging and swaying and trembling under the bulk of Alec.

This, for three days, he absolutely refused to attempt, often climbing to the top of his little ladder and then whining bitterly when he saw the perilous road which he was called upon to cross before he could enjoy that priceless romp with the man at the other end.

By this time he had been forced to attempt so many things. He had found all difficulties so easily vanquished and so richly rewarded when they were overcome. He had acquired such an actual mental taste for singular problems that, finally, he made the great effort and essayed the single rod. He fell off a hundred times at least before he caught the knack of it and learned to go across crouched low, putting out his feet one by one, like a stalking cat.

He passed that stage. He could stand erect and go across with wonderful surety. Then he could fairly run across that narrow way. This was a triumph indeed!

Massey dared not look at Calmont. The latter, he knew, was eyeing these performances with bitter glances. Not a word of praise, not even a syllable of notice came from poor Calmont, cut off and isolated from any share in these great triumphs of man and dog over the force of gravity. The whole thing was beginning to be uncanny.

Other matters, equally difficult in their own way, were taken up one by one, for Alec was proving an indefatigable pupil. Closed up as he was most of the day, he had learned to put all of his puppy energy, his impatient desire for amusement, his willingness to romp, into those man-directed games which Massey had taught him. No sooner was one thing ended, than another began.

He learned to walk upon his hind legs with absurd ease after he had had a little practice in balance, crossing the narrow bridge. He learned to stand on his rear legs and jump a surprising distance without dropping his forepaws to the ground.

He would perform that most valuable trick of lying on guard over any object for any length of time. An hour, two hours, all night, all day, he would remain camped over the bone, the cap, the glove which was given to him. No Roman sentinel could have been more scrupulous in obedience and in patient discipline.

It was truly all a prodigious game which only he and Massey understood, and for which he could be amply rewarded by one of those wild, noisy, tumbling romps that sometimes threatened to bring down even the solid walls of the igloo.

Fetching and carrying was, of course, a matter of no difficulty at all, but to fetch and carry articles belonging to Massey was a much more difficult matter. At last, by pointing to his feet as he gave the order and perhaps by some knowledge of the naked word itself, big young Alec the Great learned to carry a boot to his master. By dint of really tremendous patience and many cunning devices, Massey taught the puppy to get a flap of each boot in his mouth and drag the heavy things across the floor to him.

This, comparatively simple as it appeared in relation to the other and far more difficult tasks, was the one which cost Alec the Great the largest number of brainstorms and Massey the greatest amount of time and trouble. Then followed gloves, cap, coat, unloaded revolver in its holster, rifle dragged by its stock, the knife in its case and finally without a sheath at all! These articles were learned in rapid succession and, once learned, it was difficult to make Alec keep from bringing something in the shack to Massey, his teacher.

He had plenty of exercise from jumping over a stick, or from going to fetch a bundle of firewood and carry or drag it back across the floor. But this indoor exercise was not enough for the intentions of Massey.

As he saw that young Alec was growing up into a magnificent specimen of a dog, he determined to give him the advantage of the outdoors for the sake of his wind, his coat, his muscles, his dog senses. Therefore, every day he took out Alec for a long trek across the snows. In the face of storms he taught Alec to travel, and over ice and the crusted snows until the pads of the puppy's feet grew leathery hard.

There were perils in the earlier of these excursions, for the teams outside did not like the creature that came out to them in his white robe and his black markings and his strong scent of man. They, for the most part, were more wild than tamed, and nothing would have pleased those surly Huskies more than to sink their teeth in the throat of the upstart who enjoyed such warm sleeping quarters at the side of man, the master.

Chubby, however, was an exception. If the mother love had been somewhat dimmed in her breast by the early adoption of her son into the house, nevertheless she was able to remember that Alec was to her something more than other dogs. Gladly she undertook her share in his tuition when Massey brought him outside.

She taught him the secrets of the trail, the riddles of thin ice, of the varying strength of snow crusts, and of how, above all, to read the open book of the wind, filled with the large print of nearby odors and the indescribably small writing of the more distant scents.

In their romps she revealed to him with many a shrewd nip and many a hard bump the matchless science of wolf fighting, slashing with teeth that flash like a sword, parrying strokes with a gaping mouth, springing in to give the shoulder to an enemy with a resistless, compacted weight, feigning retreats, whirling to make sudden attacks, how to prance on lightest toe tip, being ready to leap to either side, how to slide in low as a seal to get to the legs and then suddenly whirl and grip the throat.

Alec's man-schooled brain learned with a wonderful rapidity, though he had not yet the power to withstand Chubby's rushes. But that deftness of foot which he had learned on the ladder and walking on a slender single willow rod enabled him to dodge her with a consummate adroitness. Indoors and outdoors, moreover, it was always by man that he was seen, appreciated, rewarded. Man stood by and watched these mimic fights. Man stood by and heartened him with a strong voice when he managed to catch his good-natured mother off balance and strike her floundering into the snow with a good shoulder stroke.

Therefore, it was only fitting that he should learn the other games of man outside as well as in — to range ahead and bark in a certain note when he crossed a wolf trail and in another voice when he crossed the way of other dogs, since a few half-starved creatures had been left behind by prospectors of the previous summer, not willingly but because they had run away. There was still a different call for the home trail, the sign of the home dogs.

A dog prefers by far to talk with his teeth and his tail and his eloquent paws, but he can pick up a large vocabulary of speech as well. Now Alec the Great was in the best school in the world. In that outdoor school he learned what police dogs are so readily trained to do — to attack a man. It was arranged by erecting a ridiculous image of a man out of dried, broken, or withered or worn-out skins, stuffed with moss and willow twigs. By rubbing gloves over the image a man-scent was given, and Alec the Great learned with almost a sinister ease to fly for the throat, or dive hard for the legs, giving them his teeth in a way that ripped the dummy wide, or his shoulder with a force that knocked the thing sprawling.

As for the work in harness — with his strong mother to tug at the wheel, himself in the lead, and the hand of Massey on the gee pole — he picked this up as a mere trifle and, when the weather was at all decent, they used to run away through the arctic night for miles. Young Alec would come home exhausted but happy. For never was he so petted and made much of and fed as when he had detected thin snow crust, or brittle ice, or picked his way most cleverly through wind-piled hummocks of white. He learned to swing right and left at the least word, to halt, to walk, to trot, to gallop, to race at full speed. For some reason, he gloried in this more than in all else.

Being a puppy he could enjoy twelve hours of sleep in the day, partly taken out in a solid repose of eight hours, and the rest used in cat naps and dozing. During the other twelve hours his brain and his body were constantly on the alert, constantly acquiring new wisdom or new tricks.

The eye can learn to speak, and never did an eye speak more eloquently than when Alec stood in the middle of the floor and, with head canted to one side, looked long and earnestly into the face of Massey to beg for something more to do, like a bored child weary of its old toys. He worked Massey to exhaustion with his young energy, but it was a fatigue in which Massey gloried.

Then came the crash.

Though Calmont had been growing more and more silent, yet Massey was not prepared for the end. Going out of the hut one day for a few moments, he was amazed when he returned and found the dog tied to Calmont's bunk with a length of light chain. Massey knew all too well what it meant.

CHAPTER
SIX

Danger

Human nature is made of such contrary stuff that we love a gift more than a purchase. Alexander the Great had been to Massey, in a sense, a gift. Therefore, he cherished him all the more.

In the same way, he had not been hired to teach the puppy, but he had poured out all his energy, his talent, his patience, and his time because he loved the dog and the things the dog could do. If it would be delightful to learn the language of dogs, it was hardly less so to make a dog understand so much of the language of a man.

Massey had forgotten that young Alec really belonged to Calmont. For that matter, it hardly was of importance to which of them a dog or a rifle or a sled really belonged, since they owned everything so much in common. But when he saw the puppy on the chain, he knew that the time had come when Calmont, at a stroke, intended to assert his rights and make the dog his own. When he attempted that — Massey shuddered and turned cold for in a flash he saw before him the whole dark story that would unfold!

Calmont lay stretched on his bunk, pretending to read one of the ancient, greasy magazines, but his jaw was locked so hard that a point of white stood out in his cheeks. The place of his holstered revolver had been shifted to a new peg over the bunk, and Massey knew without asking that that gun was loaded. Therefore, he said not a word.

A little later that evening, Alec the Great rose and, with a stealthy look over his shoulder at Calmont, walked to the end of the chain. The strength of it stopped him and, with a whine and a wagging of his tail, he plainly asked Massey to deliver him. Massey, looking over to his partner, detected the faintest of stern smiles upon the lips of Calmont, and at that black rage seized upon his mind. He went to Alec the Great and rubbed his head.

"Poor old boy!" he said.

Calmont lowered the magazine.

"Aye, poor old boy," he said, seeing the puppy licking the hand of his friend, "you've been through a pretty long schoolin', and you oughta turn into a useful dog, so it's time that you learn who's your real boss."

"He doesn't talk our language, Arnie," commented Massey.

"I'm gonna teach him *my* language," said Calmont.

"You've tried before, and he never will be able to understand you, or you to understand him, Arnie."

"You'll maybe have a hard time understandin' my tongue, Alec," Calmont said to the dog, "but you'll mighty *pronto* learn to understand my hand."

Massey straightened. He went back to his bunk, lay down on it, and closed his ears as well as he could to the sorrowful, impatient whining of the dog. Twice,

Alec tried to snap the thing by leaning forward with all his strength. Twice the jerk of the chain laid him on his back. And twice that faint smile of cruel pleasure touched the grim mouth of Calmont.

A brief, eloquent bark was directed toward Massey, who started on his bunk in spite of the hold he was keeping upon himself. Then Alec settled down to work upon the chain with his teeth and labored until his jaws ached. By that time he had polished six inches of it, but another frantic lunge showed him that the supple, icy thing which had broken his teeth and burned his tongue was as strong as ever.

"Poor boy!" said Massey gently.

Then Alec turned about and sat down, facing Calmont. He half guessed, long months before, that the man was an enemy. Now, with all the strength of a dog's heart, he knew for certain.

Calmont smiled with a deep, still, inward joy. He had waited until almost the very end of the winter. There was hardly a month remaining before the land would be open to incoming prospectors again. During all of this month, at least, he intended to taste and enjoy his triumph. The more the dog loved Massey, the more Massey loved the dog, by just that much would the heart of Calmont be soothed and gratified.

He knew the vastness of his revenge, simple though it might seem. He knew by his own hours of enormous weariness of soul as he had lain there or lounged and watched the intricate games and devices of the two. He disdained asking for a part where another part could not be. He had seen each day weld the two closer and closer together with the consummate knowledge that in the end, by a single stroke of the right he possessed, he could separate them again as far as the poles. Now he had delivered the stroke.

To be sure, the dog was of little use to him. He saw the eyes of the brute narrowed and green with hatred, and knew that he might break the spirit but that he never could bend it. That long association with the supple, keen, more graceful intelligence of Massey had made Alec the Great into a veritable sword for the hand of the younger man and into a useless tool for Calmont's clumsier grasp.

Yet, just as Massey had tormented Calmont through Alec, now by the same means Calmont would manage to torture Massey. The bitter pleasure of the sullen man was on Calmont. A sneer was on his lip and hatred of the world was in his heart — because he knew that he was doing a detestable thing.

From that moment forward, the men spoke no more. Now and then one of them addressed the dog, but it was only through dumb Alec that they attempted to communicate.

The trial of Massey was doubly severe in that during all of these months he literally had crowded every waking hour full with the work over Alec, with play, with teaching, with walks, with watching him as he slept, with grooming his fluffy, warm coat. Now he was stripped of all employment and, being tenfold more nervous than Calmont in temperament, in ten minutes he was in despair.

Toward evening, Calmont stood up, undid the chain from the bunk, and led the dog toward the door. Alec braced his feet, but the strong hand of Calmont compelled him. Massey suddenly turned his face to the wall and lay still, listening to the thundering of his heart, his hands aching.

After a time, Calmont returned. He must have dragged the puppy for a considerable distance through the snow. Alec was more than half choked, and his eyes were glassy. Yet his stubbornness was like that of a balking horse, and he had refused to lift a foot. He had remained braced against all persuasion throughout that strange promenade.

"Well," said Calmont, coming in, "that was a good little walk, Alec . . . a good little breather for the pair of us. You and me is gonna get on fine together, eh?"

Alec, with a sudden leap, tore the chain from the hands of his master and almost escaped to Massey. But a timely jerk snatched him out of the air and landed him upon the compact dirt floor with a force that knocked him senseless.

Massey sat with the eyes of a demon and stared at Calmont, and Calmont dragged the dog back until he could tie the chain to the bunk. But he knew the meaning of those staring eyes. If once the dog managed to get to Massey even for an instant, the latter never would give him up again. Already he was enduring more than flesh and blood commonly can sustain. But to ask for more would be impossible.

Massey, however, still said not a word, even to the puppy. His first movement was to take his rifle and revolver, wrap them up, and carry them out of the igloo. He placed them in security upon the top of the little house. Then he went back inside, remembered his hunting knife, and carried that out as well.

Calmont understood perfectly. The time had come when words would no longer serve. And this thing staggered him more than he had expected it might do. He could not help remembering, in a rush, all that had passed between them since that first gallant day when Massey had dashed so fearlessly to his rescue among the flashing knives of those Canucks. He could remember all the rest, too, with a strange vividness, as of a man about to die. He could recall the mutually endured pleasures of cold, storm, water, ice, and snow. Starvation and sickness they had endured side by side.

Now this was ended. It did not seem possible that there was between them a gulf which the bridge of a single word could not overcome. But the terrible fact remained and took his breath, as though he were staggering suddenly upon the brink of a great height.

For his own part, he followed the good example of Massey. He picked up rifle, revolver, and knife, and carried them outside. He could see the mound of the other weapons at one end of the roof. Upon the other end he heaped his own and saw the snow drift over them. Then he went back to the deadly silence of the hut.

CHAPTER
SEVEN

The Fight

He found Massey on his knees, petting the dog. At the appearance of Calmont, Massey stood up and went back to his bunk.

Calmont started at the work of dividing the pack. He made everything into two parts. There was only one fork; therefore, it was stuck into the turf wall near the stove, to be used by either in turn. There was only one axe. It was tossed on top of the house. There were three sled sheets. The third one was cut exactly in two. The dog harness too was carefully segregated and, there being an extra dog collar, this was slashed apart exactly in the center — making two strips of leather equally useless to both men.

Massey submitted. It was the way "divorces" were achieved in the Far North when partners had seen too much of one another. His irritation grew to such a point, however, that he could not endure to remain in the hut any longer, so he went out for a walk through the snow, trudging patiently on his snowshoes, as though he thought that his fury could in some way be worked out with utter fatigue.

When he came back, he heard the noise of a struggle inside the cabin, and old Chubby stood alertly on watch before the door. He heard snarling fury from the throat of Alexander the Great, the rattling of a chain, and the sound of whip strokes landing or whistling through the air.

Massey took off his snowshoes and left them at the door. He threw off his parka also and left it in the snow. He knew that he would have work to do inside that would need his unencumbered might. Then he pushed the door wide and entered, with the whiplash swishing past his face on the back stroke. It hung in the air. Alec crouched at the end of his chain with a devil in his eyes, his mouth slavering. He waited and prepared to endure, but there was no surrender in him — and for that a deep, strong thanksgiving went up from the soul of his teacher.

Massey thrust a hand against the shoulder of Calmont and spun him around, spoiling the last whip stroke. The face of his partner wore an expression he had never seen before. His mouth was locked. The lips were a depressed line that showed no red. He was a purplish color, not from exercise, but from sheer fury, and his eyes glittered almost as green as those of the young dog. No word was spoken by Massey. No word was spoken by Calmont, either. He had a more eloquent way of expressing himself and struck his friend across the face with the whiplash.

A foul blow will sometimes end a fight. Otherwise, it is a foolish stroke, because it always gives to the injured man a feeling of moral superiority — a sort of extra claim upon Fortune that will keep him all the more stubbornly to his work. Massey took the knife cut of that stroke which opened his cheek and let his blood run. Then he slid in under the blow with which Calmont tried to follow up and knocked Calmont head over heels on the floor.

The sting of the whip stroke had gone into the strong arm and the hard fist of Massey. He hesitated an instant as to whether he should throw himself on his fallen companion, but the laws of fair play were so strongly ingrained in the nature of Massey that he could not take an advantage. It was hardly a thing for which he needed praise. It had simply been ground into him during his school days.

Calmont rolled to his feet and rushed in to finish the thing with murder in his face. Neither of them made a sound. Massey, backing warily away, stopped that rush with a perfect straight left. It landed on Calmont's forehead and nearly broke Massey's hand, but the older man was checked, stopped, thrust back by a shower of stinging blows. He felt foiled and was doubly enraged. He saw now that the youngster merely had been playing with him during their daily boxing bouts and, instead of crediting Massey with honorable motives of a sporting fairness, he laid it down at once to a desire on the part of his friend to keep something up his sleeve. Therefore, if Calmont had wanted to kill before, he wanted doubly to do so now.

He came in as low as a football player charging in the line. A chopping hook struck behind his ear and pitched him on his face. There seemed to be lead in the hands of young Massey. He stood back and, seeing this, Calmont cursed more deeply in his heart and vowed that, if ever he had an advantage, he would not be fool enough to waste it in this "after you" courtesy. So he lurched up again, took three blows full in the face that split his flesh like knife strokes, and leaned in too close.

Massey, quick as a cat, dodged. He should have got free, but his leg struck against the dog, and down he went. Calmont was on him in a flash, clapping on a stranglehold that bent the head of Massey back to the point where his throat seemed just as if it were splitting. Alec the Great, springing to the end of his chain, tried to help his teacher but only succeeded in slashing the side of his master's coat.

Calmont hitched out of range and went on with his murder. He saw the face of Massey turn black and his tongue thrust out. It gave him no sense of horror but only a delicious satisfaction. Struggling to maintain his advantage, he bent his head. Instantly a hard set of knuckles rammed up against his nose and jerked his face back. Again, again, and again, trip-hammer, short, jarring blows upon the face and throat of Calmont. His grip slipped, and Massey twisted instantly out of it.

In the convulsive strength that came with the realization that he had escaped death, Massey got to his feet, but he was far gone. He knew now that he was fighting with a man who actually wanted his life, and who would stop at nothing to take it. Fair play existed in the mind of Calmont that day no more than it exists in the mind of a jungle brute. The very knees of the younger man went weak with the thought. He saw the door and turned to flee through it. Then his eye caught on Alexander the Great, and he stayed to fight to the end.

There was a difference between the men. Calmont fought for the sake of murder. Massey fought to win a human point. To slay this man with his bare hands, even if it were in his power, was impossible to his nature. Therefore, he was weakened. It was only the high disdain of defeat that sustained him and gave him the last, wonderful strength. Yet he was badly done up from the struggle on the floor. His head rang. Spots of black and of fire swam before his eyes. His lungs refused to take in fresh air and, when it came slowly, it was fire in his lungs. He staggered in his weakness.

Calmont, lunging forward, went brutally in for the finish. But, as an old pugilist once said, there are brains in a fighter's legs. They hold him up when he is about to sink. They carry him instinctively away from danger. That instinct saved young Massey now. He managed to side step. Calmont, with a swerve and a curse, almost fell into the teeth of the waiting Alex. He turned, charged again, and this time there was power enough in the arms of Massey to hit the man away from him.

Twice more Calmont charged, and twice stunning blows sent him reeling. Massey was revived. He had lost his fear of the horrible, distorted face that ran at him like a nightmare. But he had not quite lost his sense of pity. When the third time he knocked Calmont away with beautifully clean punches, he followed with a flying tackle that floored the other in a corner of the hut. One foot of Calmont, as he fell, struck the little stove and knocked it headlong. The coals and the burning wood filled the place with a thick, choking smudge. Through that smudge, Massey found Calmont face down, motionless beneath him.

He raised his clenched fist. A mere tap behind the ear would end that last tie now. And yet he could not deliver it! Across his mind came a picture all blinding white of the swirl of a dense snow storm, of sickening weakness in his knees, and of the mighty arm of Calmont supporting him through the march.

Massey rose, staggering, to his feet and stepped clear. He saw that Calmont remained prone and for a moment feared that in the fall the other had been seriously injured. Then he saw Calmont rise in turn, looking gigantic through the fog of smoke. He heard a ripping sound. He saw that Calmont with his naked hand — a miraculous feat of strength — had ripped away the willow pole that made a side to his bunk. It was a good, heavy club and, armed with it, Calmont came hurling back to the attack.

Massey sprang across the shack and wrenched at the bed pole of the other bunk. He lacked by far the power of hand or arm to tear the pole loose. Then, desperate, turning empty handed, he attempted to face the danger. It was on him at once.

Hitherto, there had not been a word spoken, or a sound made, except that hideous sound of panting that comes from desperately struggling men. But now Calmont began to laugh, through his set teeth. Twice, by a miracle of footwork, Massey avoided the strokes of the club. They came hurtling past his head. By the very sound of them, he knew that they were intended to kill.

It seemed to him that there was only one way to end this uneven battle and that was to spring close in and struggle with the bigger man for the possession of the club, though in such a struggle the superior weight and the strength of shoulder of Calmont was bound to tell heavily. Prepared with tingling nerves, he waited for the next blow. Again that laughter of Calmont rang in his ears, more horrible to Massey than the howl of a wild beast; and he saw the broad shoulders of the other charging in, dashing the smoke aside in wreaths. The club hung in the air, and Massey, dodging, raised an arm toward his head and leaped in.

In the very midst of his charge he saw, in the face of Calmont and by the motion of the club, that it was a feint that he had dodged and that the real blow was coming now. He sensed this as he rushed, far too late to dodge again. Yet he tried it. Frantically he swerved at the last moment, but the stroke came at him with unavoidable speed and strength. He had a knowledge of it in the brief part of a second which was too short to enable him to defend himself. He had the feeling of a slaughtered steer as the darkness shocked upon his brain.

CHAPTER
EIGHT

Wolves!

With his body turned to lead, Massey wakened. Cold weighted it, glued it against the ground. There was no light except an unspeakable gloom that seeped in around the edges of the willow door frame. The stove was gone or gave no heat. The light was out. For some time he must have been lying there. The chill was nibbling at the marrow of his bones. As he tried to put out his hands and to sit up, he discovered that he was securely bound. Lashings about his wrists, his knees, his ankles secured him, and the wrist thongs were bound down to the fastenings upon his knees. These bonds were not few but manifold and put on with such force that they bit deeply into his flesh. They helped to check the flow of his blood, and the sluggishness of it would shorten the length of time required to freeze him.

He was glad of that. The shorter the time, the less the pain — he saw that his position was hopeless. He rolled to the wall and worked into a sitting posture against it. This was the limit of useful motion, except in so far as exercise would increase his body warmth. He was stabbed by two pains. One was the early pang of hunger. The other was an ache in his head where the crushing blow from the club of Calmont had landed. He knew perfectly what had happened. Seeing him down, wishing him dead, Calmont had made sure of the business in this way. He had packed up the food and the essentials which were in the place and started away with the dog team. There remained for the other partner starvation and freezing.

Massey could detect the blind rage in the procedure not only by the tightness with which his bonds had been drawn but by the very fact that he had been left in this manner. If he had been bound and dragged out into the snow, for instance, cold would have ended him in an hour or so. In the spring of the year the explanation of death would have been easily arranged for no one could have suspected such an old companion to be guilty of murder, any more than one could suspect that a dog was the cause of the destruction. Now, however, the incoming prospectors were sure to stop at this igloo; they were certain to find the remains of the dead man; they would naturally send back the report to Nome, and then the days of Calmont would be measured.

Bearing this in mind, it seemed very probable to Massey that Calmont would think the matter over while he was on the trail and return to deal with his enemy in a different fashion. That was the one hope to hold in his heart. When his partner returned, Massey was fairly confident that an appeal to his good sense and reason would make Calmont set him free. But would Calmont return?

Not suddenly, Massey decided. The emotions of that wolfish man rose suddenly, but they lasted long, and the hatred which had been building so steadily that winter would not burn out and give clear, calm reason a chance until he had been many hours on the trail, most likely. The thin hope, however, was enough to make Massey set deliberately toward the preservation of his life. He rolled and worked himself to all parts of the igloo in the hope that he might find something on which to rub through the fastenings which held his wrists together. That accomplished, he quickly could set himself free. But, hunt as he would, he could find nothing. The very bunks had been torn down, and nothing remained except the heavy sod walls of the house. They and the winter snow surrounded him. He was alone!

Day brightened slowly. Prying around the edges of the door, it filtered into the place a soft, unearthly light, and by it he could describe his surroundings more than by the sense of touch. It was the end for him, unless some living agency came to help him. Even if his hands and legs were set free, how could he support existence without fire, without weapons, without even a heavy coat to keep the cold away? Despair swept over him, more chilling to the soul than the arctic cold to the flesh.

But he was a fighter and, therefore, he would not surrender for more than an instant. Another man would have fallen to hysterically begging his Creator's mercy, or else he would have laid down and given up at once when the cold would have finished the business quickly enough with its silent dagger. But Massey kept in motion enough to warm his body. Only his hands and feet grew numb and icy. Calmly he noted the progress of the freezing. He kicked his feet against the wall and squeezed his hands between his knees. The labor employed his mind and gave some small, dull circulation to the freezing places. Yet he felt more and more convinced that the house would be his tomb.

Weariness, at the last, made him quiet. He rested, trying to keep all thought away and, while he was thus silent, he heard something breathing at the door of his igloo. He thought it was Calmont at first, but then he decided it could not be a man, for the sound was too sharp. Next he was aware of a shadow at the door, which was presently pushed open, and the big head and shoulders of a timber wolf appeared. He shouted in horror, and the monster shrank back and vanished.

A moment later, however, just as his heart was beginning to beat more easily, the door swayed open again, and this time he saw not only the scarred head of the big leader but several more of the beasts behind him. He yelled again. They winced but did not jump back, and the leader raised his head and sniffed the air as though he would trust the sense of smell to tell him more than the shouting of a mere man could do. Plainly he feared not man himself, the helpless creature that walks erect, but man's slaves of iron and steel. He sniffed now and snarled as he did so, while the heart of Massey turned cold. Grinding his teeth in despair and in rage, he shouted louder. He even rolled himself a turn or two toward the door, but the ominous fighting growl of the leader warned him that the sham would not do.

Bluffs had doubtless been tried on that old traveler many a time before by various animals, and only an animal was Massey now, pinioned as he was. His movement along the ground was not that of a man but rather that of some clumsy otter out of water. Massey, with an effort, sat up, balanced himself, and tried to catch the eyes of the big wolf with his own. There had been strange stories told about the magic power of the mind of man when it confronted a wild beast through the force of eye upon eye. So he stared hard, and the leader stared back but, when the weight of the human attention was too much for the beast, he snarled and dropped his head lower. He made a slinking pace forward, and two younger, higher-headed warriors of that pack crowded behind him.

They were burned thin by long famine. They were no more than loose robes strung over gaunt frames of bones, but Massey knew that the power remains in the jaws of a wolf until he dies. Hunger merely serves to sharpen his brain and give an edge to his teeth. He looked wildly about him in the search for some weapon. Then, realizing that even if he had all the weapons in the world, they would be useless to his imprisoned hands, he turned his head toward the danger once more. The leader had come a whole stride nearer. He was scarcely a yard away, and Massey saw the bristling of the hair along the back, saw plainly the redness of the eyes, and the slavering of the mouth. The pain of death or the pain of hunger — for these creatures there was little to choose between, and they were ready to die for the sake of a full stomach.

Now the monster crouched. A shout from Massey and a convulsive movement effected nothing. The younger beasts made ready for the leap as well. It seemed to Massey that already he felt their teeth in the softness of his throat when a reinforcement came to the hunters — a white wolf, bounding high through the doorway to lead the attack. Then a wild, hoarse cry of delight came from the throat of Massey, such a sound as was strange to his own ears, for it was Alec the Great who had come back!

He would have tucked his tail between his legs and run as his mother had taught him to do after sighting the wild beasts, but here they were not in the open which was theirs. They were in his own kennel, and fear did not occur to him. They were, moreover, under the very eye of man, the god, the miracle worker. So he came in with a leap and gave the great leader a side slash as he flew past.

That old fighter could have downed the young dog in a moment, but he was taken by surprise. The ground was not his own; the freedom and the fierceness of the attack seemed to point it out as a mere vanguard of hostility. He bounded back through the door with a yelp of terror, and his host went with him. They flung away in terror, and the door slapped to behind them, while Alec the Great, giving them no more heed, flung himself on his master with frantic whinings of joy. He licked the face, the cold hands of Massey; he raced and bounded about the igloo in his perfect satisfaction.

Massey, weak and trembling with joy, could hardly see until he had shaken the tears from his eyes. Then he made out the great welts which crossed and recrossed the head of the puppy. There was an iron collar about his neck and a foot-long dangling line hanging from it. He had the picture of Calmont flogging the refractory dog and, the keen tooth slash with which Alec had divided the leather that fastened him to one of the sleds. After that, let the wind catch him, but his master could not.

The heart of Massey yearned over the fine fellow. Then his satisfaction ended with a cruel pang. Better to die in this company but afterward? He had in his mind's eye a picture of his body stiff as ice, and of poor Alec couched on his breast and licking the dead face of his teacher. Tears of pity stung the eyes of Massey, but he was not pitying himself. Alec the Great, having finished his first frantic demonstration of joy, went to the entrance of the salmon cache and uttered the low-pitched yelp which meant that he was hungry.

But there was nothing to give. Already, with a frantic hope, the man's eyes had explored that recess and seen that the thorough-going cruelty of Calmont had removed even this small hope and comfort. He had nothing. For the first time, Alec asked of him in vain. He had nothing to give. He could not even stroke the fine, proud neck of Alec. He had his voice alone and, when he said "No" to that appeal for food, Alec came over and sniffed him curiously from head to foot. Then he sat back, canted his head to one side, and looked quizzically at the man.

CHAPTER
NINE

Flame

There was a vast fund of good humor in Alec the Great. He continually looked as if he had just finished laughing or were about to begin when he confronted his teacher. They had had so many romps together; they had accomplished so many miraculous deeds; they had walked so far and talked so long that Alec the Great had learned to follow without command, to obey without fear, and to pluck danger by the beard so long as Massey were near. For that reason he had not dreaded the wolf pack with Massey's eye upon him. And, as always in the past, he had conquered at a single stroke. They had fled like so many grim ghosts and left him alone with the man he loved.

Other men were different creatures. That is to say, the other man. The population of the civilized world was, for Alec the Great, composed of Chubby, Massey, and Calmont. The rest of the dog team was on the border in a no man's land. They would cut his throat as soon as wink. Beyond this border lay the wilderness in which were rabbits on the one hand and wolves on the other. In this world Massey was the god, the benefactor, the ceaseless distributor of food, entertainment, caresses. He filled the stomach of the dog. More importantly, he also filled the mind of Alec. In the same way Calmont was the demon. His touch was fire; his voice was a roar; he was the very symbol of pain and torment. With utter singleness of purpose big Alec — for he had grown almost to his full height — sat down before Massey and worshipped, inquired, and waited for the fun to begin. With this teacher, rewards were often postponed, he knew; they never were finally denied.

The grimness with which Massey, for his part, sat there and faced the puppy could not remain for very long. They had done so many things together that even this new and more important miracle might be achieved. He wanted to have his hands free, first of all, before he could so much as think of the future. Alec the Great had teeth which were as knives. He had tried his own teeth on the tough, twisted strand of the leather bonds about his wrist, but he might as well have chewed on iron. The incisors of Alec would quickly make another story of it, if he only could use them. But how tell a dog to bite? How tell him to bite so close to the sacred flesh of man?

He thought of a way to attempt it. With his own teeth he bit at and worried the leather thong between his wrists. Then, making as much of a motion as he could, he spread out his hands and offered the place to Alec. The dog sniffed. He licked the thong and stared up impulsively at the man. He had learned long ago that there were no wasted movements with Massey, nothing

65

ridiculous, nothing absurd without a purpose. The thong was shown to him with some object, and he wondered what.

Again, Massey pretended to snap at the leather; again he offered it; and Alex, gently, playfully, snapped, in turn, but not with force enough to break the skin of a new-born babe. Then he heard a serious, cheerful, encouraging voice, and he bit the leather, kept his teeth upon it, fastened his eyes on the face of the master, and sank his grip firmer. Massey, laughing, tugged back, and instantly Alec understood. It was a tug of war, of course!

He flung himself back, writhing, twisting, jerking, fighting, and the man jerked and twisted against him, though with a strange lack of force. It was a good game. Alec, playfully snarling, struggled with all his might and actually toppled Massey upon his side. Then the thong unfairly gave way between his knife-sharp teeth!

At this, man, the teacher did a very strange thing. He got on his knees and raised his freed hands toward the heavens; then he flung his arms around the neck of the beloved dog and hugged him. It was simple, after that, to undo the other fastenings. Massey got up and jogged around the igloo, waving his arms, smashing his numbed hands together, stamping the blood back into his feet. Alec the Great went with him, bounding, panting, pretending to threaten the soft throat of man with his white teeth. After that, however, he went back to the salmon cache and asked again for food.

Massey stopped short, and his heart stopped also. He stared at the dog, and he thought of himself. His total possessions consisted of one straight piece of willow which had once been part of his own bunk rail, a few half-burned pieces of wood which remained scattered on the floor after the overturning of the stove, and the bits of leather thong with which he had been bound by Calmont. With such weapons as these he had to find food and fire or else die, and the dog with him.

There was also the collar around the neck of the dog. When he examined it, he found that it was a single piece of good steel, thin and over-supple, of course, but capable of service. He unlatched the collar at once and laid it away for future efforts. He continued his pacing back and forth, while the dog sat down to watch and barked no more. He was very hungry, of course, but his patience was equal to his trust in the man. This, like the blind faith of a child, frightened and overpowered Massey. He tried so desperately to think of expedients that his brain went blank time and again.

The only possible food which he could reach was rabbit, or at least that was all of which he could think. He thought of making a bow of the strips of leather thong and the willow stick but, if he did so, what could he use to tip the arrows except bits of fish bone? Besides, how hit such a target as a rabbit with a clumsy weapon and an unpracticed hand? Rabbits he must have, however, or else starve.

Suddenly he shouted. Alec bounded halfway to the ceiling and lighted on four braced legs, eager for a game, and Massey tumbled him joyously on the floor. He had thought of at least something to try and that was to put up some traps on the rabbit trails crossing

67

the snow. Plenty of rabbits came to nibble at iced willow shoots near the warm spring and, taking some of the fragments of wood from inside the cabin, Massey went outdoors to arrange the traps.

He had gloves, or he could not have endured the cold for a moment. As it was, the cold was like a bath of ice water to a naked man. Half a dozen times he had to run back into the igloo and warm himself with violent exercise. But he built two clumsy pitfalls by repeated trips, breaking off the tough willows to help in the rude structures and baiting them with plenty of the icy willow twigs. No matter how poor the bait, he had a profound faith in the famine which drives the snowshoe rabbit.

He went back to the cabin, always accompanied by the dog, and began his next effort to save Alec. For that began to exceed all his interest in his own life. Among the fragments of leather string, he found one piece more than two feet long. It had been used to bind his ankles. He knotted other pieces to this and with it strung a straight, tough, willow stick, bending it a little. The longest bit of thong was now in the center of the string of this clumsy bow, but it was not to be used to shoot an arrow. His plan was to attempt to make fire as the Indians had done in the old days by friction. He knew that it was a vague hope, but he clung to it. It had to be done, or he would die. The cold had already had him by the throat. The time was quickly coming when exhaustion would prevent him from keeping away freezing through exercise.

He selected a straight, narrow stick from the fire-dried pieces on the floor. With the blunt edge of the dog collar as a knife, he rubbed away the charred end of the wood to the semblance of a point. With a corner of the collar, he easily knocked hollows in two other bits. Next in a shallow trench he imbedded the larger sticks. The smaller one he held in his left hand with its notch pressed over the end of the piece which was to be twirled by the bowstrings. The string, last of all, was carefully wrapped around the last stick, and the instrument was almost ready. He needed something with which to feed the flame, however, if ever he should succeed in raising so much as a spark.

This timber he supplied, as well as he could, by shredding with teeth and fingers the small bits of willow firewood. How great a treasure this now seemed, this casual scattering of embers upon the floor. Life, without them, would not even be worth fighting for. It would be a lost hope instantly.

Then he began to work. He worked until his shoulders and upper arms were as sore as though they had been beaten. Then he saw the first sign of hope — a thin wisp of smoke. He was dizzy with effort already, but he stuck to his work. Bitterly he ground the bow back and forth, driving his muscles. Moisture stood out on his face and then turned to ice as it ran among his whiskers. He groaned with the exquisite agony of protesting muscles, until Alec the Great came before him to ask what this was all about.

Suddenly Massey had to stop. His arms would do no more. He felt the end of the stick. It was not hot enough to make fire begin. The magic point of ignition of wood was still far away. He stood up, groaning, despairing. The cold was in the pit of his stomach like a lump of ice, and he knew that the end would not be far off. So he began to stride hurriedly through the igloo, not searching for help but with the desperation of a trapped thing in its cage. In his despair he saw something like a small, yellow eye blinking at him from a corner. He thought he was going mad at first but, when he leaned over it, he found a single cartridge that, in Calmont's murderous haste, had been left behind.

Joy came so swiftly and strongly over Massey that he staggered like a drunken man. He went back to the bow. He kneaded his arm muscles for a moment until they seemed more at ease. Then he broke open the cartridge and prepared to work.

The point of the whirling stick had worn its groove deep and smooth by this time. The wood was dry, and utter desperation was keeping Massey at the work. Smoke began to rise. He sprinkled on the gunpowder liberally, held his breath, and instinctively looked upward. Then he began to work the bow as never before. There were thicker fumes. The sting of the gunpowder smoke touched his nostrils, and there followed a little spurt of flame. Snatching the stick away, upon that flame he scattered gently the tinder he had heaped around, but the fire turned to a red coal at the touch of the wood.

CHAPTER
TEN

Thirst for Vengeance

It was as though the gods had smiled on him only to show him how easily they may snatch away their gifts. Throwing himself on his stomach, he began to blow. He saw the whole outer edges of the fire spot go away at the first blast of his breath, as though there were a curse in it. He blew again, and in the center a single point of white remained. Under steady fanning, it grew a little, and then a little more. It spread. He heard a light crackling sound that was to him like a divine music. Brighter shone that star of hope. Smoke went up, thick and more thickly. He pressed the last of the tinder above it, and now a meager little tongue of flame flickered in the smoke. It jumped out of sight, choked, as it were, by the fumes of the burning wood. It began again. It danced up and down like a malicious, small demon, taunting poor Massey with continual hope, and all the while the cold of the ground was stealing into his bones.

At last the flame took a firm foothold. It raised its small head with a proud steadiness above the heap of tinder. It was a tiny thing, yet it was no longer an unembodied ghost but a true servant and slave of man.

It was a gift stolen from heaven, and the joy of heaven itself was in the heart of Massey as he got to his knees and began to feed the flame. There was only a handful of timber, and he was afraid that it might not have sufficient strength to ignite the larger bits of wood. Prayerfully he laid them in place and watched. The flame struggled, shrank from the new food, wavered, dwindled, and then gave out that cheerful crackling sound which was finer to Massey's ear than organ music and angelic violins.

He ran out from the cabin to the willows, cursing himself for not having done this before. In this way he saw two rabbits in his falls. They mattered not. The cold sprang like a demon on his back and sank its invisible teeth in his vitals, but he gave it no heed. He had hope before him, and he was blind to all else. Even the frantic bounding and barking of the dog beside him was as nothing. He broke and ripped and tore down the willows. Close to the spring they were shallow rooted, and he plucked them up bodily. He carried a great armful back into the igloo and, pushing open the door, was greeted by a vast cloud of smoke through which no fire at all was visible.

Massey, hurling the willows down, went staggering back from that spectacle. Misfortune, he felt with a profound conviction, was hounding and baffling him on this day. He propped the door open. He climbed to the top of the house and smashed in his great invention, the window of seal bladder with its encrustations of frost and ice. As he broke it down, he saw the white smoke rise upward like a ghost, and through the deadly fog of it there was the red eye of the life from heaven. Down he went again.

The cabin was clearing rapidly of the fumes, and around the flame he distributed the willow wood carefully. He knocked the ice from it. The larger pieces he laid close by to dry. The smaller he extended straight above the fire.

Massey was himself half frozen, but he could not help laughing, now, at the sight of the dog seated by the fire, hungrily lolling its tongue. For when did man make fire among the snows of that country except to cook food? Alec the Great was already slavering in anticipation as he watched the yellow power writhe and gather strength and feed itself.

Massey got the two rabbits, reset the falls, and hurried back into the house. With the sharp corner of the dog collar he opened the tender skins between the forelegs, but with his bare hands he skinned, cleaned, and divided the hares. Fingers can become knives to the skillful or those who are desperate. The dog's raw share disappeared in a moment. Massey's smaller half was soon roasting on three small spits made of willow twigs.

The smoke billowed about him, sagging away from the weak draft of that most improper chimney. Cold still iced all the edges of the cabin. Compared with this means of heating, the little stove was as the sun of a hot summer's day, but Massey was grateful and content. How short a time before he had lain tied hand and foot, with wolves standing over him.

"You're my luck!" said he to Alec the Great.

Alec licked his hand then lay down by the fire to sleep, as though he realized that the day's work was ended. It was ended for him, but not for Massey.

He dared not sleep without covering on the naked, icy floor of the cabin. Therefore, he went back to the willows and broke down enough branches, enough saplings, to carry back and make a bed of a sort which would at the least raise him from the floor. This was wet. The melting ice dribbled in little streams across the floor, but eventually it would dry. While he waited for that to happen, he fought away the fatigue that kept rushing over his brain in tingling waves.

At last, he could stand it no longer. Body and soul were crying out for sleep, so he built two fires and heaped the willows in between. Then he lay down to sleep. It was a wretched slumber. The cold was defeated on each side, but it dropped on him from above, and it breathed at him like ice from below. As he slept, he had to keep turning and several times, choked with the smoke, he sat up, coughing. But he slept again.

He only wakened definitely when the heaps of fuel had been exhausted, and the actual sinking of the fires let the cold wave flood back upon him. It seemed as though he were wearier than when he first lay down, but by degrees his brain cleared, his heart beat stronger. He would set his teeth and tell himself that he would endure. Three weeks would bring the first prospectors into the region. In three weeks he would be able to get some help, no doubt, and start back across the open country. Life would be a wretched existence until that time, but life it would be nevertheless.

He had dreamed of Calmont in a strange way. He had dreamed that it was he who had struck down Calmont with a foul blow. That it was he who had bound the other hand and foot. That it was he who had stood sneezing and laughing over the body of the fallen man and keeping back his hand from outright murder merely because he wished Calmont to taste death by slow degrees and with the more exquisite anguish of loneliness. It was he who had taken the bundles of guns down from the roof of the cabin.

As he rehearsed that portion of his dream, his mind flashed back to actualities. Certainly Calmont would be a fool if he weighed himself down with the burden of an extra revolver and an extra rifle on the way to Nome. Somewhere he had thrown them into the snow, of course.

Opening the door, he shrank from the icy hand that pushed in at him, but now he studied the footprints. His own were easily distinguished. They headed always straight for the willows, but those of Calmont wandered here and there. Snow had fallen a few hours before the fight. Therefore, it was only a recent story that the footprints told.

Massey gathered the embers of the fires into heaps and fed them afresh. Then he went out to examine the tracks. One line led around the corner of the shack, and there he found the trail to end at the face of a snowdrift which had been broken into in the center. He kicked into the snow and nearly broke his foot on a solid bulk. He heard the clink of metal and, stooping, he picked out his own gun bundle. It was intact, just as he had wrapped it in the half of the sled sheet and carried it out to the top of the house — rifle, revolver, and ammunition.

His troubles suddenly became small. There was even a knife, and the miserable necessity of grinding the steel collar of the dog to an edge was removed. A most excellent rifle, revolver, ammunition, and knife. The sled sheet would do far better than nothing worn as a cloak to turn the edge of the wind. It seemed to Massey a miracle. But he could see with a little afterthought that from the first it was patent that Calmont would do exactly this.

He had taken away to a sufficient distance all that Massey could possibly reach, bound as he was hand and foot. Certainly he would not burden himself with such extra weight. It would have been madness, when trekking to Nome over such a distance and such terrain. Yet a flavor of the miracle was about it still.

That flavor wore off by degrees as the warmer, brighter weather came on. No matter how warm, it was always cold in the igloo. When there was sufficient fire to keep Massey comfortable, his lungs were being choked with intolerable masses of smoke. The weeks went by him like laggards. There was no starvation, but simply steady discomfort. Wolves that had been dangerous neighbors before still haunted the place and paid dearly for their temerity. He shot that same gaunt leader which had nearly torn the flesh of his throat. He shot three more of the same pack, as well — two of them within ten seconds of one another. Of their skins he rudely tailored himself a coat and a sleeping robe.

The manufacture was clumsy, but the need was served. He made himself a pair of the worst snowshoes that ever were devised. Over the fire in the cabin, he jerked enough rabbit meat to make a pack of it.

In the middle of one night he sat up and decided that he must move. It was well enough to play safe and wait for the summer and the new crop of prospectors, come out to explore this terrible playground of storms and dreariness. But there was something burning in him that demanded food, and food immediately. It was the consummate hatred which he felt for Calmont that always spurred him. That had been the one occupation of his mind since the fire began to burn. Certainly, since he had found guns in his hands again, there was nothing else worthy of occupying him. So he had given his mind by day and his dreams by night to some perfect revenge.

He had devised for days ways of killing Calmont. But neither gun nor knife nor choking hands were enough. There was nothing in such pain that would equal his own moments of agony when he lay hopeless and helpless on the floor of the igloo until Alexander the Great came back to rescue him. His soul had been drawn to two focal points — love for the dog and hatred of Calmont. He could not tell which was the more gripping emotion, but he knew that he could not endure the suspense any longer. He stood up and prepared to depart.

CHAPTER
ELEVEN

Tod Regan Goes Out

In one sense Doctor Borg was an honest man. That is to say, he looked what he was, and that was a tower of battle. He was only thirty years old, but he appeared forty. His forehead was fleshy as though cushioned to withstand shocks. His nose had been hit so often while he was on his feet and kicked so often when he was on the floor that it was a loose, shapeless thing. His mouth had no red showing. It was a straight line, nearly always compressed. He wore his hair long to cover a missing ear but, since the hair was thin, the terrible scar continually showed through. His eyes were half baffled and half thoughtful. He had the appearance of one who has just received a blow and is about to strike back. Few people waited to receive the weight of his fist.

He was dressed night and day in the same manner, as he stalked about his combined saloon, gambling hall, and dance pavilion in Nome. He wore on his head a tall, peaked Mexican hat which he never took off and which, together with his thin, dangling hair and his block of a face, added fifty per cent to the evil and unearthly tone of his appearance. His coat was a short mackinaw with a checked pattern. It was very dirty, and most of the nap was rubbed off. The colors had faded in spots. It was his *luck*, and men said that he slept in it. Certainly it looked as though he did. To match his hat he wore the high-heeled boots of a cowpuncher, with his trousers stuffed into the tops of them.

Doctor Borg was as hard as he looked. Every man who got drunk in his place was in danger of being rolled for his wad. And since men constantly got drunk there, his income was large.

This was a time when Nome was at its wildest and meanest. There were said to be five thousand men in the town out of work that winter, and men out of work are not hard to please in the work they are asked to do. Doctor Borg always hand-picked the five thousand and kept the best five. They were the ones who were quickest on the trigger, hungriest for a fight, and with a special appetite for a murder.

No other saloon keeper in Nome would have tried to run such an extensive place with only five bouncers, but Borg's men were known and, whenever they hove into view, each wearing a small, visorless cap as a badge of office, they spread peace around them faster than the ripples in a pool around a dropped stone. The average life of these men was said to be something like three weeks. They melted away in the strong currents of emotion which poured through Borg's establishment. They disappeared, and no one asked questions, for their faces were hardly regarded — only the small, round black caps which they wore. Their pay was as high as their duties were precarious, and there was never a lack of applicants for such positions. Some member of his corps of five was always at the elbow of the doctor as he stood behind the bar or stalked through his extensive rooms. In a certain sense one might have looked on the doctor as a spider and his five henchmen as five strands in his web.

It was a mystery to the casual observer that men would flock to such a den, but there were reasons. It was true that many men were rolled in this place of vice and amusement, but it was also true that no beggar ever was turned away empty handed and that no one got less than a dollar. That being true, why did not the whole five thousand parade past his door every day? A good many of them did, but shame takes the place of virtue, and most men prefer to eat pride if they can't pay for their meal with cash. Pride is a thin diet, but it has kept many an unlucky fellow going. Honesty, however, was even a greater virtue with the doctor than charity. He was honest about everything. He was even honest when he was asked if he were a robber.

"Of course I am," he would say. "Why else should I be here? I dig gold. The Joint is my beach claim."

Part of his honesty was shown by the fact that his place was called The Joint and had that name painted in large, bullet-sprinkled letters outside his door. If it were true that terrible things took place beyond that door, it was also true that the man made no pretense. Every man who saw that sign looked on it as a place of evil, a place of danger. It was a perpetual challenge hung out before his eyes, and no dare could go long untaken by such men as thronged Nome in that early day. Evil was then so familiar that the mottled character of the doctor sometimes appeared almost bright. Murders were committed every day. It was said that at one time during this year every sheriff and deputy sheriff in Nome had a prison record. Where it is impossible to find virtue, men are apt to cling to facts, however bad. And the doctor was a fact. No man could say that he was familiar with the life in this wild town unless he had been in The Joint. They went slumming and became a part of what they went to see.

The honesty of the doctor appeared most startlingly at the bar. Behind this appeared several kegs of whiskey besides a number of bottles. The prices were not high. In fact, they were surprisingly cheap compared with the headline robberies of other saloons of the time. There were three kinds of whiskey. Over one keg appeared this sign:

This costs a dollar a glass. It is old and good. It might be too good for you, and it won't get you drunk as quick as the others.

Over a second keg appeared another sign:

This is good enough for you to get drunk on. It costs you only sixty cents a glass. It is real whiskey, but not old enough to be wise.

Over a third keg appeared:

This is dynamite. Drink it if you don't give a damn.

It cost twenty-five cents a glass only, and most of the patrons of The Joint didn't give a damn.

The doctor kept office hours just before the evening rush. That was when his day began. In that time he hired new entertainers, new dance-hall girls, new bartenders, new bouncers. He took on new gamblers, distributed stakes for the different tables, gave change to the bar money boxes, raked the cooks over the coals — there was a restaurant attached to make The Joint complete — and performed other duties of an executive nature. During this time he never lost his temper, never raised his voice. He was as cold as steel — or water dripping on ice. Few men asked a question twice of the doctor, and no man had been known to argue and live.

It was at just this time that a young man stepped through the front door of The Joint. His face had the familiar starved look that comes from long exposure to cold which burns the body as dry as Arizona heat. There were bluish patches on his face. He was wretchedly dressed in wolfskins, clumsily put together. His boots were rags. He limped on one leg. He looked on the whole as though a storm had passed over him, after lingering a while about his person. Behind him stepped a tall dog, obviously young and peculiarly marked. He was all white, snowy white, except that the ears, muzzle, and tail tip were sooty black. He was so beautifully made, with such promising quarters and shoulders, that the eyes of expert dog drivers dwelt upon him fondly. They would have him at a high price in spite of his youth, because he had the wise eyes and the fearless bearing of a leader.

No sooner had the man in wolfskins entered than Tod Regan stepped up to him. Tod was a known man. He had been with The Joint for five months, which was almost, if not quite, a record. He was equally good with knife, gun, and hand because he had been educated in the New York prize ring, Chihuahua, and the Texas cattle range. He was six feet two, and his two hundred odd pounds were all bone, muscle, and mule-hard sinew. He would have stayed at The Joint for nothing because he loved the life there so well. He would have been at home in a cage with wild cats. In short, he was the right man in the right place.

He looked at the frost-pinched face of the stranger with a shade of sympathy. Then he said roughly because sympathy did not know how to get into his voice: "Outside with that dog, friend!"

"Ah!" said the other, "don't you like dogs?" He smiled almost timidly at Tod Regan.

"You heard me the first time," declared Tod. "Get that dog off of this here floor!"

The stranger turned a little to the dog. "You hear him, Alec?" he said.

The dog lifted his bright, speaking face toward his master.

"He says for *you* to get out," said the stranger.

"You're a joker, are you?" asked Tod, all business now. "This ain't a place for jokes. Take your dog out, and stay out."

The man in the wolfskins said: "You seem to be a hard young man."

Tod Regan ordinarily would have knocked the stranger down and heaved him out into a snow bank, then he would have kicked the dog after him. But this was early in the evening, and he was not yet in exercise, so he warmed himself up with half a minute of selected swearing. At the end of it, the stranger had not left. He was nodding with admiration. He looked thinner and smaller than ever as he smiled.

"You could drive mules pretty well with lingo like that," he declared, "but I'm not a mule."

He had a pleasant voice, and a pleasant smile, too, until one analyzed it for a moment, and then it seemed as cold as ice — or the eye of the doctor. Tod Regan considered the stranger for an astonished moment. He was not exactly vain. He was too seriously interested in fighting to have any small vanity on the subject. Champions who are vain are fools, and Tod was not a fool. However, it was clear that his name and fame were unknown to this man, and he decided that it would not be worth while to waste time in explanations.

"You poor boob!" said Tod and made two quick, short steps forward — the steps of a gliding prize fighter — to knock the stranger through the door.

The latter was perfectly at home it appeared. He spared the time to say: "Steady, Alec!"

Alec, already leaping for the throat of the bouncer, clicked his teeth on thin air and sailed harmlessly past him. This did not upset Tod Regan. He was too seriously bent upon his professional duties which half a dozen men had turned to watch him perform. They were only mildly interested, and so was Tod. This job was so easy that he almost smiled, and the result was that he was foolishly careless. His guard was low. He was only thinking of what he might give and not of what he might receive, which is a charitable but often a silly attitude in this hard world.

The result was that a fist flicked out to the point of his chin. It was so fast that it looked like a light blow, but it clicked against the bone like a hammer head. Tod rose and then dropped heavily back on his heels, while the man in the wolfskins stepped in and turned his back. His arms reached behind his head and caught poor Tod by the back of his. After this, the stranger leaned forward, and Tod, irresistibly impelled, sailed over the wolfskins, struck the door, and went on through it into the outer night, leaving his glorious reputation behind him.

CHAPTER
ELEVEN

Man to Man

If Calmont had seen that done, he would have recognized the hammer hold instantly. Calmont was not there, but a sufficient crowd saw and admired a new technique. Young Massey could have had twenty drinks without asking, but he disregarded waved hands, cheerful salutations, and even the bar itself as he marched back to find the office of the doctor.

That good man sat behind a small window past which the faces which were his business filed at this time every day. Massey did not wait. The red-faced Swedish cook was about to step into place at the window when he came up.

"You have my place in line, I think," said Massey and smiled at the Swede as he stepped in front of him to the window.

The Swede was a cook only by accident and balled his great fist instinctively. However, he did it slowly enough to give himself time for reflection and, when he reflected on that smile and saw the wolfskins, he changed his mind. Those who think twice live longer lives in the arctic.

The doctor, when he saw the stranger there, did not ask who he was. He never had to ask questions because he sat there to tell, not to demand.

"I was just wondering," said Massey, "if you have a job for me as a bouncer."

"Give your name to the red-headed bartender," said Doctor Borg. "I'm full up." He waved his hand for the stranger to pass on.

"I beg your pardon," said Massey, "but a vacancy has just occurred."

"The hell there has," said the doctor without emotion. "What one of my boys has taken time off?"

"I don't know his name," answered Massey. "A big young man with very black eyebrows . . . ?"

"That's Tod Regan. You're drunk," said Doctor Borg.

"Aye," said Massey, "he had that sort of look."

"Break his hand on somebody?" asked the doctor, interested more than usual.

"No, his head," said Massey.

"On what?"

"The door," said Massey.

"He broke his head on the door? Whatcha talkin' about, and who'n hell are you?"

The doctor was growing impatient. He was almost attached to Tod Regan — he had enjoyed at second hand, as it were, so many of the beatings that young man had delivered at a small charge in The Joint.

"He didn't like my dog," said Massey, "and he was about to throw me out on account of him."

"Did you bring a dog in here?" asked the doctor. A vein stood out in his forehead.

87

"I take my dog everywhere," said Massey.

The anger of the doctor rose so high that he stood up. He was big. He towered above Massey outside the office window. "Nobody sent that dog out?" he demanded.

"My dog is the exception that proves the rule," said Massey gently.

"There ain't any exception," said the doctor. "You got the dog with you now?"

"Yes," said Massey.

"And Regan let you get in?"

"He made a little argument," said Massey.

"I reckon that he did. With his fists he'd do his arguing, and I don't see no mark on you!"

"I had to throw him through the door," said Massey.

"You lie," said the doctor without heat. "He'd eat you in two bites."

"Come out to the door," said Massey, "and I'll show you how it happened."

He smiled still. He was always smiling. A second vein now stood out on the forehead of the doctor. However, he was a man not above pride, it might be said, but beyond it. He had fought so many times, had left so many crushed lives or ended ones behind him, that there was no point to him in sheer battle — chiefly because it might spoil his business at The Joint. Fighting was to him a luxury. He saved it for his days off, and this was the middle of his business hour.

"Call Bob," he said.

Bob came. He was small. He looked like a building, and apparently he felt like one. He could only talk through one corner of his mouth, it seemed, and even in that corner one saw two teeth missing and a broken one.

"Where's Regan?" asked the doctor.

"Regan, aw . . . he got hot and went out to get cool."

"Where?"

"In the snow."

"What's the matter with him?"

"Aw, nothin' but a cracked head and a sprained neck and a twisted back and a lump on his chin," said Bob.

"How did he get that?"

Bob said explicitly: "He got the lump on his chin from a right cross. He got the sprained neck when this guy slaps a hammer hold on him. He cracked his head when he hit the front door and busted it open, and he twisted his back when he fell into the snow."

The doctor looked back at the applicant for a position.

"You reckon to work in The Joint?" he said.

"I'd try to please," said Massey

"With a dog along?"

"He'd be a help."

"The dog would help?"

"Yes, he's that kind of a dog."

"Help at what?"

"Fetching and carrying."

The doctor sat back in his chair. He always had plenty of time to spend with real characters.

"I'd like to see that dog," he said.

"Here!" replied Massey and slapped the small shelf which extended outside the office window.

Upon that narrow ledge leaped Alexander the Great and, since it was too small to permit him to stand there and retain his balance, he acquired more room by thrusting his head through the window and snarling bitterly at the doctor.

The latter regarded him with a critical eye. "That's a young dog," he said.

"Yes," said Massey.

"You've trained him?"

"I've trained him."

"You only get half pay if you come on with a dog along with you."

"What's half pay?"

"Ten dollars."

"I'll take that, then."

The doctor drummed his big fingers upon the desk surface. "Who are you?" he asked.

"I'm a man with a dog."

"Whatcha want here?"

"A place to wait."

"For what?"

"Christmas," said Massey gravely.

The other nodded, as though he had heard exactly this sort of talk before.

"I'll tell you the name of the dog, though," said Massey.

"Let's hear it, then."

"It's Alexander the Great."

"He's great, is he?"

"Yeah, he's great."

"At what?"

"Doing what he's told . . . by me."

"He's a one-man dog?"

"That's what he is."

The doctor leaned forward. "Wrestling holds ain't the only thing that we need," he said.

"I wear a Colt," said Massey.

"Can you use it?"

"Yeah, I can use it."

At this, the doctor actually smiled. "I think I can use you, young feller."

"Thanks," said Massey.

"I might take you on at full pay."

"That's still better."

"Will this dog behave?"

"He'll do what I tell him, and nothing else."

"Go out and see the red-headed bartender and tell him that you want a black cap."

"I don't wear a uniform," said Massey unexpectedly.

"Hey?"

"I don't wear a uniform."

"Are you too good for that?" growled the owner angrily.

"Yeah," said Massey with that cold smile of his which was a new expression on his face.

The doctor looked him over with the utmost gravity. "You're wanted on the outside, I reckon," he said.

Massey smiled again. "No," he said, "I'm wanted for nothing."

"Is that gospel?"

"That's gospel."

"All right, then, you go out and tell Redhead that you're on the payroll as a bouncer. How long d'you think you'll stay?"

"Until I've done my job."

"Look here, son, are you a spider in a web?"

"Aye," said Massey, "and this is the right web to draw my fly."

Suddenly the doctor leaned back in his chair, and a strange thing happened. His straight line of lips parted. His head went back. His mouth opened to a tremendous cavern. His eyes closed. His thick jowls wrinkled, and he laughed.

There were two men inside the office. One was Bob, and the other was a poor, mangy-looking clerk. Both of them stared as though the earth had opened at their feet. That sound of Doctor Borg's laughter grated like rusty hinges. It was a note that no one in Nome ever before had heard from his lips.

"God," said the doctor, "if you don't make me feel young again! Go, get away from here and see Redhead."

CHAPTER
THIRTEEN

The Talking Dog

When Massey went to the designated bartender, he found as tough a man as one would expect even in The Joint of Doctor Borg. But Cliff Anson was a smiling, pleasant-mannered fellow. Massey was now also a smiling man. He recognized in the other something of the cold steel which he felt in his own heart. Cliff Anson offered his hand and a drink. Massey took the hand and not the drink.

"Don't you trust liquor?" asked Anson genially.

"I don't trust myself," said Massey. "I want to get the hang of this job, Anson, and to have my name put on the payroll. Can you manage that?"

"I'll do both," said Anson. "Your job is to keep wandering through the rooms spotting trouble and throwing it out the window before it explodes. The doctor ain't so interested in bouncers that stop a big fight as he is in bouncers that check out people before they get into a fight at all."

"He wants mind-readers, then," Massey suggested.

"No, but you get a line on people pretty quick, if you're on your job. You foller the folks in Nome, and soon you get to know the friends and enemies. Mix mighty little enemies together, and pretty soon you got stuff that will blow the roof off the house. Then you can usually spot drunks that are heading toward a fight and sometimes, if you step soft enough, you'll overhear what's meant to be a private word that will tell you what to expect at a table."

"What about the dance-hall end of the business?" asked Massey.

"That's where you have to step extra light. There'll be a little trouble in there for a week but, when it starts, it's likely to mean killing."

After that, Massey took on his duties enthusiastically. He often went back to the white, lean, smiling face of Cliff Anson with the fiery hair above it. Anson knew a great deal. It was not for nothing that he was executive lieutenant for the doctor. He could generally tell the history of visitors at a glance if they were old-timers in Nome, and for strangers he had a peculiar ability in reading character. There was a studious, constant concern in the glances which he threw toward the door when people entered. He told Massey a good deal which simplified his task as bouncer. After the first evening, they even became friends, as far as the cold heart of Anson could admit of friendship.

On that first night an overly enthusiastic partaker of the twenty-five-cent brew picked up an extra bottle and tried to split Anson's skull. He would have succeeded, since Anson's back was turned, but by the grace of good luck Massey was near and laid the length of his revolver barrel alongside the skull of the drunkard. It chimed merrily on that thick head, and the man went down. For this service Anson made no rendering of thanks. His eye remained as frosted as ever when he met the eye of Massey, but later on in the evening he said: "What's your drift here, stranger?"

"I'm doing a little waiting," said Massey.

"For a face, eh?"

"Yes. That's it." Then he added: "What are you here for?"

"To have my back against the wall," said Anson with his usual cold smile.

"But you're turned away from the crowd half of the time," said Massey, suddenly seeing that Anson was being literal.

"I have the mirror in front of me to show me what they're doing then."

"What about the fellow with the bottle?"

"Why, I was pulling my gun as he raised the bottle, but the hammer caught in my coat lining." He was as calm as could be saying this. "I'm waiting for murder, and it's pretty sure to come quick. Fixed here, the way I am, I have a chance to dodge it for a while. That's all." He touched a thin red scar on the side of his temple. "That was the time before," said he. "Last week it was."

"D'you mean," exclaimed Massey, horrified in spite of himself by this remark, "that they're trying to get you, and you don't know who?"

"I don't know who."

"That fellow with the bottle . . . you think he wasn't just a drunk?"

"Of course, he wasn't just a drunk. He was one of them, all right!"

"Why didn't you let me know? He ought to be in jail."

"Yeah?" said the bartender carelessly. "I dunno. The more heads that I lop off, the hotter the fire would get. No, I'll just go on taking chances, I reckon. How's the dog coming along?"

This ended the serious part of the conversation, but Massey went off almost bewildered by the complexity of the situation of this man who knew that murder must be looking him in the face every day of his life, but who yet could not tell what face it was wearing.

It made his own position and task seem ridiculously simple. He wondered what power lay behind these attacks upon the bartender, and he could not help guessing that there was likely to be an adequate reason for them. If ever there was a man with the face of the coldly calculating criminal, it was Cliff Anson. He helped, however, to make the new bouncer's position an easy one from the start.

It had seemed to Massey a spectacular way to take his revenge, but a very good one. With the dog shown to the public every day, it was certain that Calmont, if he were in Nome, would hear of Alec the Great's performances. He knew Calmont's nature well enough to be sure that no power in the world could keep him from trying to reclaim the dog which belonged to him. To meet Calmont there before the crowd, to beat him and humiliate and crush him before a thousand pairs of eyes, that was the plan of Massey.

It was also necessary that he should establish in the eyes of all men his claim to the dog, and that could only be done before numbers. So he waited there in The Joint night after night, until he began to despair of finding Calmont. He began to suspect that the other had pulled out of Nome so as to be farther away from what he must have considered his murdered man.

In the meantime, there was plenty of employment. He had his hands full, and Alexander the Great was occupied in all four feet and his teeth as well. He became such a favorite that he could have drunk nothing but wine and eaten nothing but sweet-meats if Massey had chosen to let him. But it was not hard to teach Alec to refuse food from all hands except his own.

It was at this time that there grew up the superstition, widespread to this day, that Alec the Great could understand human speech. There were hundreds and thousands of men in Nome who vowed that the dog had the wits of a human — or of a demon. They were rather inclined to accredit him with the latter. This strange suggestion, much more remarkable than the legend of the thinking horse in Germany, grew up in the following manner, and for the following cause.

Deeper than all other lessons, poor Alec the Great had learned the meaning of anger in the human voice. What the words might be, of course, he could not tell, but the note of anger itself was brilliantly engraved on his memory. During the earliest months of his life, there never had been a harsh word between the two partners. There never was a single inflection that seemed to show an enmity, for the pair were such old friends and such wise ones that they avoided disagreeable words. Therefore, when on the day which was the beginning of the end the dog for the first time heard a snarling tone come into the voices of the two, he had stopped and cocked his ear as at a miracle. It was a thing unprecedented. It was almost as though two new beings were presented to his eye.

He learned familiarly the same sound when Calmont, in a fury of impatient anger, had spoken to him and cursed him during the season of lessons. Finally, he had heard the harshest and the loudest yells of anger. But the undertone snarl was the thing with which he was most familiar and which was printed with the profoundest shudder in his soul. It was this which gave him his uncanny reputation in Nome, more than all of his tricks, his beauty, his courage, and the rest. Sensible men swore that the brute had communicated with either angel or demon.

On the very first night, as Alec trotted across the floor ahead of his master, he had spotted with his keen ears to the left of him the soft-pitched snarl of angry men. There are various pitches of fury. That which was heard so often at the bar was a roar as loud as a column of soaring fire and as irresistible. Sometimes from the tables there was a ringing word or two, usually in curses. It was too late, by far, to interfere then with the troublemakers. But the beginning of rage is almost without exception the cold, snarling murmur which may be reduced to the most polite softness but which has one quality, loud or soft, in man, woman, or in child. That was the sound which was heard by

Alexander the Great in his first walk through the rooms.

He halted and turned his head directly toward the corner table. That table was almost lost in dimness, but Massey, straining his eyes, could make out the attitude of the two men and saw that they were stiffly strained. Men about to strike are apt to be in that pose, leaning a little forward. He made for the pair and came up in time to hear the last nameless insult, whispered no louder than a most vital secret. Straightway, he took those gentlemen by the arms and led them to the door.

"You'll have more room to drop each other!" he told them.

They were utterly amazed by this interruption. They slipped off into the night in opposite directions, the cold air having blown the liquor and the murder out of their hearts.

That was not the last time the hand of Massey fell like fate on the arm of some man in an ugly humor. He did not always make sure that an actual fight was in the air. Sometimes the thing was much too subtle for that. But he could very well be sure that only one sound would make Alec the Great halt suddenly with a quiver of his ears. Usually Massey could step up to the table and tell them quietly that they were being watched. It was enough. There was a rule in The Joint that bouncers opened fire the instant they saw a gun drawn. So these quiet little reminders were enough to prevent many a budding fight.

On the second night Massey was cursed and told to go about his business by a powerful young miner.

About his business, accordingly, he went, and the youth went out the door via the same hammer lock which had almost sprained the backbone of Tod Regan. After that, Massey was a known man for his own qualities as well as those of his dog.

CHAPTER
FOURTEEN

A Question of Ownership

In a sense, it was a peculiarly delightful interim in the hard life of Massey. He was in from the bitterest privation and the near shadow of death, and here were warmth, ease, comfort, good food, and admiration for the beauty and the wise ways of Alexander the Great. Massey could not help showing him off at every opportunity, like a child with a new toy. Sometimes Alec walked along with tiny little steps on his hind feet alone, like the silly gait of a toe dancer. Sometimes he went on his forepaws only. Sometimes he was seen carrying his master's hat before him. When charitable organizations wanted to take up a collection for the unemployed, they soon learned to give a wooden-handled bucket into the teeth of Alec, for his bright eyes and wagging tail, as he went about among the tables, persuaded more ounces out of money belts than all the human eloquence in the world.

By the third night of their stay with Doctor Borg, Alec showed that he was something more than a decoration. Two men ejected the night before by

Massey loaded up with bad whiskey in another place and returned for vengeance. They came at Massey shoulder to shoulder, and Massey took his gun butt to one and sent the dog at the legs of the second. In truest wolf style, Alec the Great floored the rascal and stood over him with his paws on the man's breast, ready at a word to slash his throat from ear to ear. It was immediately after this event that a man offered Massey twenty-five hundred dollars for Alec, and the offer alarmed Massey without tempting him. Twenty-five-hundred-dollar dogs need a bodyguard.

He took this high bidder aside and said to him seriously: "I'd sell this dog to you, but you couldn't do a thing with him. He's a one-man dog. If I sold him to you tonight, you'd come back gunning for me tomorrow."

"Hold on," said the dog handler. "I've had about twenty strings in my day, and I've had my hand on Alec's head my own self."

"Aye," said Massey, "and did you watch his eye while it was resting there?"

The other, without a word, placed his strong hand on the head of the dog and thoughtfully looked into the eyes of the Husky. They were like green glass! At this he stepped back and nodded to Massey.

"You're a white man, stranger," he said. "That dog knows only one boss, I reckon."

The story went the rounds, and Massey was more envied but less jealously than before.

So he came to that night which was to tell the tale of the ownership of Alec the Great, once and for all. He had the word from Cliff Anson behind the bar, as he paused there in answer to a signal.

"Deputy Sheriff Sam Binney is in here," said Anson. "He's just come in with a husky fellow that has the look of wanting trouble. Binney's a mean one . . . up to anything. Take a look at that pair. They're over around the corner, sitting in a poker hand, but the cards don't seem to mean much to them."

Cards did not mean much to them. They sat at the table, when Massey came in view, as though they cared more about wasting time than making money. Sam Binney was six inches over six feet in height, narrow as a rail, and tough as a hickory switch. He had a great long nose and buck teeth which gave him a half-amiable, half-foolish look. As a matter of fact, he was as hard as nails, and only smiled as he talked because he could not help it. His face never was still, since he was continually struggling to cover his long upper teeth.

Deputy Sheriff Binney would have been rather an aspirant to jail than to a legal office in any place other than Nome, but here men were more "open minded." One gunman was considered as good as another at this time, if he were willing to take the oath to defend the law. So Binney, in spite of his long and lurid record, was duly installed. He was said to wear two pairs of guns under his lower clothes, and in a pinch he could be depended upon to use a knife like a Mexican, both for science and bloodthirstiness. The fighting qualities of Sam Binney were celebrated, but they were as nothing, whether with knife, gun, or hand, compared with the repute of the broad-shouldered dark-faced man who sat at the table beside him. For that man was Arnold Calmont.

Alec the Great, at the first glimpse of his owner, leaped fairly behind the legs of Massey. Then Calmont turned his head and stared at the man and the dog with a deathless malice. The long silence in the winter igloo, and the competition which had begun as such a simple thing now showed this as the ripened fruit. As for Massey, he looked at Calmont as though he were seeing not the face but the bleeding heart of the other.

"There's your man," said Calmont, and pointed toward Massey.

Tall Sam Binney arose, unlinking his height bit by bit. Then he strode toward the new bouncer of The Joint. Calmont came close to him, a little behind and to the side, walking like a hunter who fears to make a noise, his eyes upon his goal. Massey knew with perfect surety that Calmont would die with the greatest joy in the world if only he could send his enemy to death before him.

This sense of the blind hatred of Calmont qualified the savage detestation with which Massey looked on the wolf-faced man. Not that it made him hate him less, but it forced more thought and calmness into his mind. He remembered, as he had long ago decided while he sat in the smoke of the igloo fire, that merely to dash the life out of Calmont with the stroke of a bullet would be as nothing. So he stared at Calmont and tried to see the future, and how he should deal with the man then.

Sam Binney stood before him. "Your name Massey?" he asked, scowling blackly.

"That appears to be my name," agreed Massey.

"I'm dep'ty sheriff, name of Sam Binney, and I'm arrestin' you in the name of the law."

He had a hand on the revolver beneath his coat as he spoke. His eyes searched the eyes of Massey deeply, looking for the first flicker of the fire of resistance. Resistance there was none. Massey simply smiled back at the tall deputy sheriff.

"What's the charge, sheriff?" he asked cheerfully.

Sam Binney had a large vocabulary, sometimes used very loosely. He was fond of talking, and he elaborated on every possible occasion.

"This here," said Sam, "is kind of a cross between grand larceny and goddamned battery and malice aforethought . . . which it's a mighty serious charge, Massey, and right from now on every word that you say is likely to be used against you. Shove out your hands. I've got a set of bracelets for you to wear."

"I don't mind the law," said Massey, "but I'd like to know exactly what I'm charged with having done."

"You swiped Calmont's dog, and you damn' well know that you did!" said Sam Binney. "Now, shove out your hands or I'll . . ."

"Hold on," said Massey. "You're a reasonable man, Sam, I know. I've heard that you've a good, logical head on your shoulders. If you look around you for a few seconds, you'll see that you're not going to take me out of The Joint without a good deal of trouble. Look about and use your eyes."

Sam Binney for a sharp second suspected the speaker of trickery but, when he looked right and left, he saw that there was truth in the warning. A black-capped bouncer stood keenly alert against the wall at one side, and around the corner of the bar appeared the lounging form of the red-headed bartender, Cliff Anson. A known man was Cliff, to say nothing of the other two.

"I kinda hope," said Binney, "that you ain't gonna put yourself in the position of resistin' the law, my young feller?"

"That's a serious offense," said Massey. "But about the stealing of the dog . . . this is the one that Calmont means, I suppose?"

"You know it's the one I mean," broke in Calmont in his snarling voice.

Alexander the Great growled behind the legs of his teacher, where he was skulking.

"Is this the dog that Calmont is talking about?" said Massey politely to Binney.

The deputy sheriff scowled more blackly than before.

"Why, you certainly hear him say so," he said.

"I can't hear him talk," said Massey. "It's a peculiarity of my ears that I can't understand what a snake says, Binney."

The deputy sheriff stepped back a little, glanced askance at Calmont, and saw on the face of the latter a hungry grin of uttermost rage and hatred. Binney stepped in again.

"There ain't any use, Massey," he said. "I've heard a right promisin' lot of things about what you've done here in The Joint, but this here is a plain arrest, and you gotta plainly come along with me."

This conversation had lasted long enough to attract attention, and a crowd had gathered at a discreet distance to either side of the central group. If Binney and Calmont were known men, so was Massey, to say nothing of the dog. Hopes and expectations ran high. Inevitably, there were a few soft-voiced bets, here and there and then the droning, drawling, loose-lipped voice of a drunkard, saying: "My money on Mashey. Whatcha say, boys? Got hundred dollahs fo' Mashey . . ."

The doctor suddenly appeared, tall hat, high-heeled boots, and all. He approached the center of argument with a long and heavy stride.

"Now, what's all this here damned nonsense about?" he demanded.

Even Binney looked with a certain amount of respect on the celebrated proprietor of The Joint.

"Here's a bouncer of yours that's charged with the stealin' of a dog, Doctor," said Binney. "I gotta have that man and take him away with me. Sorry to bother you, but it's gotta be done."

"It's gotta, has it?" said the doctor. "Well, we'll see about that. You, Massey . . . you steal that dog?"

"You ask the dog if I own him," said Massey.

The doctor scowled. He did not like frivolous answers.

"He's gone and trained that dog right slick, by what I hear," said Sam Binney, "but that don't make Alec his. Belongs to Calmont, here, a friend of mine and an honest man."

"He looks honest," said the proprietor. "He looks honest like a hungry wolf is honest. Is that dog your dog, Calmont?"

"Yeah," said Calmont. "That's my dog."

"You can prove it?"

"Yeah, I can prove it."

"We'll hold a court right here," said the doctor soberly. "Massey's a mighty useful man to me, and his dog is a mighty lot more useful than Massey. We'll make a court."

"Who'll be the judge?" asked Binney doubtfully.

"I will, you loon!" said the doctor.

CHAPTER
FIFTEEN

Hard but Square

"What kind of law is this?" asked Calmont savagely. "I want a judge to decide this."

Binney shrugged his shoulders. "You get a new gent to do the arrestin', then," he said. "The doctor is hard, but he's square. Everybody in Nome knows that. He'll give you a square deal, if it's a square deal that you want."

Calmont tapped the deputy sheriff on the shoulder with fingers as hard and as heavy as steel. "You and me, we'll have a talk about this, a little later on," he said.

"Sure we will," answered Binney readily, "night or day. I'm the man for you, but I ain't gonna try to mob the whole Joint for you, my son! Talk up and tell the doctor your proofs. You'll find him square."

"We'll sit right now and hear out this case," said the doctor. "C'mon into the dance hall where we'll have room, for there's gonna be a crowd that'll want to hear this case!"

He was right. Everybody in The Joint wanted to be close to the arguments and to the judgment. The rumor flying out onto the street — since rumor can pierce walls however thick — brought in fresh crowds to the

109

great advantage of the bar and the great detriment of the dance floor because wet snow was stamped onto it from scores of rough-shod feet.

In the center of the dance-hall wall, on the east side, there was a sort of red-plush throne where the duly elected queen of the dance used to sit later in the night or on festival occasions. On this throne the doctor assumed his place as judge and solemnized the occasion by pulling his great hat further forward upon his brow, giving his appearance a more weird and unearthly caste than before. Packed around the sides and pouring into the center of the big room were all the people of Nome who had been permitted to jam their way through the front door this evening.

Calmont and Massey faced each other. Calmont was black with his hate. Massey was smiling.

"You wanta get this dog," said the doctor as judge. "Now, what's your lingo, stranger?"

"I got the father and I got the mother of this here dog," said Calmont. "I can show 'em."

"D'you admit that?" asked the judge of Massey.

"I admit nothing," said Massey.

"Well, that's reasonable too," said the judge. "How you gonna prove that you got the pa and ma of Alec the Great yonder?"

"Well," said Calmont, grinning with satisfaction, "I reckon that the dog was born in our igloo this winter, and I reckon that my Chubby was the only bitch in our two strings."

This statement caused a catching of breath all around the room. There was no doubt that Calmont had scored heavily, and the peculiar smile of detestation with which Massey looked at his former bunkie grew colder and colder every moment. Massey was favored by the crowd, if not for his own sake, then at least for the sake of the dog.

"What have you got to say to that?" said the judge, Doctor Borg.

"I say nothing," said Massey gloomily.

"Not sayin' nothin'," remarked the doctor, "is the same as admittin' that he's right."

Massey was silent, staring at Calmont and Calmont at him.

"Then," said the doctor with terrible calm and logic, "if the pup was born to one of Calmont's string, Alec the Great, so far as I can see, ain't your dog at all."

Massey looked at the dog and then at the dog's owner. "Dogs can be bought," said Massey.

"You claim that you bought him, eh?" said the doctor.

"I do."

"He lies," said Calmont.

"Wait a minute," said the doctor. "The first of you that gets impolite, I'm gonna chuck him out the door, and he'll never get inside again to lay hands on Alec the Great. He's a good dog, and a damn' smart dog, and he's worth a pile of any man's money that can run him. How much did you pay for him?"

Massey answered slowly with a most deadly effect: "I paid for him with blood."

It seemed as though Calmont did not dream that the other would humiliate himself by admitting how he had been beaten and left tied up like a cur. Now he started violently and sneered, as he looked at Massey.

"What you mean?" demanded Borg. "Did he offer to trade you the dog for his blood, or something?"

Then Massey, in words which never left the minds of those who heard him, told the tale of that tragedy.

"We were buddies, Borg. We're old-timers. We've done the Klondike, and Circle City, and the rest, down to Nome, and last summer we went up to the circle prospecting. This pup was born there and, when he began to like me better than he liked Calmont, Calmont began to hate me. Finally, he tied the dog up, when it was able to all but talk to me. He wouldn't let me come near it.

"We had a spell of silent treatment. We put our guns outside on the roof. We laid the axe and the knives there, too. Yet every time that I heard him turn over at night, I felt sure that he was going to try to steal across and strangle me. There were just the pair of us, and the dog tied to the bunk . . . by him."

He stepped aside suddenly, as he said this, and pointed full at Calmont. Alec the Great, as though at an order, bounded half way toward his owner and stood suddenly revealed in the middle of the floor, showing all his teeth in a most evil grin of hatred. It does not seem much, but the effect of this rush at a man by a dog was so horrible that two or three of the dance girls shrieked, and there was a general stir even among the hardy fellows listening.

"I came back one day," said Massey, slowly lowering the arm which had pointed out Calmont — for on Calmont's face there was no remorse but only a smile of the most brutal satisfaction — "and found him beating Alec. We fought then. I fought him fair and square and was beating him, but he picked up a club and hammered me across the head with it."

"You lie!" shouted Calmont.

Massey smiled as he went on: "I have the mark of it on my head, Calmont. Then you tied me hand and foot while I was unconscious, and you took the stove, the food, and the clothes. You cleaned out the igloo. You spoiled and threw away the salmon that you didn't want to carry off with you. You left me there to die of cold and the madness of being alone."

Someone groaned. There was not a man there, perhaps, who did not know the old horror and dread of being deserted by one's traveling partner in the middle of the night. They stared back at Calmont, and they saw Calmont grinning with a savage joy.

"Yeah," said Calmont, "and I'm telling you I'm mighty pleased with what I done."

"Now, then," went on Massey, "after I'd lain a good while, some wolves sniffed their way through the door of the igloo. They were hungry enough to eat human meat, and I was half a second from my finish when in comes my friend. Not that one . . . but the dog. He scattered those wolves. He chewed through the thongs that held my hands. He'd escaped from Calmont and came straight back to me. He was ready to die with me, and how I managed to keep going and make fire and snare rabbits, and how I finally found the place where Calmont had thrown my guns . . . that doesn't matter. What's important to me is only that the dog came back to see me through. I've told you that I've bought that dog with blood, and I say it again. Is there anybody here that says no to me?"

"I say no," said Calmont.

"Words never would answer between us," said Massey utterly calm.

His meaning became suddenly plain to every one in the room. He hungered and thirsted after the life of Calmont. Have it he must.

"You hear him talk," said Calmont to Borg. "You gotta see that he's admitted that the dog's mine."

"He'd choke sooner than take even a fish from your hands, and you know it!" exclaimed Massey. "What can you do with him? But he'd walk a tight rope as wide as this room for me, and you know it."

The judge, dropping his chin upon one ponderous hand, considered these conflicting claims in a silence so profound that one forgot the evil in his face and became aware of the judicial effect only.

"What good would the dog do you, Calmont?" he asked at last.

"He'd do me the good of spitin' Massey every minute that he stayed in my hands!"

This frank avowal caused a little tinkling outcry from the women, and the men growled. But it was not in total disapproval of Calmont, for there was something about the thoroughness of his hate that caused understanding if not sympathy.

114

"He'll never be likely," said the doctor, "to do you no good in a team or around your house, except to tear your throat for you, if he gets a fair chance?"

"The dog's mine," said Calmont, "and I'll have what's my own."

"Wait a minute," said Borg. "The dog's yours by right in his birth, but it ain't a sensible thing that you're talking about, man. That there dog is worth five or six thousand dollars in hard cash to me, right here in The Joint. He's the best entertainer that we got! Now, man, lemme buy that dog off of you at the top figure and go along about your business."

It was an astonishing offer from Borg. Not a man there but felt surprise and pleasure tingle down his spine at this generous announcement for all knew, somehow, that Borg never intended to take the dog away from its teacher.

"I'll see you damned," said Calmont. "I want justice, and I'm gonna have it, Borg, and if I don't get it . . . I'll take it!"

A very big and ugly man he looked as he stood there, his anger and hate swaying him a little.

"The dog's yours," said Borg, "and justice is what you oughta have, and justice is what really I aim to give you."

Calmont laughed and stepped toward the dog, and the hair of Alec the Great bristled. No one breathed but watched the young Husky, the savage grin of Calmont, and the white, terrible face of Massey.

"You oughta have the dog," went on Borg, "but you got no right to what he knows. He's been taught and

115

trained and learned by Massey. Massey and him have been through death together. Speak to him, Massey!"

"Alec!" said the man hoarsely.

Alec slipped back to his side and, sitting down, looked up into his face with unutterable joy and love.

"You oughta have Alec," said Borg, "but you got no right to that. You gotta right to kill Alec even, but you got no right to kill that!"

He pointed as he spoke to the pair. In fact, the affection between the man and the beast seemed as real as sunshine.

"And so," said the doctor, "I've gotta give a judgment; and I'm gonna give one. It's gonna displease you both a damned lot, but you'll likely take it from me."

CHAPTER
SIXTEEN

Verdict

Of this famous judgment of the doctor's men still speak, and there are a hundred at least who can repeat the exact words of it, which were as follows:

"Here's the case, ladies and gents. Here's two men that claim one dog. Money can't buy that dog. It's a matter of hate and love. No matter how the dog goes . . . to Calmont, or to Massey . . . the end looks to be the same. If Massey keeps the dog, Calmont is gonna burn until he gets a good chance to cut Massey's throat. If Calmont gets the dog, Massey will get Calmont's life as sure as duck hawks can fly and ferrets run down rabbit holes. Now, what I say is that the two of them ought to be stopped. What I say is that the two of them are gonna be stopped. Here, you, Calmont, if you got this here dog, would you lift up your head and your hand and look the boys in this room in the face and swear that you'd never try to kill Massey?"

Calmont's lip curled. His eyes glittered with emotion. But finally he said: "All right. Gimme the dog, and I wouldn't mind swearing!"

"And you, Massey?" asked the doctor.

In spite of the question which already had been propounded in his hearing to his rival and enemy, Massey started, stammered, and then burst out furiously: "No, no, no! Whether it's with the dog or not . . . Calmont, you're going to die, and I'm going to taste the killing of you."

There was something so grotesquely horrible in the word *taste* that the hardiest old-timers in that room quaked somewhat inwardly.

"All right," said the doctor, "if you ain't gonna swear to that, take the dog, Calmont."

"Wait!" shouted Massey.

"Wait!" commanded the imperturbable doctor to Calmont.

Massey, in the meantime, was in a visible agony which made him writhe and sent drops of sweat rolling down his face. The salt of his daily existence had been the sweet daydream of murdering Calmont. His disturbance was so great that Alec, noticing it, licked the hand of his teacher and whined a little. At this, a sentimental girl burst into a loud boo-hooing, and Massey surrendered with a groan.

"All right, then," said the doctor. "Each of you hold up your right hand and repeat this here oath after me. Whoever of you gets the dog, he swears by his honor, if he's honest and by his manhood, if he's a man, that he'll never try for the life of the other. Now, swear that after me."

Hesitantly, with pauses, they took the oath, Massey for love of the dog, purely and simply, and Calmont because it was only by possession of the dog that he felt

118

he would be able to torment his old partner thoroughly enough.

"Now, then, for the judgment," said the doctor, nodding. "The dog belongs mostly to Calmont, but Massey has a right on him by my seein' of it."

There was a vast shout at this, showing clearly where the sympathies of the crowd were located.

"Shut yer faces!" said the doctor, rearing himself up straighter upon his throne. "It ain't to please you but to please justice that I'm settin' here. The dog is gonna do the judgin' himself!"

Calmont turned yellowish white.

"Massey's brought the test on himself," said the doctor. "He said that there dog of his could walk a forty-foot tight rope. Well, we've seen that dog do a pile of smart things but a tight rope I reckon he can't walk. If he can, Massey gets the dog. But if the dog should happen to fall off, he goes to Calmont."

Massey groaned loudly, his self-control almost gone.

"Borg," he said, "why don't you give him to Calmont outright and stop the fooling?"

"I stick by my judgment," said the doctor. "When I once make up my mind . . ."

"Will you give him three tries?" begged Massey. "He's walked a short rod but never a rope . . . and forty feet . . . Borg, for heaven's sake, give him and me a chance!"

The iron face of the doctor did not change.

"Tie a rope from the bar rail to the window and make the dog walk it. Otherwise, he goes to Calmont. I've said it. I stick to it. And one trial is all that he gets!"

The apparent injustice of this trial brought many murmurs, but the excitement even increased as they went into the big bar and gaming room and the length of a heavy, rawhide lariat was strung the full distance of forty feet and then pulled tight to the trembling point.

Massey, while this was being done, walked up and down restlessly, trying to gather courage. He put poor Alec the Great through a few tricks simply to rouse his expectations and steady his own nerves and, now as the crowd was placed and the rapid betting ended, he waved Alec up to the top of the bar and took his own place at the farther end of the line.

He called to him then, cheerfully, pleasantly, though a very sick face was that of Massey in his suffering and his fear, while Alec the Great, well aware of what was expected of him, tried the lariat with one paw and then sniffed the bottom of his foot for information about this new game. This brought a great shout of mirth from the crowd, and Alec, lifting his head, laughed back in his own bright way.

"Poor boy, poor pup," said Cliff Anson, "he don't know what depends on this here draw!"

Called again, the dog suddenly stepped out along the rope, not with the care which he showed in walking even the shortest and steadiest rail, but as though he actually felt no fear about the tenuous footing which the rope afforded to him. He glided straight out fully fifteen or twenty feet, until he was almost in the exact center of the rope. He moved with such skill that it seemed as though he must have thoroughly rehearsed for this.

However, good beginnings do not always mean good endings. In the center of the rope, a vibration began, and the dog staggered. Poor Massey cried out tensely, like a dying man, and Alec the Great, by way of answer, gave one pitifully small waggle of his tail.

He was terribly intent on his work, and the swaying and shuddering of the rope seemed actually to increase. Massey, his face a mask of dread and of hope, stood bent over with his arms stretched rigidly out to either side, in his effort to help the dog balance. Cliff Anson said afterward that Massey looked like a mother watching her child burn alive. Calmont, with a snarling satisfaction, watched the reeling dog and the staggering rope.

And yet Alec the Great did not fall! He went on. The rope quieted. He was suddenly six feet from the outstretched arms of Massey and the end of the journey, and people were standing on tiptoe with tense and eager expectation, when he began to stagger on the rope again. He was close to the end now, however. He made two or three little reeling steps, then hurled himself forward and barely was scooped up by the iron grip of Massey.

There was a wild yell from Calmont that the dog had not finished the journey entirely unaided. The arms of Massey had shortened the distance. But a universal shout of rejoicing drowned this protest. There was a whirl of enthusiasm, and Massey was seen holding the big dog in his arms, regardless of how his face was licked, and whirling him in a wild joy and shouting.

Calmont was seen like a dark rock around which that enthusiasm boiled. He had only one want now and that was the life of Massey, but the doctor smiled with an iron self-content. He knew that he had been Solomon on this day.

Riding into Peril

Although he had written a short novel and a serial for Street & Smith's *Western Story Magazine* in late 1920, Frederick Faust's fiction did not become a major presence in the magazine until the next year. The Bull Hunter stories appeared that year, including "Outlaws All" with which this trio concludes, as well as the first of the Ronicky Doone serials. It was, incidentally, a convention of this publication's editorial policy in the 1920s that Western stories were often presumed to be set in the contemporary West so that no modern contrivance was really to be regarded as an anachronism. "Riding into Peril" appeared in *Western Story Magazine* in the issue dated November 19, 1921. This is the first time it has been reprinted.

CHAPTER ONE

Justice Bland's Plan

Let it be understood at the outset that no alibi is offered for the Kid, not even the oldest one — his youth. Young as he was, he was old enough to know better. In a word, he was nineteen. To those over thirty that seems mere infancy, but anyone under twenty can appreciate how really old nineteen is. Therefore we say again, and with emphasis, no alibi is offered: he was old enough to know better. Under no circumstances should he have broken jail.

But as to how he came to be in jail — well, that is quite another matter, and there are excuses in plenty. In the first place, he stood in his stockinged feet exactly the romantic height of six feet, and he had possessed that stature since his fifteenth year. In the second place, he was cursed with a crop of light-yellow hair, very thick and silken; his eyes were large and of the mildest blue; his features were delicately and well chiseled; his skin was a pearly white which the burning sun of the Southwest never had been able to tan, and his only color was, in time of excitement, a spot of pink which appeared and disappeared in the center of each cheek — in Jorgenville people called it "the Kid's red flag of danger!" In the third place, his name was Kantwell Irving Dangerfield, hence the sobriquet Kid.

Surely enough has been said to give a picture of one of those "pretty" youths who cause such hardy men as flourish in the West to smile, and smile broadly, and sometimes to sneer. Such terms as "mamma's boy" and "mamma's pet" came naturally to the tip of the tongue when the Kid appeared. Now, if the only people to associate with the Kid had been those old inhabitants of Jorgenville who really knew him, there would have been no trouble at all after he reached maturity and his qualities became known. But unfortunately Jorgenville was one of those tiny communities which are called towns by courtesy and not in fact. It lay where three important roads crossed, and there was a continual drift of strangers through it. Naturally there could not be a sign on every road coming in and going out: **Beware of the Kid!** The result was infinite complications — infinite indeed!

Ordinarily, the Kid would have been as harmless as his looks — that is, if he had been like the general run of folk. But he was not like the general run. He detested exercise above all things and was passionately devoted to sitting still and rolling cigarettes with his long, white fingers and to smoking them, one after the other. Indeed, he did not have to work at all because, though he was early left an orphan without close relations, he was also left the possessor of a large and prosperous estate handled by a large and prosperous manager who could have made money out of pasturing cows on a thistle patch. The Kid, therefore, was left master of his destiny and his time, so far as the workaday necessities of this vale of tears were concerned. He chose to spend his time in sitting.

It was an occupation that should have made him disgustingly fat and disgustingly flabby, but it did neither. There live, from time to time, singular individuals who are born strong and remain strong to their death day. Exercise is not needed; practice is not required to perfect the nice coordination of mind and nerve and muscle. Every college, for instance, has its legends of lazy, quiet fellows who never lifted a hand until their last year and then sauntered out on the football field because ennui drove them to it — and literally ripped and tore their way to fame and endless glory to the alma mater and endless bruises to the opposing teams. Kantwell Irving Dangerfield, in a word, was one of this type. Indeed, that lithe body, rippling in easy lines of strength up to the shoulders intended by Providence for striking and lifting, would have been sufficient advertisement in itself of trouble ahead. But, as has been said, he was cursed with that baby complexion and those large, mild blue eyes. Besides, a handsome man is despised instinctively by every other man.

Now, when all this is borne in mind and when the nature of Jorgenville's transients is further considered, it might be imagined that the Kid was the spark which set off many and many an explosion. In fact, he was just this. He had not only his cunningly devised muscles, but he also had three natural penchants. One was a love of man-killing broncos. Another was a hungry desire to use his fists, an art which he early mastered and of which he had even exerted himself to learn the fine points. The third was that dominating passion which, to a greater or less degree, must appear in every man. In the Kid that super passion was the love of guns, and more particularly of the long, heavy forty-five caliber Colt with which the Southwest has shot itself into history.

The exact nature of the spark which the Kid contributed to so many explosions may now, in some measure, be understood. Moreover, nature had furnished him with a face that roused the ire of other men and had completed the work of art by endowing him with other qualities that acted as a lure to brutality and bullying. When strangers sneered at him, he looked the other way. When they insulted him, he merely expressed a wish in the gentlest of voices that they betake themselves to other occupations. It was only when they cursed his "baby eyes" or laid hands on him that the Kid responded with action. The action was generally short. Usually it began and ended with one of those white-fingered hands. But often, too often, it passed into the realm of powder and shot and ended with the Kid putting up his gun and looking at a sprawling, writhing form in the dust or on the floor in front of him.

Not that he had ever killed a man. To a consummate artist with a revolver, a death is not necessary. There are too many knock-out points, such as the thigh of the leg or the right shoulder or, to the finest of the fine, the gun arm of the opponent. The Kid placed his shots neatly and sauntered carelessly on his way. So that it may be seen that he was a menace to the health of transients and a blessing to Jorgenville's two doctors. In the old days Jorgenville's percentage had run high in doctors and saloons and now, although the saloons were no more, the doctors remained.

Naturally people divided into factions — that is, the men did. Some men said that the time would come when the Kid would forget caution or go red eyed with rage and would shoot to kill. But the older men said: "Aw, give the Kid time. He'll grow out of those habits. There ain't nothing wrong with his heart!"

For three years things had continued in this manner, ever since the Kid came home from school or, to be more exact, from schools for he had never been able to stay in a boarding school more than six months at a time. During that period he became involved in so many fights and inflicted such an array of black eyes and broken noses that, although it was ever admitted that he did not start the quarrels, the principals usually gave him a polite but urgent invitation to pursue his studies elsewhere in the ensuing term.

But to return to the point. The Kid came back unchanged in lazy manner and speaking good English, which was another irritant to the hardy-handed transients who crossed his path. For three years his list of casualties inflicted grew steadily. Then two fellows jumped him in front of the general merchandise store. Now, it may have been that the Kid obtained so much impetus in shooting down two that he could not stop, or it may have been that, in the whirl of action that followed, he thought more than two were involved. At any rate, he not only dropped the two assailants, but he continued by drilling a perfectly innocent bystander through the thigh of the right leg and crumpled him up in the dust.

No sooner was it done than, like one who makes a slip of the tongue in polite company, the Kid was full of apologies. He picked up the third man, conveyed him to the nearest doctor, and handsomely paid the bill. But the matter did not end there. The family of young Tomkins took it up. There had been, they declared, "too much Kid" in Jorgenville during the past three years, and it was high time to popularize a diet of lamb! All must agree that a slip of the tongue is one thing, a slip of the gun is quite another. In a word, a warrant was duly sworn out, a charge of manslaughter laid, and the Kid was put in jail. Of course, he should have been out at once on bail, but here the justice entered.

A word about his honor, Steven Bland, justice of the peace. He was one of those public-spirited men who take office, not because they want either power or notoriety, but because they feel they can give to the community something that the community needs. He had a large ranch and a profitable one, but he chose to give so many days a month to the service of the big, sprawling county, and the county, in turn, accepted Bland as a benefactor. For it was he, in reality, who directed the administration of justice and made the district frightfully unhealthy for gunmen. He even led posses, the sort of posses who do not gallop wildly in all directions for ten hours and then return and declare the criminal has mysteriously disappeared. Bland's men used to go out and follow a wisely laid plan of campaign which brought back two out of three of the guilty parties nearly every time. Breakers of the law hated Bland with a consummate hatred, and the community in which he lived, aware that cattle rustling and other crimes was distinctly rare, blessed his name.

Naturally the one black spot on Bland's horizon was the career of young Dangerfield. It was a singularly difficult spot to remove because, as every one knew, the Kid never by any chance started a fight. Finishing was his particular specialty. Lacking legal footholds against him, the justice had tried the power of suasion, always to be met with a gentle blue eye and a gentler voice which assured him that he, the Kid, would never dream of attacking anyone — that he was far from hunting trouble in any form — that these disagreeable affairs insisted on recurring, and that no one deprecated them more than he. This was not exactly true, but the Kid really did not know that he loved fighting, or at least it was a thing that he would not admit to himself.

So the three years went on until the shooting of Tomkins. It must also be known that Bland loved young Dangerfield — had loved his father before him and had honored his mother, that he would gladly have given a leg or even an arm to serve the Kid in any vital manner. Yet, when he heard of what had happened, when moreover Mr. Tomkins senior arrived, hot under the collar and hotter in his vocabulary, Mr. Bland actually sat back and rubbed his hands, and his expression was: "I've got him now!" One might have thought that he was the most bitter personal enemy that young Dangerfield had, instead of his heartiest friend.

"I want that man," said the elder Tompkins, "put behind the bars to ripen!"

"And how," said Mr. Bland, "can he be put behind the bars?"

"By a jury of twelve men, sir," exploded Mr. Tompkins, whose white imperial wagged with his emotion. "A jury of twelve of his peers, sir!"

"And where in this county," said Mr. Bland, "are you going to find twelve men who will convict the Kid of anything more than a bit of carelessness?"

"Carelessness?" yelled Mr. Tompkins. "And my boy lying at the point of death!"

"Hardly that," said the justice, a trifle dryly it must be admitted, "though I allow you have cause enough for being excited. But even if the men of this county wanted to put the Kid out of the way and behind the bars for a period of what you justly call ripening . . . even if they wanted to do that . . . I give you my word that the women wouldn't let 'em! That's the trouble with women. They have no imagination. They see the face of things and nothing else. And having seen the face of the Kid, no power between earth and heaven can convince them that he could do a wrong thing if he lived a hundred years! Every woman over thirty wishes she were his mother, and every woman under thirty would fall in love with him in two winks if he gave her a chance. So bear that in mind, Mister Tompkins, and remember that there isn't a ghost of a chance of laying a finger on him if this case comes to trial."

Mr. Tompkins would have argued with anyone other than Bland. But, before Bland, he could only grow purple and gasp: "And in heaven's name, then, what can be done to punish him?"

"Very simple. Don't let this case come to trial."

"Punish him that way?"

"Mister Tompkins, leave that to me. I'm not going to admit him to bail. It isn't exactly legal, but I think, if I make the ruling, no one in town will question it. Extra legal actions must be taken now and again. This is a case in point. Mister Tompkins, you go home and rest assured that I'll give young Dangerfield the worst week he has ever had and, when I'm through with him, he'll come out under oath never to wear a gun again. This is the only way, I'm convinced, that the pest in Jorgenville can be ended."

Mr. Tompkins was hardly convinced, but he had not sufficient morale to maintain the field against the justice in person. For him the matter came to an end at this point. For young Dangerfield, alias the Kid, the matter had just begun, and for the justice, good man that he was, the final ending was one which, if he could have guessed it, would have made him set fire to his own house rather than go to the Kid and talk to him as he did that afternoon.

CHAPTER
TWO

Misguided Diplomacy

Mr. Bland was, being a lawyer, rather akin to Epimetheus than Prometheus. He was rather practical than prescient. Therefore, how could he guess that his upbraiding of the Kid would lead to the first jail break that Jorgenville had known in years?

He went straight to the jail. He went straight to the cell where the Kid reclined comfortably on his bunk smoking cigarettes one after the other and studying the pattern of cracks on the ceiling. The jail was simply an old dwelling made into a fortress of the law. Mr. Bland regarded him for a moment in silence. Then he raised his voice and, in a tone of thunder that he could summon on occasion, he roared for the jailer. When that worthy came, he said severely: "How does it happen that this door is unlocked?"

"Eh?" said the jailer.

"You heard me the first time!" bellowed the justice. "Do you realize that the man in that cell is under a capital charge?"

"The Kid?" gasped the jailer. "Capital charge?"

"Kantwell Dangerfield, alias the Kid," said the justice, "is in danger of a long term in the state prison.

See that the door is locked hereafter. And see that you keep a close watch over the Kid. I shall hold you responsible. I am going into that cell in person. While I am there, remain within call. You know the reputation of this gunfighter."

The jailer staggered away with the gait and the facial expression of one who has been struck over the head by his own son. He had been working in the elder Dangerfield's stable when Kantwell was born. He had seen the nurse walk out with the bundle in her arms. He had been invited to lift the edge of the silky blanket and peep at the red morsel beneath it. The rest of that day he had groomed horses with extra vigor because, it seemed to him having seen the heir apparent of the estate so soon after his appearance in the world, he had become in some strange manner an intimate part and portion of the Dangerfield possessions. Now the first glimmering of real thought that came to him was a feeling that Mr. Bland had lost his reason. He was crazy, in fact, if he dared suspect that there was anything really criminal about the Kid. Had he not, Jim Sloan, taught the Kid to sit a saddle, whether English pad or range? Had he not taught the Kid the points of a horse? This was proof positive that there could be nothing wrong with the youth.

In the meantime Mr. Bland had stepped into the cell. His denunciation of the jailer, instead of making the Kid start to his feet, had merely induced him to turn his big, handsome head and lazily regard the two. He said as the justice stepped into the cell: "That's pretty hard on poor old Jim. He knew perfectly well that I

135

wouldn't leave the jail as long as he didn't want me to. You know it, too, Uncle Steve."

Uncle Steve, on the verge of smiling, summoned a prodigious scowl. He pulled the glasses lower on his nose. He glowered above them at the culprit. It was that expression he assumed in the courtroom when he heard a piece of evidence which he considered particularly damning.

"I know, young man," said Uncle Steve Bland, "that you are charged with manslaughter, and there are few more serious charges!"

"Really?" said the Kid, and he sat up — to roll another cigarette.

Mr. Bland set his teeth. How could he get through that thick layer of indifference?

"A charge which might place you in state prison for many years."

"H-m," said the Kid. "That sounds bad."

Here, as he lighted his cigarette, his big blue eyes rose so gently to the face of the justice that the latter had a sudden vision of the lad's mother as she had been some twenty-odd years before. He was so moved that he cursed tremendously and hastily assumed a seat on a stool which stood in a corner of the cell — though, of course, such a movable article should not have been in the jail at all.

"Kantwell . . . ," he began when he was interrupted by a sigh from the prisoner.

"I suppose this means a lecture?" said the Kid. "They generally begin that way . . . with Kantwell.

Why, under heaven, Uncle Steve, did they pick out a fool name like that for me?"

"It was a name," said the justice severely, "that suited your mother, sir!"

The Kid winced and murmured in his soft voice: "I didn't know. Of course, that's different."

"I thank heaven," said the justice brutally, "that she is not here to see her son lodged in the jail."

The red flag of danger flared in the cheeks of the Kid. Though the justice saw it, he thundered on his way: "Kantwell Dangerfield, I have come to talk with you seriously. Is it possible for you to be serious?"

"I shall do my best," said the Kid gravely, and with this he sat erect on the cot and looked the justice in the eye. He had a peculiar ability to straighten his glance so that one forgot his youth. It suddenly made him all man in every sense of the term.

"I don't mean simply to keep a straight face and refrain from going to sleep. I mean, can you listen and use your brains? By heaven, sir, I sometimes think you have no brains to use!"

It was a little far for even the justice to go. The Kid swallowed.

"I'm sorry you think that," he said.

"Think? I almost know it!" cried the justice, delighted to see that insult was at least waking the Kid. It was more than he had accomplished in any other interview. At least, felt the justice, there was something in a downright pounding with words. He continued: "I have thanked heaven a thousand times that Major

137

Dangerfield did not live to see his heir . . . his sole heir and supporter of his old and glorious name."

It was a bit thick as an oratorical effort, but it brought the Kid to his feet. He glared at Mr. Bland for a moment, took a turn about the cell, and then sat down again.

"I have tried to keep the name untarnished," he said with that mildness of voice which had deceived so many strangers.

It did not deceive the justice, but it was exactly the reaction he wanted. "And how," he asked, "is a fine old name kept from tarnishing?"

"Sir," said the Kid, "I have never deliberately hurt any human being or any beast in the world. I give you my word. I have had many troubles with men, but I think you know that I have never hunted for fights."

There was a dignity about this speech that staggered even the headlong Steven Bland. He was deterred for only a second before he continued: "Your father was my dearest friend."

"Sir?" murmured the Kid, very straight and very bright of eye. That was a subject, as the justice knew, on which he was always touchy. Everything which affected his parents affected him.

"Because of your mother," said Mr. Bland, "I have never married."

The Kid rose a second time. He strode to the justice. He towered above him, swelling, literally, until he dominated the room.

"Sir," he said, "tell me what you want of me, but don't torture me any longer. My father I hardly remember. And . . . have only my mother's picture and the memory of her in other people. Uncle Steve, talk to me about anything else . . . I'll listen with respect. But on that one subject . . ." He paused.

"Kantwell," said the justice, "there is one thing that, if they were alive, would gladden their hearts. Swear to me never to wear a revolver again!"

The Kid stepped back again, graver than ever. "You have no right," he said, "to make that request and especially in such a manner!"

"Is it much to ask?"

For answer the Kid raised his right hand. Then he raised his left and stared at both curiously as though he were seeing them for the first time. He dropped his hands to his sides. "I've always fooled about with revolvers," he said.

It was a most indirect answer but, to the justice, a most convincing one.

"And for the sake of toys . . . ," thundered Bland in a last effort of persuasion.

"They are more than toys," said the Kid, his forehead wrinkling with the unaccustomed effort of thought. "I've never tried to work it out. But when I have a gun or two guns at my hip . . . well, I'm a different man, Uncle Steve. They make me free. Do you understand? Think of it! I have only to whip out a gun and there . . . if I wish . . . I have a man's life in my hands. I have only to crook a finger ever so little, and I can beckon the soul out of the man's body . . . the strongest man that ever lived."

The justice was learning more than he had expected to learn. Now he blanched and actually gaped. "Murder?" he muttered. "Is that what you're headed for?"

"For heaven's sake, Uncle Steve," said the Kid, "be reasonable! It's the possibility that fascinates me. It isn't the fact. Of course I'm not going to kill anyone. But why do people want to have a hundred million dollars? They can't spend it all. The burden of managing it wears them away, but they cling to it because it represents power over others. And that's what my guns mean."

"A fine comparison," the justice sneered, "between a revolver and a hundred million dollars."

"Nevertheless, I would not change."

This was, indeed, serious. The justice determined to play his cards — all of them. If he could not persuade the Kid, he would try to frighten him into compliance. And there he made his great tactical mistake.

"Kantwell," he said, "do you know where you are headed?"

"Well?"

"To ruin! As straight as I ever saw a man. Listen to me! Have you ever lifted your hand in your life?"

"Do you mean to ask me if I have worked to make money?"

"I do."

"It didn't seem necessary."

"Have you ever built or made a thing that would be useful to others?"

"I made a bridle for that gray mare of mine," said the Kid after some thought. "Have you seen her, Uncle Steve? I broke her myself. Wild as a hare, beautiful as an angel, and fast as the wind. I call her Tippety. That seems to fit her. Let's go up and have a look at her now. And that bridle of mine with the leather-covered bit is the only one . . ."

The roar of the justice cut him short: "A bridle for a horse! The total product of a life now perhaps one-third spent. Kantwell, don't you see the tragedy in this?"

"I suppose I'm not much account," the boy sighed. After all, he was really not much more.

"No work . . . nothing made . . . nothing done . . . a blank in society! Ah, my boy, but if that were all. It's not all. You are headed to the place to which idleness has brought millions before you. You love horses . . . you love guns. And a death will be the end of it."

"Do you think it's as bad as all that?" muttered the boy.

"Worse! So much worse than anything I can say, that I have made up my mind, Kantwell, to have you removed from society for a space of years. I am going to have this case pressed home. I have refused to admit you to bail. I shall have your case pressed before a jury. I shall myself represent the Tompkinses. I'll have you committed to prison. Five or six years there will bring you to maturity with some quiet sense in your head."

The crimson had flared into the cheeks of the boy. Now it went out and left him deadly pale, the more so by contrast. "Of course you don't mean that?" he breathed.

"Don't I?"

"Prison?" muttered the Kid. "Inside of four walls? Never a chance, hardly, to see the sky? You're simply threatening me."

The justice, incredulous but overjoyed, saw that the Kid — the fearless, the nerveless Kid — was trembling like an hysterical girl. But it was not really unique. He had known the bravest of brave men to tremble at one fear, that of incarceration. To have their life threatened was nothing. To have their liberty threatened was torture beyond reckoning. He saw all of this staring at him out of the wild eyes of the Kid.

"You know, Kantwell," he said, "that I would only do it for your own good."

"I know," said the Kid, "that, if you do this, I'll detest you and despise you to the end of my life. If you were younger . . ."

"You'd go gunning for me, eh? Well, my boy, that's the whole point. In prison you'll have a chance to see where a fondness for guns brings people. You'll have a proper awe for the law instilled into you. And, Kantwell, there is only one way in the world by which you can escape serving your term, that is by giving me your promise now that you will never wear a gun again."

The words of promise tumbled to the pale lips of the boy but hung there unvoiced. His eyes wandered and then came desperately back to the face of his tormentor. "I can't do it," he muttered. "I can't do it. Not that the guns mean so much . . . but, if I give that promise, it means I have stopped trusting myself. I can't start that way. If I fear to trust myself with guns, before long I stop trusting myself with other things. It would be cowardly. It . . . it makes me ashamed merely to think of it."

There was a little more reason in this answer than the justice had expected to hear, but he stuck by his guns. "I give you a last opportunity," he said. "I am about to leave you. Before midnight I'll have the jail wagon here. I'll send you to the county seat. I'll follow you with Tompkins to press the trial. For the last time, Kantwell, will you give me that promise?"

No doubt, if he had used a trifle more of diplomacy, he would have wrung the promise from the Kid for the latter was literally shaking with dread. Six years in prison. It seemed an eternity. What devil had possessed Uncle Steve? But he was known to be a bitter, hard man at times. Six years! The gray mare would be ten by the time he got out. Here was a direct threat to which in honor he could not submit.

"Sir," he said coldly, "I shall not consent."

In place of answering, Uncle Steve turned on his heel, slammed the steel-barred door behind him, and strode down the corridor. Once around the corner he stole back and peeked. The Kid had dropped back on the couch, his face buried in his hands.

Justice Bland turned away, rubbing his hands, and chuckling to himself. He had struck twelve that time. He had got under the young idiot's skin at last. At midnight he intended to come back to continue the bluff and have the wagon at the door. But just before they entered it, he would renew his proposition. He knew perfectly well that it would be accepted. There was only one trouble with the plan — at twelve midnight the Kid was not on hand.

CHAPTER
THREE

Riding into Outlawry

At five that afternoon poor Jim Sloan, slipping back into the corridor of the jail, paused to drop a word or two of comfort. When he spoke, young Dangerfield turned upon him a wild and glaring eye which had no understanding in it. Sloan shrank backward as though a leveled gun had been thrust at him. He was no coward, but there was something in the face of the Kid that discouraged words, discouraged even bodily nearness. Other men would come to feel the same thing later on and for various reasons.

At six that evening Sloan received not a word when he brought the dinner to his prisoner, and this time he was so frightened that he dared not open the cell door but shoved the meal through the small opening which was arranged in the center of the door for this purpose. At nine he came again and found the prisoner walking up and down with a long, soft stride. There was something decidedly wrong.

Indeed, there was much that was wrong. Had the Kid known anything about the law, he would have understood that he was not in the slightest danger so long as he remained quiet and let the law take its course. But he did not know the law. Neither did he pause to reflect that there were five thousand men and women in this county perfectly willing to swear away their souls to save him from the shadow of danger. All that he could think of was that Uncle Steve had stated his ability and his purpose of committing him to prison for six years. Like everyone else in the district, he had been raised to believe that nothing but inescapable verity issued from the lips of Steven Bland. In fact, he stopped thinking about any possibility except that he was going to prison, to be herded like cattle with others, to be branded forever with ignominy, to blot the luster of the name of Dangerfield. He shuddered at the thought.

He waited till ten o'clock in the evening. Then he began to act. His actions were direct, simple, to the point. Now, the bars which fenced off the jail cells were fixed in the wooden flooring below and in the plaster ceiling above. They looked strong as rock, but in reality they were not. It has been said that the Kid was naturally strong but, when he was excited, he was a giant. He went to those bars, laid hold of one, and wrenched it loose. Another he grasped and tore away. Then he stepped into the corridor.

Now, indeed, he had passed into the danger of the law. To be sure, everyone is apt to look on law as a thing apart, a danger to be shunned, whereas it is designed and supported for everyone's protection. The easiest way of paying for a crime, the easiest way for a criminal to live, is to submit to the dictation of the law and to pay his penalty. But the Kid was not thinking of anything save that the air of the jail was damp and close — a foretaste of the prison — and that the stars outside would be free and beautiful to see.

He slipped down the corridor, cat-footed in his deft steps, and opened the door of Sloan's room. Here he entered. There was Sloan, fast asleep in his chair, but to the Kid came the utter surety that he could move about the room at will without waking a soul. He went straight to the wall and took down his own belt with his own pair of guns swinging from it in their holsters. This he strapped around his waist. He leaned over the desk and scribbled boldly on the blotting pad:

Awfully sorry. But if you want me come and take me!

The Kid

Then he walked out of the room, closed the door with equally calm surety that it would not click, stepped out of the front door of the jail, and looked up and down the narrow street. Spots of light and life were here. Children were playing before the Masters' house, raising clouds of dust and laughter. Men moved, great black shapes, into the flare of the gasoline lamp over the general merchandise store, and their low, muttering voices rolled across to him. It was like the voice of all society, now become a menace to him.

Then he turned and, cutting to the right behind the row of houses, he began to run. As he ran, his clear view of things grew. He must keep straight on until he came to his own place, but there he must not enter the house because the alarm might have been given and riders might have sped there ahead of him. But in the pasture he would find Tippety.

So, in twenty minutes of steady running, still amazingly fresh, he reached the big pasture where he kept Tippety by herself. Over the fence he leaped without laying hand on a post. He whistled softly, and a gray ghost galloped up to him out of the darkness, a gray head was thrust close to his, and he saw the bright, starry eyes glistening. Of a sudden he passed his arms about that beautiful head and drew it close to him. She, at least, trusted him absolutely and uncritically — she alone — for, since Uncle Steve Bland had turned on him, it was perfectly clear that he had not a friend in the world. They had been hating him all the time and disguising it with smiles. That, of course, was the most convincing proof the Kid was young indeed.

Did he dare venture to the stable for saddle and bridle? No, that would be folly. That would be the very place where they would lay the ambush for him. He vaulted onto Tippety's back. He called to her, and in a trice she had swept lightly over the barbed-wire fence and landed in the road beyond. He turned her with a pressure of his knee and a sway of his body, and she set off at a gallop — such a gallop as only Tippety had at her command, a joyous, heart-stirring thing. After all, it would not be so bad. What did he want of old friends when he had her to comfort him, to lift her head when he spoke, to prick her thin ears when he whistled? That was conversation worth more than a thousand hours of the windy talk of man.

Straight for the nearest county line he headed, for his impulse was to get out of that district of enemies as fast as he could. There was some logic in his deduction. If Uncle Steve hated and despised him, how must the rest of the men in the county feel toward him?

An hour of steady work brought Tippety across the line. At the first house he paused, knocked on the door, and heard a stir of life above him. Then a light was scratched and a head thrust out of a window above him.

"I'm Kantwell Dangerfield," said the Kid.

"Oh, you are," drawled a voice above him. "That's considerable name for a gent to carry."

Obviously this must be a newcomer in the country.

"I lost my saddle down the road," said the Kid. "I'd like to get another from you."

"Better go back and try to find the one you lost," said the other. "I got no spare saddles."

The Kid paused to consider. "Partner," he said in that almost femininely soft voice of his, "I'd like to talk to you a minute about it."

"And I," said the other, "would like to go to sleep. Trot along, Kantwell Dangerfield. I ain't got any time to stand joking with you."

"Friend," said the Kid, "if you don't open the door, I'll open it for myself."

"The door's locked," said the man above. "And it'll stay locked. Besides, unless you want to rile me, you'll move along. When I'm riled, I ain't no angel, son. Trot along before you get all mussed up."

For answer the Kid tried the knob of the door. It was, as the host had said, locked. The Kid kicked the door

149

from its hinges and strode inside. The crash of the falling door, however, was followed up by a number of swift echoes above — a volley of curses, a thudding of bare heels — and, as the Kid stepped back from the lamp which he had just lighted, he saw, coming down the stairs a pair of long legs attired in long, pink, cotton underwear. Then came the upper portion of a raw-boned Yankee type. The man's face was prodigiously thin. His hands were of vast proportions, and each of them carried a forty-five.

"Well, cuss my eyes black and white," said the rancher, stalking across the floor. "D'you know what you've done by busting down my door? You've entered my premises by force. You've committed burglary. And I've a mind to have the law on you. As it is, pay for that door, tell me you're sorry, and I'll think it over. But . . . are you plumb crazy?" He peered earnestly into the mild blue eyes and the pale face of the Kid.

"I haven't a cent in my pocket," said the Kid.

"Who's you're dad? Or who's your keeper, I'd better ask?"

"I've come for a saddle," said the Kid quietly. "Do I get it?"

"Well," gasped the householder, overwhelmed by this insolence.

"If I don't get it, I'll have to take it. Make up your mind."

"Take it?" shouted the other, as one taunted beyond endurance. "You'll take this, too . . ." He finished his sentence by jerking up his guns — not to shoot but simply to cover his visitor.

150

At the first twitch of his arms the Kid had acted. He did not draw a gun. Instead, he brought his right arm up, across, and in, in what is known as a short inside right hook. It was delivered with a technical perfection that would have delighted the heart of the tough old ex-pugilist who had given him many a drubbing and many a lesson some years before. It was delivered also with a hundred and eighty pounds of bone and muscle surging behind it in perfect time. The tall man whirled about, his guns spinning to corners of the room undischarged, and pitched upon his face. The fist had caught him squarely in the stomach.

"You see," said the Kid without pausing to wonder at his lack of emotion, "the fist is sometimes faster than the hand."

This philosophical comment brought forth no reply. He dropped on one knee and listened. The householder was still breathing, faintly and regularly, like one fallen into a sound sleep.

So the Kid rose, went into the lower back room of the house, selected from among six the best saddle. From among a dozen he took the bridle with the nearest approach to a straight bit then left the house. Before he left, he scribbled on the deal table which stood in the corner of the room:

I promise to pay, when I have the money, the price of a good saddle and a fair bridle, to the fellow I knocked down tonight.

The Kid

151

This done, he issued into the night, called Tippety, and threw the saddle over her back. And so he galloped into outlawry. On this one night he had broken jail, stolen two guns — for they were not his until the law restored them formally — committed burglary and assault and battery, and was now riding off with the stolen goods.

In Jorgenville they still remember that night; the alarm at the jail — the coming of the long, gaunt fellow who recited a tale of a blond giant and an iron fist and demanded a posse to pursue him — the white face of agony which Steve Bland wore — and finally the starting of the posse, very unwillingly, and without the presence of the justice. But, willing or unwilling, they had to admit that the Kid had stepped beyond the pale of the law.

As for the justice, he went to the jail and sat down on the bunk where he had last seen the Kid bury his face in his hands. The justice did the same thing and finally looked up to see Jim Sloan glowering above him.

"And now that he's gone wild, Mister Bland," said Jim, "he'll go plumb wild, you can lay to that. It's the Dangerfield way. They don't do nothing by halves. And if what you've made the Kid start, don't bring you to ruin, nothing will."

"Yes," said Bland brokenly.

The next day he resigned from the position which he had held for twenty years.

CHAPTER FOUR

Vanquishing an Idol

The posse accomplished what it started out in the hope of accomplishing — which was, to be exact, nothing! They had known the boy's father. They had known his mother. They had known him. They knew nothing bad of any in his family except what had happened on this one night. Besides, he was the Kid, the pride of Jorgenville. For it has not been mentioned that he actually was the pride of the town. And what Western village would not have been proud of a man who never hunted for trouble but, once being in the hole, never failed to climb out of it? What town would not point with pride to the fact that they had, among their law-abiding citizens, one who had overmastered the toughest of the tough men who came their way?

The Kid was lost, and Jorgenville, in short, mourned bitterly for him. When it became known through Jim Sloan, rather vaguely, that the former justice had in some way been responsible for the driving of the boy from the village, half of Steve Bland's popularity was stripped from him in an hour. If he had run for justice again the next election, he would have been defeated overwhelmingly.

153

Before long reports began to come in from the trail of the Kid. For two hundred miles the reports drifted back from point after point. Descriptions had been wired ahead. In one place a sheriff had attempted to arrest him and had been shot through the arm for his pains. In another a bank had been held up and robbed of a hundred dollars — a hundred dollars when he might have walked off with ten thousand just as well. But no, he had demanded only that sum, and he had received it at the point of a revolver. He had left promising to pay — some day.

That story made a stir in Jorgenville. As usual, they could see nothing wrong with him. He was their spoiled child. He could do no harm wherever he went, or whatever he undertook. Finally there were no more reports. In vain Steve Bland sent message after message to be broadcast, stating that all could be arranged peacefully if the truant would return. When he heard of the bank robbery, he had to cancel the messages which were still unsent. The rolling stone that he had started had gathered such impetus that he was powerless to stop it or to control its flight. And now the Kid had disappeared.

As a matter of fact he had passed out of the farthest district where the name of Dangerfield had ever been known, and he was now to the north, well to the north. If he wished, there was every chance for him to change his name and settle down to a new life in new communities where questions were not asked of newcomers and where every man's entire past would be generously judged by what he had performed on yesterday or, at most, the day before.

The Kid did not think of settling down. The one enchanting thing which he found in this new life was the very fact that it was unsettled. Each day brought him to new outlooks and to new horizons. There was only one worry — how was he to get enough money to live? Of course, he could have written home and obtained all that he wished, but that never occurred. If he had thought of it, it was only to feel at once that, by sending an address, he would simply pull the hounds of the law on his traces. So he rejoiced in the new country around him, and he even rejoiced in the new people he met from time to time, always taking care to have his back to the wall and to make every man pass in front of him.

One day he rode into Morgantown and threw the reins over the head of Tippety. He left her standing near the watering trough, while he took a chair in the line of idlers who sat in front of the hotel-store combined. This is the Western social center. To be in that line men ride long distances, sit half a day, rise, mount, and ride back again. Gossip is exchanged, friends meet after long separation, politics are discussed gingerly, and in general nothing is done with great placidity. But the Kid had a definite purpose. When he first stepped up onto the verandah, he had swept that line of faces with a swift glance. Then he sat down and awaited the arrival of such a man as he wanted.

At length he came, a fellow in the younger prime of life, straight backed, clear eyed, hard of face and

155

hand, and with those visible signs of prosperity for which the Kid was on the lookout — above all with that air of command which he wanted to see. He threw his reins with a careless jerk. He told the horse to stand still with the manner of one addressing a hired man. This fellow, as he mounted the steps, the Kid rose to meet and stop.

"And what do you want with me?" asked the stranger.

"Work," said the Kid tersely.

The other looked him in the eye. It was the mildest and bluest eye he had ever seen. Personally, he detested mild eyes. His own were as hard as shiny flint. His wife, whom he loathed, had eyes of just that dull sort which he now confronted. Even if he had tried, he could not have helped a sneer.

"D'you know me?" he snappily inquired.

"I'm afraid I don't," said the Kid.

"How d'you know then that I have any work to offer?"

"Because," explained the Kid, more mild than ever, "you look prosperous, and you have the air of one who employs men. That's all I can say to explain it."

"Huh!" The rancher turned to the line of idlers. "Any of you tell him who I am?"

"Nope," came the answer in a chorus. They were leaning forward to watch — anything was worth watching by that line.

"Huh!" said the other, and he regarded the Kid with a more lenient eye. "You seem to see more than I'd've expected out of you." He swept his interlocutor from head to foot. "Lemme see your hands."

The Kid obediently held them forth. The rancher rubbed his thumb over the soft palms.

"What can you do?" he asked. "Use a rope?"

"Ah . . . not very well. No, I really can't use a rope."

"I thought you couldn't. Can you ride herd?"

"I can ride," said the Kid innocently.

It brought a guffaw from the listeners and a sneer from the questioner.

"You can, eh? Know anything about cattle? Feed, flies, screw worms?"

The Kid considered. "No," he murmured at length. "I'm afraid I don't."

"Ever work in a round up?"

"Not exactly."

"Ever use a branding iron?"

"Can't say that I have."

"Then what do you mean by asking me for a job, young fellow? What can you do?"

It brought another guffaw from the line of idlers. The red flag of danger flared in the cheeks of the Kid, but that red flag always seemed to other men the mere blush of shame or of fear.

"Well, I can ride a little," said the Kid.

"You can, eh?"

"Yes. And I can shoot."

"A little, eh?" The big, lean man sneered as he spoke, and his eyes narrowed to scornful slits.

"About average," said the Kid.

"What d'you call average?"

"Why," said the Kid with the same unbroken gentleness, "I'd say that being able to shoot about three times as well as you can shoot would be about average."

The laughter hushed. The grins froze to astonished gapings. The big fellow with the dark eyes flushed to his hair and set his teeth. He became aware that the mildness was gone from the face before him. Two pink spots burned in the cheeks, and the Kid seemed to be growing steadily in size.

"That's a fresh thing to say," the rancher remarked, moving his lips but not his teeth. "Got any more like it up your sleeve?"

"Down in my part of the country," said the Kid as softly as ever, "there's one thing that people don't talk about. They simply keep away from them."

"What you driving at now?"

"Skunks," said the Kid.

In the technology of rapier days this was beyond doubt the "offense absolute." Still the other paused. His repute as a fighter was too well established for him to be afraid that his name would be besmudged by not instantly taking up a fight. He even allowed his eye to run up and down the line of those who waited tensely now and, when he was sure that every man there knew him, he turned his head leisurely upon the Kid.

"In these parts," he said, "there's one rule we have for young fools. We horsewhip 'em till they know manners. Understand?"

"Perfectly," said the Kid, and his smile showed a row of even, white teeth. "Perfectly," he repeated. "I'm now waiting to see the whip."

"You young hound!" snarled out the rancher, and instantly the quirt whirled above his head.

There was a spurt of light at the hip of the Kid. It was the long barrel of the Colt catching the sun as it came into his hand. At the same instant it exploded, and the rancher, bringing his hand down with a yell, found it shorn of the weight of his quirt. The bullet had blown it in two, three inches above his hand. He leaped back, but the gun of the Kid was already restored to its holster.

In the pause the rancher looked first down at the ragged edge of the quirt and then at the empty hands of the Kid. Slowly realization broke upon his mind. He grew white as paper. Then he threw aside the loaded butt of the quirt. He had recognized finally that he was dealing with a fighter, and he had recognized, also, that he himself had to fight. He had drawn it upon himself. He had placed himself in the corner and now, if he wished ever to hold up his head again among his fellows, he had to draw a gun on the man of the blue eyes who stood before him. Not that he had a hope of success. He knew perfectly that there had been no luck in the shot that had severed the quirt. If he had doubted, he could have found confirmation in the wonder and growing fear in the faces of those on the chairs — those who had been on the chairs. Every man of them was now on his feet.

He remembered, then, that there was one thing he must do before he died. "I'm coming out in a minute," he said courteously to the Kid and turned on his heel.

Inside the hotel he took a scrap of paper, and there, in fifty seconds, he had written what must serve as his will. His death would legalize it and make it strong as a stone wall in the eyes of any jury in that country. He stuffed the paper into the pocket over his heart and came again onto the porch. The terrible stranger was rolling a cigarette and, leaning against a pillar of the porch, was looking across the country to the hillsides beyond where the lodgepole pines clothed every slope with yellow-green verdure.

"I'm ready to take a little walk with you," said the rancher. "Suppose we step around the corner. Bill . . . Harry . . . will you come along?"

They rose, nodding, stiff with excitement and apprehension.

"Wait a minute," said the Kid. "It looks to me as if I've got to ask a favor of you. I suppose a blind man could tell what you want. You figure on going around the corner and shooting this out with me. Partner, it's no good. Now and then I get mixed up in a little fight, but killing goes against my grain. If I stand up to you, I'll kill you as sure as there's a sun in the sky."

It was very strange talk. No one there, in reality, quite understood it but, if they imagined that the Kid were unwilling to fight, they were quickly undeceived. He stepped a pace closer to the rancher, and they saw that every muscle in his big body was trembling. It made them think of a hound on the leash with the game in sight.

"Friend," said the Kid, "I asked you a white question, and you gave me a dirty answer. I treated you

160

like a gentleman, and you ought to be treated like a dog. The reason I don't take your invitation up and go around the corner with you is that I don't shoot dogs. Now get out of my sight. I've shown this town what you are. They'll know you after I pass on. And the job that's too small for me to take up, one of them will do."

The rancher swallowed, then his hand froze over the butt of his gun.

"What you did and said before was enough," he said. "What you say now is too much. Come out with me, or I'll draw on you here. I know you and your breed . . . gunfighters for the money there is in it. Now pull your gun, or I'll shoot you where you stand!"

The words had hardly left his lips when he jerked the revolver clear. Of what followed, those who were not diving for cover were able to describe in only the broadest manner. They caught, so to speak, the general trend of the events but not the details. In those details the left hand of the Kid snapped out and caught the gun hand of the other at the wrist, twisted it till the Colt fell from the unnerved fingers, forced his antagonist to whirl to keep his arm from being broken and, when his back was turned, the Kid picked him up by the nape of the neck and the belt, carried him to the edge of the verandah, and dropped him face downward into the dust.

After that, he took forth his inevitable papers and tobacco, while the rancher leaped to his feet, saw at a glance that he had been hopelessly shamed, sprang onto his horse, and spurred out of the town, leaving his revolver on the floor of the verandah. The Kid picked up the weapon.

"Gentlemen," he said, "I need money, and I need it bad. How much do you bid for this curio?"

CHAPTER
FIVE

To Investigate
the Phantom

If a tribute to the power and influence of the humiliated rancher were needed, it was supplied by the absolute silence which greeted this proposal. There was not even a smile. The Kid, looking them over one by one, tossed the gun into the dust where its owner had lain.

"Or if anyone knows," he said, "where I'm apt to find a place to work around here, please speak up, and I'll be grateful."

Still no one answered. As a matter of fact there were many men there who would have been glad to take him aside, shake him by the hand, and bid him into their confidence. The humbled rancher was, no doubt, the most detested man in the community. But he was feared even as much as he was hated, and there was none who dared make a friend out of the rich man's enemy. So the revolver was not bid for and the question remained unanswered. The Kid drew up his belt two notches and swung again into the saddle on Tippety. There was a peculiar grimness about his expression as the mare took him north again out of Morgantown.

He had done his best, he felt, to play "evens" with the law-abiding element of society, but plainly they would have none of him. He had passed unnoticed. No, not entirely unnoticed for a horseman, now that he was out of sight over the hill, was hurrying after him. To turn and stare at the pursuer would not by any means be manners. The Kid waited until the other was comparatively near, then he made Tippety seem to shy at a rock, so swinging her sideways. From this position he took in every detail of him who was coming up behind. It had long since become necessary for the Kid to allow no one to approach him, particularly from behind, without the closest surveillance. The fellow who now came on at the brisk gallop he recognized as one of those who had been in that line of idlers in front of the store — and consequently his gorge rose at the sight of him. Was he one of those who dared not speak in public but would sneak around out of sight to do his congratulating?

The man was small, wiry, with shoulders disproportionately broad. His face was similarly broad across the cheeks and forehead but came down in almost straight lines across the cheeks to a pointed chin, so that the outline of the head was that of an inverted pyramid when he came on full face. In this triangle there was a wide mouth and a wide, large nose. In contrast the eyes were exceedingly small and active. Described in detail, he might seem a caricature of a man, but in reality he was hardly beyond the common run. His short legs jutted out on each side of the barrel of a large horse. Nevertheless, the little man, who on foot would probably not be more than five feet and an inch in height, managed his formidable charger with great address. When he presently came alongside of Tippety, he took advantage of the superior bulk of his nag to look down into the eyes of the Kid and wave to him a sort of superior greeting.

At least this was the manner in which the Kid interpreted it, and in accordance he returned a gruff monosyllable and fixed his eyes on the road before him. He had quite worn out his supply of courtesy against the granite bluntness of this Western world, and now he was prone to take neither first step nor second but let all men do the leading, so to speak. For this the other was, it seemed, quite ready.

"I was at the store," he said. "But perhaps you saw me there in one of the chairs?"

"I did," said the Kid.

"Good," and the other nodded. "You saw me?" He smiled and nodded as though it greatly pleased him to have been noticed by the formidable fighter. "Well, what chair was I in, partner?"

"Second from the end," said the Kid.

"You're sharp with your eyes, right enough," said the little man. "By the way, my name is Justis . . . Hal Justis. Maybe you're heard of it?"

"I haven't," said the Kid, still blunt. "My name is the Kid. Perhaps you've heard of it?"

"A pile of times," said Justis. "Yep, I've heard of you and a whole menagerie full of your cousins. There's the Texas Kid, and the Arizona Kid, and the Windy Kid, and the Buffalo Kid, and the Montana Kid, and Kid Porky, and Kid . . ."

"That's about enough," said Kantwell Irving Dangerfield. "I see you know the rest of the family."

"Suppose we go back a ways then, now that we know each other?"

"You know me, Mister Justis. I haven't pretended that I know you. As for going back, I am constitutionally averse to it."

The little man returned with unabated good humor: "I don't mean to turn the hosses around. I mean to go back a ways in our talk."

The Kid shrugged his shoulders.

"What I wanted to say, was . . . ," began Hal Justis, but he paused to murmur: "Look at that sassy bunch of feathers on the wire over yonder. Can you hit him?"

It was a tiny bird balancing on the top of the three strands of barbed wire.

"I hate to waste lead," said the Kid, persistently gloomy.

"Well, I'll try my hand," said the other.

So saying, he drew from a saddle holster a Colt which looked peculiarly long and heavy in his small, claw-like hand. He balanced it, dropped it carefully on the target, and then the explosion tossed up the muzzle of the gun. The bird, untouched, darted away with a sharp volleying of frightened chirping, but the wire on which it had perched parted with a twang.

"Missed," said Hal Justis, grinning. "But as long as I started another job I might as well finish it."

So saying, he twice again took careful aim and with two successive shots he cut the strands of wire beneath the top. Then he shoved the revolver into the holster. The Kid, smiling for the first time, looked at him in admiration. His own consummate marksmanship made him appreciate this truly beautiful bit of work. For the wires, though close, were only glimmering streaks of light.

"That looks like blowhard shooting," said Hal Justis, "but I wanted to show you that I know enough to be a judge. What I wanted to go back about was that of all the pretty bits of gun play I ever seen, what you did with Borden's quirt was the neatest and the snappiest."

His eyes, with their Oriental slant and their yellow-stained pupils, became steadily fixed upon the Kid, and the latter was astonished by the change. He began to guess that his companion was gradually approaching a proposal of one sort or another.

"Thanks," muttered the Kid. "What you think means more than a dozen of the common run."

"You're right," said Hal Justis. "It sure does. There are gun-fighters that are good and fighters that are better and fighters that are best. Some are handy at a target but go to pieces when they have a man under their gun. Some ain't much good at a target but, when it comes to a pinch and they have a man in front of them reaching for his gun, they're fast as greased lightning and straight enough with their bullets to fill the other gent full of lead."

He paused in the midst of his dissertation, but his glance never wavered from the face of the Kid. The latter was beginning to grow a little uneasy, and his companion continued: "Take me, for instance. I'm a pile better than the pretty good shots. When I got plenty of time, I can figure with most of the fancy shots. But for all-around speed and making his gun talk my foreman, Charlie Queen, makes me look like a greenhorn. You see Charlie work, and you figure him to be as fine as any man that ever pulled a gun. But there's The Phantom who's better still, I guess. Ever hear of The Phantom?"

"No. But . . . you have a foreman. You're a ranch owner, then?"

"I got a place up in the Black Hills. Why they call 'em black I dunno, unless it's because the first gents that tried to get across 'em gave 'em that title back before they got through to the clear country on the other side. That's their name to this day — Black Hills. It's a hard country, Kid. Nothing very high in the line of hills, but you get a highland here and a lowland there, a strip of forest and strip of meadow, a strip of bushes and a strip of marsh, all mixed up. You go bang through open forest. First thing you know your hoss is up to his knees in a bog. You get covered with dust all morning, and you get covered with mud all afternoon. That's the life my cowpunchers have up there. I keep a big buckboard running back and forth to town all the time. Take in a bunch that are quitting and bring out a gang that's so hard up they'll even go and work a while in the Black Hills. But sometime they get so tired of the country and the work that they don't wait for the first of the month but just slip out without stopping to collect wages."

He impressed the Kid as a man who was not probably very talkative. There must be something behind all his chatter of today. He waited to find out what it might be. He said: "I asked if you were a rancher. That's because I hoped you might make up your mind to be different from that fellow I had words with back in Morgantown . . . he couldn't see any place for me in the world."

"That's about it," replied Hal Justis. "Jim Borden sometimes makes the mistake of figuring that his ranch is the biggest part of the world. If he ain't got any use for a thing, he don't see how anybody can have a use for it. Trouble is that Borden owns about half of the range around here, and everybody gets out of his way. You're the first gent I ever seen or heard of that stood up to him. You can lay to it that a pile of the boys was tickled to see what you done, and you can lay to it that about a thousand folks will be talking tonight about Jim Borden getting what was due him . . . and overdue, too!

"If he wants anybody's land, he offers a price and, if his price ain't taken, he starts raising ructions with that gent. How he does it, I dunno. But bad luck starts coming. Take me, for instance. He wanted to buy me out to connect up two chunks of new range that he'd bought. He didn't have no way through the Black Hills except by cutting through my fences. So he wanted to buy. I told him to go to thunder. My folks have been around these parts running onto thirty years, now.

169

"Well, ever since I turned him down and his money with him, he's been giving me the worst of the way for traveling. Nothing turns out right for me. If I get a good cow hand even, he steps in and buys him away from me with higher pay than I can offer. He's taken all my good hands except my foreman, Charlie Queen. Charlie ain't a very pretty gent to look at, and he has his bad ways, but Charlie's sure faithful! As I was saying . . . everything has been going wrong, one bad luck on top of the other. And I charge everything to Jim Borden except The Phantom. Borden didn't have nothing to do with him, unless The Phantom seen that I was backed up by the rest of the folks around here, and so he set out to ruin me."

"And who's The Phantom?"

"The Phantom? Well, he's a cross between cutthroat, bandit, sneak thief, and cattle rustler. He's been around here, off and on, about five years. Got his name by the mask he always wears when he's working. White mask with a black cross in it. Queer thing to see. One arm of the cross is the open strip across his eyes. Another arm runs down his nose and across his mouth to the chin. No chance of ever making out what he looks like with that mask."

"But it sounds like a good target," muttered the Kid.

"Target? No live man ever got close enough to The Phantom to do real shooting. He drops 'em too pronto! I was talking about fine shots? Well, The Phantom is in a class by himself. Some of us got together, and first we hired Gregory to come up from Texas and try a hand at getting The Phantom. Gregory worked five months

170

with ten experts, and then Gregory went back home with three men killed out of his crowd and one of his own arms shot off. Then we went a step higher and got old Sheriff Woolwich. He lasted only a week of action. Then he bumped into The Phantom. Three men seen the fight from a distance. Woolwich had the name for being one of the fastest and straightest shooters that ever pulled a gun. The Phantom beat him terrible easy and left him lying full of lead."

"Mister Justis," said the Kid suddenly, "are you looking for someone to send against The Phantom?"

"Well . . . ?" said Justis, his voice grown suddenly harsh.

"Well, sir, I'd like to try my hand."

"Are you talking," said Justis, in that same grim voice, "for the sake of the square meal you need, or do you mean business?"

The red flag of danger burned into the cheeks of the Kid. "Mister Justis," he said, "I'll have you know this: even if I come to work as a hired man, I'll have to be treated as a gentleman."

He was astonished to see the claw-like hand of the other suddenly proffered to him. Justis was laughing silently.

"Don't you see, son," he said, "that I been leading up to this all the time? That it's been in my mind ever since I seen you stand up to Jim Borden? D'you think I been doing all this talking for my health?"

"I didn't guess it," and the Kid sighed. "I'm afraid I'm stupid at working out puzzles."

"You're young," said the other. "That's all. And you're honest. That's why I want you, my friend. Some folks say: 'take a thief to catch a thief.' I say, take an honest man, and in the end he'll run down any thief that ever lived. Charlie Queen is honest enough, but he has all the faults of a thief. He thinks everybody in the world is crooked. Only makes one exception, and that's in favor of my girl, Marianne. He worships the ground she walks on, and that's what keeps him faithful. Also he's got to hate The Phantom, because The Phantom has fooled him so many times. You see? So he stays on. He'd stay for nothing, just to be near Marianne and to have a whirl at The Phantom."

"Will you tell me," asked the Kid, "why all the ranchers in these parts don't get together and run The Phantom out of the country or kill him?"

"That's easy. First place, it costs money to run down The Phantom. Second place, they don't suffer now. The Phantom ain't raiding anybody but me. He rustles my cattle a bit at a time. He leaves everybody else alone. What's the result? The other ranchers say, 'What's in it for us? Justis is bound to go to the wall, anyway. Borden is out to get him. If we help Justis, Borden will turn on us. Now, The Phantom is living off of Justis and not bothering us. If we tackle him he'll make things warm for all of us. Let well enough alone.'"

The Kid flushed angrily. "In my part of the country," he said savagely, "folks like that wouldn't get on very long or very well. We'd run them out."

"What is your part of the country, Kid?"

"Over yonder," said the Kid pointedly, and the wave of his arm included half the points on the compass.

The rancher looked him squarely in the eye. "All right," he said, "if you don't want any questions asked, I won't start the asking. I'm glad enough to have you."

"And do you really think," said the Kid curiously, "that I'll have a chance against The Phantom?"

"I been wondering how you feel about it?"

"Well, I've been thinking that I'd like to take a try. I'm sort of curious, Mister Justis."

"Me, too," said the rancher. "I'm a pile curious, son. So we'll let it rest at that."

CHAPTER
SIX

The Household of
Hal Justis

The afternoon had worn late before they climbed the long and gradual grade of the trail which brought them, at last, fairly into view of the Black Hills. It was a district northwest of Morgantown. The Kid at the start had noted the rolling clouds which were bunched over this corner of the horizon, and now the same clouds covered half of the sky and brooded over the hills, as though the very atmosphere were different in this gloomy region. One glance at the rolling landscape taught the Kid the reason for its name — dark evergreens swarmed everywhere across the hills, and even the hundred crooked creeks which twisted among the valleys were a tarnished silver, perhaps because of the dark sky above. It seemed to the Kid that the very meadowlands were covered with a blue-black grass. No wonder that this place was called the Black Hills.

Glancing at his companion, he understood also what had made the little man seem so out of place, so unearthly in other regions. It was because that Oriental and mysterious eye, that swarthy skin, that broad, singular face, that expression of mystic dreaminess, and a cruel, practical sense so oddly combined — all of these things fitted in perfectly with the atmosphere of the Black Hills. Such a man would be at home here, and he alone would be in place.

They passed fat cattle on the down trail. At least that rank-growing grass had plumped the flanks of the shorthorns and, where on a level section the plow had recently turned the soil, a rich loam in itself black enough to have named the hills was exposed to the air. This region was cut with an infinite criss-cross of ravines, creeks, marshes, and strips of shrub and forest, so that the main road to the farm house tossed up and down and crossed a hundred bridges within five miles.

Presently they came to the house itself. It squatted close to the black earth. Climbing vines trailed over it; shrubs bordered it; the forest, which had been cleared away on all sides, had still kept sending in green waves of vines and bushes and trailers to reclaim the lost ground. It seemed to the Kid that the house, unpainted and weathered to a deep drab, had pushed itself out of the ground and grown of its own accord. Yet there had been an attempt at architecture, an attempt to introduce the English farm-mansion type. But the small windows, the overhanging eaves, the low walls, were given a dark homogeneity with all the landscape around them. Just as the master of the Black Hills was a fit lord of such an estate, so his mansion was a proper castle for that sullen region. It seemed to the Kid that out of the darkening windows — for the afternoon was now faded to evening — there looked an atmosphere of deep

175

sorrow, hopeless dismay. In spite of himself he began to think of murders and shameful sins.

None of this atmosphere was apparently noticeable to the owner. He enlarged with cheerfulness as his home came under his eye. To his companion he pointed out the good features — the hill on which it stood, affording perfect drainage, the massive tiling on the roofs which the storms of a hundred years would never break, the solidity of the walls themselves so that each window was as deep-browed as a feudal casement, the extent and perfect order of the barns and stables behind the house, the immense range of the winter sheds for the cattle, the lofty straw and hay stacks with winter provisions, it seemed, to care for a world of cattle, the granary in itself a notable building, and the tank house which drew from a hundred-and-fifty-foot well water that, according to Hal Justis, was of unrivaled purity and coldness. All of these features and more he dilated upon. But the gloom which had fallen upon the Kid at the first glimpse of the establishment continued and was even hugely intensified when he discovered that a normal human being could indeed take joy in such a domain.

At least one thing was clear. The Phantom, daring robber that he must be, had here discovered a prey on whose vitality he could subsist for an indefinite time. Fallen into brooding thoughts, the Kid dismounted in front of the stable, but he would not allow the stableman to care for Tippety. Instead, he took the gray himself to the place allotted for her, and apportioned her feed. Then he rejoined the master in front of the barn, and they proceeded to the house.

The inside of the mansion was far more cheerful than the exterior. Someone with a good eye for color had established a warm harmony of wall tints, had splashed bright notes here and there and, in spite of the sprawling bulk of the house, the individual apartments were never of barn-like dimensions. Where size was needed or desired, it was gained by length, but great breadth was never encountered. The beamed ceilings were ever homely and low, and the furniture arranged in attractive groups here and there. Yet, notwithstanding this technically pleasant decoration there was, throughout the house of Justis, an air as depressed and unrelieved as that of a childless dwelling. It seemed that the house had been standing five hundred years, wrapping about itself the gloomy memories of twenty generations of tragedy and failure, even though the Kid knew that those walls had been built not more than twenty years before at the most.

Justis conducted him through the dwelling rooms — the well-stocked library, the living room with its two fireplaces, the hall which rose through two stories with a circular stone staircase swinging around it to the second floor, and the sun parlor over whose windows a dense overmatting of vines had been allowed to grow. Then he took his guest to the second floor and showed him the room set apart for his use. It had its own fireplace. It was furnished with a great dormer window, and comfort filled it. It was prepared for instant occupancy.

"But," said the Kid, "I must be depriving someone of his place."

"No," said Justis, "it's all fixed up for somebody, but there ain't been anybody in it for a good ten months. You see," he paused and eyed the Kid narrowly, "this is where I've put the gents that took up the trail of The Phantom."

The Kid, in spite of himself, could not refrain from shuddering. Here, then, they had been housed, those hardy fellows who had come here to venture neck or nothing for the fame and the money prize of taking The Phantom or shooting him down.

"When Charlie Queen come," said Justis, "I offered him this room because he was running the hunt for The Phantom but Charlie, being foreman too, wanted to be out with the men. So he took his place in the bunkhouse . . . or, rather, in the little stone house off to one side of the bunkhouse. Matter of fact, I don't think it was the reason he give for it. He didn't want to be among the men. Nope, he didn't want to live with anybody. And that little house at the end of the men's quarters is all set off by itself. There he stays and don't want nobody to disturb him. Half the time he won't even answer the door when we want him.

"'I work regular hours,' says Charlie, 'and regular hours don't take in the night time. If I can't do enough between sunup and dark, I don't want the job.'

"Which is fair enough because I got to admit that I never had a foreman that tended to business as strict as Charlie and, beside running the cow business, he took care of the hunt for The Phantom . . . or he did till you come. And he's the only gent we ever had that's had the nerve even to go after The Phantom single-handed. He's a queer sort, is Charlie. Sometimes he don't light no lamps in his house. Just sits there in the dark of an evening. Sometimes he stays up all night walking up and down, and the girl in the morning goes in to make his bed and finds it ain't been slept in. How to figure it I don't know, but Marianne says that maybe Charlie has stepped over the law sometime or other, and he's got something on his conscience which he can't forget. But I think he's had money of his own once, and that he's lost everything. Now, when you meet him, you'll find him queer. But you'll make allowances?"

"Of course," said the Kid.

"If you want to wash, there's all the things you'll need. Then, if you want to come down, I guess dinner'll be ready. You and Marianne and Charlie and me . . . that's who sits to table in the house. The men eat in their own dining room."

Obviously the little man was proud of a household so complicated, and he was eager to have the Kid understand at once that he was working for no common man in no common capacity, since he had been admitted to the intimacy of the family. And what a queer family it must be — this mask-faced Hal Justis, his daughter, the gloomy Charlie Queen, and now him. At least it was very pleasant to be so received and, in this isolated region of the Black Hills, he would be effectually cut off from the rest of the world. There would be little or no chance that rumors out of his past should pursue him. Once this thought had come to him, he lost some of his aversion to the ranch of Hal Justis and began to feel that, after all, he had been singularly fortunate in coming to this corner of the world. Best of all, he could here put two of his great passions to their utmost use and in an honorable and praiseworthy purpose — for horsemanship would be never so much needed as in pursuits through the chopped-up valleys of the Black Hills, and skill at gun play would never be so much required as in the hunt for The Phantom.

When the Kid had finished his washing and brushed his hair, he went jauntily downstairs and walked, humming, into the living room. Hal Justis came to meet him.

"I been talking a pile about you," he said to his new man. "And now you got to prove that what I said was true." He took the Kid's arm and led him down the length of the long, narrow room. "I been telling Marianne all about you. But now you can start talking for yourself."

The Kid saw what he had failed to notice before, that a girl was rising from a chair in the corner shadow of the apartment. She had been so invisible because her dress was a peculiar shade of dull lavender, indistinguishable except when the light struck it. Her hair, too, was a smoky black, her complexion olive, her very eyes unlighted, and there was nothing about her to catch the eye in a quick glance. She stepped out to meet him, however, with a touch of color coming into her cheeks.

180

The Kid saw that she was indeed the daughter of her father. There was the same dark hair, the same broad, low forehead, the same slanting, Oriental eyes with the slightly discolored pupils, the same air of mysterious reserve, no matter how much she talked, and she was incredibly refined to suit her femininity. Among notably ugly men her father would have been one of the ugliest and least attractive but, even among very attractive girls, Marianne Justis would have been notably beautiful. The olive of her skin was transparently clear. Her nose, mouth, and chin were molded with consummate delicacy.

Instinctively he waited for her voice to complete the personality. It came as softly as the running of water.

"My father has told me a great deal, sir," she said, and he was grateful because she did not insist on finding out his name — though perhaps that gratitude was due to her father's warnings on the subject. "But you need not worry about the proofs. He has also told me that you are hungry. Shall we go in at once?"

The Kid looked at Hal Justis, and the latter chuckled. "When you got on your horse, I saw you take up a couple of notches in your belt," he said. "Couldn't help seeing, partner. But here we are!"

They had turned into the dining room. It was lighted with oil lamps hung from brackets in the wall, but so shaded that only a soft glow focused on the table. The Kid, looking curiously at the man who already waited for them in the room, was not able to make out clearly the features of Charlie Queen. He could discover only that the man was of medium height and spare in body,

181

and that he carried his head a little to one side and leaning forward — a position which gave him an air of the utmost gravity and even a touch of thoughtful sadness.

He nodded to the Kid, looking up with a startling flash of eyes, but he uttered not a word of greeting to the others. So they sat down in complete silence.

CHAPTER
SEVEN

The Phantom - Plus Charlie

That silence continued almost unbroken through the meal. Justis made a few attempts to open conversation, but he was not aided by his daughter. The Kid was entirely occupied with his food, for he had not eaten in thirty-six hours. Charlie Queen was like a wet blanket to put out any spark of cheer. It was not until the closing moment of the repast that the Kid began to notice a subdued and singular little three-cornered by-play among the others.

In the first place, every minute or so the girl was looking straight across the table at him, dwelling upon him with a dreamy intensity, as though he were a new type of human being. In the second place, Charlie Queen, who was now revealed as a rather darkly handsome fellow of thirty-five, was silently looking from the girl to the Kid and back again to the girl, where his glance would remain a moment, burning, and then flicker back for a suspicious instant toward the blond newcomer. In the third place, Hal Justis making his vain efforts to lead the conversation was observing his daughter and his foreman with much anxiety.

If the Kid had been an older man, or even if he had been a vainer man, he would have understood instantly, but he had not the slightest idea of what the trouble was about. He had already made up his mind that he would not be disturbed by the strange people he might find in this still stranger dwelling. Neither did he pause after dinner to sit around and chat. Charlie left at once, and the Kid instantly followed his example and retired to his room. All the weariness of the long trail he had ridden from Jorgenville, all the exhaustion of adventurous hours and, of late, little food because he had no money, now overcame him. Here was a safe haven of refuge for the night, no matter what lay before him the next day. He hardly waited to undress but, throwing himself on the bed, was instantly asleep.

He awoke the next morning stunned by the soundness of his slumbers. After he had plunged into a cold bath — icy cold that well water was! — he dressed in better cheer physically and mentally than he had been for many days. But, when he picked up his sombrero from the table, a small bit of paper which had been laid under the hat fluttered to the floor. The Kid scooped it up carelessly, looked at it with sudden interest, and then went frowning downstairs.

No one was in the lower living room. It was far past the early hour of the ranch breakfast, and that which the Kid held in his hand had taken his appetite anyway. So he walked out of the house and, turning about the corner of the building, he found himself in the presence of the girl of the house. She was standing in the midst of a little garden, a bright anomaly in the Black Hills. A thick-growing fir hedge set off the garden from the rest of the estate, and within these boundaries Marianne Justis had contrived a small riot of colors — golden-yellow, crimson, lavender, and shadow-places of blue blossoms. Against this background she herself was so changed from the drab figure of the night before that the Kid hardly recognized her. There was bloom in her cheeks, a smile of happiness lingering at the corners of her mouth, and such a joyous light in her eyes that the Kid forgot the paper in his hand and stared in wonder. The unusual cast of her face might have come from her father, but her beauty, and something beautiful in her spirit, must have come from her mother who was dead.

She called her good morning to him and then swept him into her confidence as though he had been out there with her for a long time — as though he had seen the planting and the growth of the garden from the plans. She pointed with her trowel.

"Wasn't it a blessed idea to get the goldenrod?" she said, pointing to the tall border, doubly brilliant against the dark hedge. "I wanted to get the sunshine effect, you know? I've been trying for years. And finally I remembered goldenrod, and here are double handfuls of sunshine just dropped down, hit and miss. Don't you like it?"

"It's fine," said the Kid. He had quite forgotten his paper now. "And what's that feathery stuff, the lavender and all that?"

185

"You aren't much up on gardens, I see," she remarked. "That's cosmos. I don't know why men care so little for gardens. Dad never comes here. Only Charlie Queen now and then, but he'll be thoughtful even here. Gardens aren't meant for thinkers, I guess."

"I begin to see the idea behind it all," said the Kid. "There's your sunshine. The larkspur yonder is for your shadow, eh?"

"That's it!" she cried, delighted. "I'm glad I'll have someone to talk to about this place."

"And to work in it when I can," he suggested, "if you'll let me."

"There's no end of work," said the girl. "The weeds, you know, keep coming. They'd have the whole garden dark and dreary in a couple of weeks if I didn't watch them like a hawk all the time. Once the morning-glories got a start and nearly swept the whole garden. Morning-glories are terrible things, you know. They twist all the way up a long stalk in no time and, when they get to the tops, they put out little flowers, but all the time they're strangling the life out of the stalk they grow around."

"But how did you get them out?"

"With work. You should have seen the calluses I grew! But weeds are thieves, work is honest and, in the end, you know, the copybooks are right. Honesty always wins."

She laughed at her own moralizing. The Kid thought her delightful. Indeed, he began to look at her and listen to her as he had never looked or listened before.

Women had been simply existent facts before — not important ones.

"How old are you?" he asked suddenly.

"I'm nineteen."

His handsome face darkened.

"What's the matter?"

"What month were you born?" asked the Kid tersely.

"In May."

He sighed with relief.

"I was born in February," he said. "That makes me a quarter of a year older."

"What's a month or two?" said the girl.

"A lot, when it's a month or two the right way. D'you know, it seems to me that you're about the only person I've ever met who was younger than I. And I'm sick of always being the Kid!"

"Well," she said seriously, "I shall not call you that, of course!"

She paused and looked at him with an absent-minded smile.

"You're looking right through me," said the Kid uneasily. "What are you thinking of?"

"Of what a happy life you must have led. And wondering if you'd learn how to frown and be gloomy up here. Every other person gets that way before they've been long among the Black Hills. This is not a happy place, you know?"

"That's because of The Phantom," he said. Which reminded him of his paper. He showed it to her. "What do you think of that? Does the cross stand for The Phantom?"

She read a childishly clumsy scrawl across the ragged fragment of paper:

You won't have far to look.

Beneath the message, in place of a signature, there was a cross. She was instantly pale. Her color was gone as the color goes from a garden when a cloud shadow sweeps across it.

"It's The Phantom!" she whispered and glanced over her shoulder and came a step closer to him. "Oh," she cried eagerly, "why do you stay? Why don't you go at once? You can never catch him, where so many others have failed. I don't see what Dad was thinking of when he asked you to come and take that work!"

"It's the only sort of work I can do," said the Kid soberly. "I'm no good at ranch work, you see. And I have to live."

Words struggled in her throat, on her lips. The Kid watched the effort, saw the passing of thoughts across her eyes. Then she bent her head.

"I'm selfish enough to be glad you'll stay," she said frankly. "For the sake of the garden, you know."

"Yes, we'll have fine times here. And as for The Phantom . . . why he's only a ghost in name. Bullets will bring him down just as they'll bring down other people."

"I'd pray that you might never meet him," and she sighed. "But it seems that he's going to hunt for you himself. And he always keeps his promises. Always!"

188

"But isn't it a little strange that he'd come to the house and leave this warning? It isn't hard to explain how he got in. He could have climbed up the side of the house and left the paper on the table simply by reaching through the window."

"He's everywhere," said the girl. "He comes and he goes wherever he wishes to. He reads our minds. He . . . he is really a phantom, you know! No one has ever seen his face. Even his own men haven't seen his face. We know, because we've taken one or two of them."

"He doesn't work alone then?"

"Oh, no. He simply directs and does the fighting when his men are hard pressed. They rustle the cattle. They commit the robberies. And all they know is that The Phantom comes now and then, in his mask, gives directions in a low voice, and goes off by himself once more. The ones that have been caught have confessed that that is all they know about him."

"He's chosen a fine stamping ground," said the Kid gloomily. "A hundred thousand men might hunt for him and his followers in this chopped-up country and never find them."

"But you won't try to find him? You'll wait till he fills his promise and comes to you?"

"Wait for a thief to fill a promise? No, I'll go out and scout for myself."

"You got a pile of ambition," said a quiet voice behind them, and they turned and confronted the foreman. Charlie Queen leaned against the side of the house, sneering, his eyes glancing quickly from the girl to the Kid and back again. "You got a pile of ambition," he repeated. "And a lot of others before you have had just as much. But all the rest of 'em have wanted a gang with 'em when they started out after The Phantom."

"Except you, Charlie," said the girl with warmth. "You've shown plenty of courage, single-handed."

"Me?" said Charlie Queen. "I don't count. Sure, I've done what I could, but your father don't figure that I've done enough. So he's brought in this . . . kid . . . to do what I couldn't do."

"Charlie!" cried the girl.

"I ain't mad," said Charlie Queen. "Only I'm thinking maybe he'd be more at home working in the garden than out riding the trail of The Phantom."

"And what makes you think so?" asked the Kid, that red flag of danger flaring in his cheeks.

"I got a pile of reasons," said Charlie. "Anyone of 'em is good enough for me. First place . . ."

The girl ran between them and, facing the foreman, she stamped her foot. "Charlie Queen," she cried, "don't you say another word! Aren't you ashamed to pick a quarrel with one of Dad's men? Aren't you ashamed to start it for no good reason at all?"

"I'll talk it over some other time," said Charlie darkly. "You and me'll have words, son. You can lay to that!"

"Whenever you wish," said the Kid, trembling with one of his sudden passions. They had come over him more and more frequently of late. When they came, his eyes were dimmed with a thin film of red. He saw all things clearly. His heart thundered, but his brain was cold as glass. "Whenever you wish," he repeated. "Day or night, with anything from fists to a gun, I'm ready to talk to you. But I'll tell you this, Queen. Down in my part of the country people do their hard talk when the women aren't around."

"If you like their ways," said Queen as he turned on his heel, "why don't you go back to 'em? We could do tolerable well without you up here."

He was gone. The girl turned slowly back to the Kid. He saw that she was white so that her eyes, which at length met his, were unnaturally large.

"Do you see what you've done?" she asked.

"Well?"

"You've not only The Phantom on your hands, but you have Charlie Queen. I suppose The Phantom is bad enough, but I'd almost rather have him than Charlie."

"What's the record of Queen?" asked the Kid.

"We don't know. Dad picked him up in Morgantown just the way he did you. He put him on the trail of The Phantom. We do know that he has ridden out day and night and hunted The Phantom alone. We know also that he has kept a stern hand over the men here on the ranch. Only rough, hard men come here and stay in the Black Hills, but Charlie can rule them all with a rod of iron. Twice there were fights, and twice he nearly killed the men who raised their hands against him. Now they dread him."

"As matter of fact, aren't you about the only person who likes him?"

"I pity him," said the girl, "because he is so unhappy. I can't help being touched because . . ." She stopped and considered the Kid gravely. "You see," she explained at length, "I want you to overlook some of Charlie's insults. He's been very kind to me. I . . . I think he likes me, in a way, more than he likes anyone else. And he's terribly jealous. You've no idea. It's because he found you talking to me here that he was so outrageous."

"Jealous of me?" breathed the Kid. "Jealous of me?"

His astonishment was so real that in spite of herself the girl smiled.

"I'm afraid so. But you will try to keep out of his way?"

"I'll try," and the Kid sighed. He turned away — he turned back again.

"But I'd like to know . . . ?"

He paused, and she said cheerfully, "What?"

"Nothing," said the Kid abruptly and went his way.

CHAPTER
EIGHT

An Important Capture

The question he had wished to ask was simply: "What on earth grounds did the fool have to make him jealous, or think he had a right to be jealous?" The reason he did not ask it was that he had decided to conduct a little investigation for himself. He would experiment and discover.

The next week was a busy one. Although he was scouring the most hidden recesses of the Black Hills, he never could find a vestige of The Phantom's men. Yet he found ample evidence several times that the agents of The Phantom were scooping up the cattle in small bunches and driving them off through the forests where all traces were soon obliterated. To watch the ground adequately and in detail he would have had to have a thousand men riding hard and constantly under his orders, but he had only his own guns and Tippety to carry him hither and yon.

In the meantime, he spent all his spare hours with the girl. By dint of much observation he discovered that the same things which made the girl happy were the very things that sent the foreman into a black frenzy of jealousy. If he smiled at her, for instance, she was very

apt to smile back and even to flush. Then Charlie
Queen grew dark with silent anger. Or if he worked
with her in the garden, the foreman was sure to pass by
and pause to watch and sneer. A dozen insults a day
were the diet of the Kid but, for the sake of the girl's
anxious pleas, he overlooked them all, even when
Queen affronted him grossly before half a dozen of the
cowpunchers.

That was the most disagreeable feature of his stay in
the Black Hills. For the rest he was very happy. The
element of danger during his explorations of the woods
was simply a pleasant seasoning, and it grew to be a joy
to ride through the green lanes never knowing from
what corner danger might start, or from behind what
tree trunk the eyes and gun of an enemy might appear.
He came to the point when every twinkle of sunshine
on the foliage was noted, when every sway of a bough
was searched for a hidden meaning. He looked back to
the life in Jorgenville as a long dream, stupidly pleasant,
from which he had been wakened by a great good
fortune. If there were pangs in the thought of the good
friends whom he had known so long and who were now
lost to him — the townsfolk and, above all, he who had
betrayed him in the end, Steven Bland — these losses
were more than compensated by one hour of swift
riding through the Black Hills, aye, or by five minutes
of talk with Marianne Justis.

It was during the seventh day of the hunting that he
came on the first active sign of his goal and that was a
very concrete sample. As he reached the top of a hill, he
saw a horseman flash into the woods in the vale below

him. No trail led that way. No cowpuncher was riding to cover that district. There could be only one explanation.

Obviously it was dangerous to follow headlong. The fugitive — if he were indeed one of The Phantom's men or even, by lucky chance, The Phantom himself — might wait in shelter of the tree trunks and shoot him down when he advanced. Or else the fellow might use his long lead and escape scot-free through the woods. But another strategy was possible. The valley was really a little bowl with the ground pitching up in a rough circle on all sides of the hollow. This top level, moreover, was comparatively clear of trees, and along the edge of the circle the Kid sent Tippety at top speed, the big mare running as she had never run before, as though she scented ahead of her the possibility of life or death which hung on her speed. Though he was traveling two feet and more for every one the fugitive might be coursing through the woods, the cleared ground and the speed of Tippety more than made up the difference.

Coming about on the far side of the hollow, he was in time to see the stranger gallop over the lip of the bowl and spur away through the level, tree-spotted plateau beyond. At sight of the Kid he winced flat along his horse, jerked out a revolver, and loosed a random volley of shots.

They went wide. Even sitting straight in the saddle, it is hard enough to balance a revolver for accurate shooting with the jerk of a horse's gallop to throw the hand off. The Kid, knowing in detail exactly how difficult the feat was, sent Tippety away like the wind in pursuit, disdaining to answer the fire. The stranger fled at the top gait of his horse, but this was only a common cow pony, and Tippety began to walk up the other, stride over stride. Every bound diminished the distance and at last the leader, who had now looked back and made sure that he was being hunted by only one man, shouted his defiance, drew the long rifle from its case under his knee, and wheeled his horse in a rapid circle entirely by the use of his knees. His hands were occupied with the weight of his gun.

Once let him get into position, once let him bring that rifle to bear, and the Kid knew that he would have small chance of escaping without a desperate wound, even death. Yet he could not strike with his revolver from this distance — at least with any pretense at accuracy. He must charge on, spurring Tippety to her super best. So he swept in, closing fiercely to pointblank revolver range. The rifle spoke, but the swerving cow pony was still in mid-circle, and the bullet went wild. Now, however, the active little animal had faced squarely about, the rifle became rigid in the hands of the rider — and the Kid whipped up his revolver and fired.

He had saved his fire to the last possible instant. Even now he was not close enough, but luck favored him. The rifle, indeed, exploded, but it had wavered before the shot. Plainly his bullet had told. He was convinced of it now as the fugitive twitched his pony about and, shifting his weight far to one side and riding with his other thigh bearing on the saddle, the fellow

196

drove his spurs home. Before the cow pony had sprinted ten yards, Tippety was shooting past. The fugitive had dropped his rifle as he turned his mount. Now he whirled in the saddle and replied to the Kid's command to halt with a savage curse. At the same instant he drew his own revolver.

Plainly he preferred death on the spot to capture, for the Kid's gun was only a yard away when he reached for his own weapon. But in place of firing — it was sheer murder to shoot at that range — the Kid swayed to one side, caught his man about the arms, and wrenched him from the saddle. Only a strong man could have even attempted it, and the effort nearly tore the shoulders of the Kid from their sockets. Yet his power of arm and back sufficed to swing the other across his pommel and hold him there with his arms trussed helplessly to his sides. Then the Kid called Tippety to a halt, and he slipped to the ground with his burden.

His captive had allowed his revolver to fall even as he had dropped his rifle in the first impulse to flee. Now he lay on the ground white with pain, his left leg bathed in crimson, his small eyes, bright with terror and agony, fixed on the victor. He was a middle-size fellow and of middle age also, hard as nails, brown as a berry, with a lean, rather handsome face. He stirred neither hand nor foot while the Kid ripped away his trousers from hip to knee and examined the wound. It was a clean bore through the fleshy part of the thigh, well toward the outside and away from the bone. It would heal in three weeks with quiet and proper care. A bandage, made out of strips of his own shirt and tightly wound, enabled the Kid to stop the flow, and then he rose, perspiring from his work, and looked down again at the fallen man. The latter spoke for the first time.

"And you're the Kid, eh?" he said.

"I'm the Kid," said Kantwell Dangerfield gently. "And I'm sorry this had to be done."

"Like fun you are," and his captive sneered. "You and any other of Justis's bloodhounds would like to run down Bill Jeffrey. That's me, Kid. If my hoss hadn't side-jumped when I turned loose at you the first time with the rifle, you'd be where I am now. But like a fool I had to be fancy. The body wouldn't do. Not for me. I had to try for your head. And here I am! And a girl-faced kid has put me here!" He groaned at the thought.

"I can get you to the house where you'll be taken care of," said the Kid, "but it will mean that I'll have to take half an hour to get there, a few minutes to hitch up a buckboard, and another hour to drive around through the hills and pick you up."

The small eyes contracted cunningly to points of light. "If you do that," he said, "you're pretty much all right, Kid."

"I know what you mean," said his conqueror. "As soon as I'm gone, you'll start shouting for help. But I'll have to take a chance on that. I'll have to take a chance that none of your friends are around. So long, Jeffrey."

He swung into the saddle again and took the straightest cut back to the house of Justis. There was no wait for the buckboard, however. One was hitched in front of the stable and, with half a dozen willing and excited hands in the body of it all armed to the teeth in case some of The Phantom's men had laid an ambush with their wounded comrade as bait, they put their team to a dead run and followed Tippety and the Kid to the scene of the encounter.

Jeffrey was gone. A trail was drawn distinctly to the first bunch of shrubbery, and there they found him lying. He had crawled away like a wild beast, though any man should have known that the trail could be followed. Like a wild beast, too, he cursed them when they picked him up and carried him to the buckboard. They started back for the house.

The Kid had never heard that name before, but the cowpunchers in the wagon were jubilant. They assured him that this capture had drawn one of The Phantom's teeth that probably could not be replaced. They clapped him on the back. They cheered him to the echo and swore that the end of The Phantom's reign was approaching. These were the same men who, a day before, had sneered and mocked when he was patiently enduring the insults of the foreman.

It was a triumphant procession they formed as they reached the house and entered it, two men carrying the captive, the others strung out before and behind. They put him down in the living room, at the direction of Justis who was walking about rubbing his hands, chuckling to himself, and acting in general like one beside himself with happiness. When his foreman came hurrying in, he could not resist clapping Charlie Queen on the back and crying: "What d'you think of the Kid

199

now, Charlie? Ain't he done more than all the rest put together?"

"Is it Jeffrey?" asked the foreman, grim of face and moved as no one had yet seen him. He advanced to the couch where the victim lay and stared down at him. Truly his name and fame must have been well known to The Phantom and his tribe. Never was a tribute so sincere paid to Charlie Queen as that which was paid by the wounded robber as the other stood above him. He turned pale, his eyes grew wide and dull, and finally, quivering through all his body, he threw up his arm to shut out the glare of the foreman's eyes. It was rather a terrible thing to see.

"They know me," said Charlie Queen savagely as he turned away, "and they'll know me better before I'm done with The Phantom and his tribe of cutthroat sneaks." He walked straight to the Kid and took his hand. All malice had left him apparently in the instant, and only an honest enthusiasm showed in his face. "Kid," he said, "I don't need to say that you and me ain't been very thick since you come. I'll even say why, with all these to listen to me. I was a jealous fool. Made me sore because a younger gent than me was brung in to do what I couldn't do, though I sure give that crowd some hard runs. Ask Jeffrey there if I didn't. But you've done better, Kid. You've got the number two man of the crowd. That means the end of The Phantom is pretty near maybe. I sure congratulate you. The next time you start on a trip for him I'm ready to start with you . . . under your orders. I take off my hat to a better man when I see him."

There was deep murmur of applause for this generous tribute.

The Kid answered hastily: "Not a better man. A luckier man, Charlie. If you and I team it, I think we may give The Phantom a run for his money."

The foreman waved his hand in graceful acknowledgment, shook hands with Justis as a sign that he appreciated to the full how great a blow had been struck in the cause of the rancher, and then drew the happy owner to one side.

CHAPTER
NINE

When Men Talk

"I take it kind of hard," said Charlie Queen, "that you didn't talk up and tell me plain what the Kid could do. They's only one harder man than Jeffrey in these parts, and that's The Phantom himself. I know! But there lies Jeffrey, and the Kid's the gent that landed him. Justis, why didn't you tell me he was up to this sort of work?"

"I tried to tell you what I knew," said Justis, "but you wouldn't listen."

"D'you mean to say," said Charlie Queen argumentatively, "that you took him on the score of that lucky shot that nipped off old sour-face Borden's quirt? You took him on that without knowing how he'd size up playing a lone hand ag'in a gent like The Phantom?"

"Charlie," said the ranch owner, overjoyed at the prospect of the close union between his two great fighting men which this evening seemed to have been brought about, "I'll tell you what I really know about the Kid. I couldn't tell you before, because I wasn't sure how you'd take it. You're a pretty hard gent to figure out, Charlie. I never know just what way you're going to jump. There was a while back there when I figured that you plumb hated the Kid."

"Because I figured that you'd cut in front of me by giving him the job of working on The Phantom's trail."

"And wasn't it maybe a little because you figured the Kid was standing in with Marianne a bit too thick?"

"Eh?" said Charlie Queen, breathing heavily. "Justis, d'you think that I figure on being sweet on Marianne? Ain't I got more sense? Don't I know my own position better'n that?"

His eyes were afire as he spoke, and the rancher, seeing nothing, said kindly enough: "Your position doesn't matter, Charlie. Not to me. I want Marianne to find a man she can love. That's all. And if you turned out to be the gent, why, I got enough money and position, I guess, to furnish out a husband for my daughter and no questions asked."

"Do you mean that?" murmured Charlie.

"Sure," said the rancher hastily, and he continued: "But you see how the wind's blowing? Look at her and the Kid. They're the same age, Charlie, but she's about ten years older for a girl than he is for a man. He don't know nothing. She's standing him on his head and spinning him around, and he can't see it. Ain't you noticed it, Charlie?"

"Sure," said Charlie, turning his head toward the younger pair. And what he saw made him set his teeth as though in pain. Yet he managed a smile when he faced the rancher again. "Sure, I've seen that going on. And you're pretty glad to have him for a son-in-law, eh, Justis? You know anything about him?"

203

"That's what I'm going to tell you, Charlie. I couldn't before. A while back I thought you were sort of aiming at Marianne yourself. But when I seen you go up and shake hands with the Kid tonight and treat him white that way, I seen that I was wrong. It was just that you thought I'd cut in front of you with him, as you put it. Am I right?"

"Sure you are," replied Charlie Queen, lying with admirable smoothness. "But what you got on him?"

"A lot, Charlie, a lot! You remember I used to live south when I was a kid?"

"Yes."

"Well, down at Jorgenville the king-pins are the Dangerfields. Old man and his wife died. Left one kid. He has the whole estate. Kantwell was his name, as I got it later on. I've kept in touch with those parts . . . even since I come up here to live. And a while back I heard in a letter about how young Dangerfield had got put in jail on a sort of a joke charge. Seems he was always handy with his guns and always getting jumped by strangers that thought he looked soft. They were always getting mussed up, and finally in a fracas he downed another gent that was just standing by. Bland, the justice, tried to throw a scare into the Kid, put him in jail without bail, and said he'd send him to prison for attempted murder unless the Kid would promise never to wear a gun again. Well, the Kid was scared . . ."

"Young Dangerfield is the Kid, eh?"

"That's right. The Kid was scared, but he wouldn't promise. That night he busted out of jail, got his hoss, rode into the next county, swiped a saddle and bridle, and hit north. They tried to head him off and sent messages that, if he'd come back and give himself up, everything could be fixed. But he traveled faster than good news.

"Now things are pretty black for him. If he'd ride in and give himself up, they could get a pardon for him through the governor. The Dangerfields are an old family, and Bland is a power. But if he gets run down and arrested by some sheriff or other, they ain't a chance of getting him off without some sort of sentence. Even if the bank he robbed won't prosecute, he'll probably still have to go up for a few years. You see, it's a pretty ticklish thing, and it all hangs on how he acts.

"Well, when I seen him shoot that whip out of Borden's hand, I begun thinking. It was pretty work. And soon I remembered what I'd heard about the Kid and his looks. Nobody else up around these parts has ever heard of him at all. So I figured on using him to grab The Phantom. Then, when he'd finished, I'd tell him the whole news of just how he stands. He thinks he's outlawed for good. Matter of fact he ain't at all. Nine chances to ten he'll be pardoned. But I didn't want to tell you while you seemed to be ag'in him, Charlie, because you got queer ways sometimes of showing up a spite. Afraid you might tell the sheriff, and there'd be an end of the Kid."

"How come?"

"Because if a sheriff jumped him, he'd fight like a tiger. And if he fought, there'd be a dead sheriff. And after that . . . well, a man has to hang for a murder. That's pretty clear."

"So," said Charlie Queen, "that's how it stands? Well, Justis, I sure congratulate you on that son-in-law you got coming up."

"When I seen how white you acted to the Kid tonight, I knew you'd feel that way. Meantime, don't say anything. I want The Phantom. And if the Kid finds out that he ain't in danger of a jail sentence, he'll most likely go back home and forget all about The Phantom . . . and maybe about Marianne, too. But there you are, Charlie. Now let's go over and see what we can get out of Jeffrey. He ought to be able to let us in on a pile of The Phantom's secrets."

"He'll never talk, Justis."

"To save his own neck? If he turns state's evidence, he'll come clear. And I'll prove it to him. Matter of fact, Charlie, The Phantom has been playing tag with us so close that I begin to think he must have an agent right here on the ranch tipping him off to our moves to get him. I'd like to get that out of Jeffrey. Anyway, I'm going to try."

"Go after him," said Charlie Queen. "I've got to get my pipe, and then I'll come back and see part of the party. Talk straight to the skunk."

Justis nodded and grinned and approached the wounded man. Jeffrey was, by this time, in the first stages of the fever which comes with wounds, but his face cleared as the rancher leaned above him. For five minutes Justis talked steadily. He showed Jeffrey how perfectly the net of the law had closed around him, mentioned one by one half a dozen of the hideous crimes which he had committed before and after joining The Phantom, assured him that his trial would be brief and to the point and his execution certain, and then showed him the one door open to him for escape — which was, briefly, to confess everything he knew. Certainly information which procured the capture of the master criminal, The Phantom, would go a long way toward setting Jeffrey free.

When Justis ended, the wounded man grinned into his face.

"And how long," he said, "d'you think I'd live if I blew on The Phantom?"

"And how long," said Justis coldly, "d'you think you'll live once the law starts you for the hangman's rope? But if you talk up, Jeffrey, I swear I'll do all in my power to protect you from The Phantom. You shall stay here in my house until you're well. In the meantime, your information should be enough to enable us to locate and kill or capture The Phantom. Is that logic? Talk up, man!"

Jeffrey stared at the ceiling, stared at his interlocutor, moistened his white lips. A gun exploded outside the room. The head of Jeffrey snapped to one side. His stare grew fixed. A purple-rimmed spot stood out on his temple where a bullet had entered, and from the window there was the tinkle of falling glass at the same time that a second shot was fired. This second shot struck no living target. It merely clipped through the front of the Kid's coat and then buried itself in the wall.

Instantly every man in the room rushed for the door. Voices clamored here and there. The Kid, with the hum of that bullet still loud in his ear, rushed here and there with his two revolvers drawn, wild for fight. But he who had fired the shots had vanished. Doubtless he had fled into the woods which were within twenty yards of one side of the house.

So into that wood they plunged and raced back and forth through it, but there was never a trace of the murderer. Not a man but knew The Phantom had been at work. None but he would have dared to follow so close to the center of danger. None but he would have dared to fire the shot which saved his own skin at the sacrifice of the traitor. None but he could have melted into thin air, apparently, so soon after the shooting.

Hal Justis was mad with vexation and disappointment. The Kid was ravening for action. But most furious of all was Charlie Queen. He had appeared on the scene with his pipe packed but unlighted between his teeth when he heard the shots. In his hands he carried his revolvers and, when he heard what had happened, his anguish was a terrible thing to see. These many months he had hounded the footsteps of The Phantom; and now the destroyer had dared to slip up to his very door and strike down a man in the house of the rancher. The others returned to the house, but Charlie Queen flung himself on his horse and rushed off into the night.

CHAPTER
TEN

Prisoner of the Posse

The dead man was cared for by the servants. Quiet came over the house of Justis. In room after room the lights went out. There was only the lamp burning at the Kid's window, behind which he stalked furiously up and down and again felt the bullet hole through the front of his coat, a scant fraction of an inch away from his heart, and there was a lamp also in the room of Justis. He hurried to the door when a light tap came there.

He opened upon Marianne who stepped hastily inside. It seemed that the tragedy of the night had been as nothing to her. She was flushed with a happy excitement, and her first words gave the clue to her father.

"Dad, I've found out his name!"

"H-m," said Justis, forgetting his own worries in an instant. "Kantwell Irving Dangerfield, eh?"

Her astonishment made him smile.

"I know the whole story, my dear," he said.

"Then," she cried, "why, why haven't you done something for him? Do you know that he's liable to be arrested at any moment . . . that . . . ?"

"I know the whole story," repeated Hal Justis. "But before I do something for him, I want him to do something for me. The Phantom, my dear."

"Is that fair?" asked Marianne, hot with anger.

"Let me tell you," said Justis calmly, "in twenty-four hours or less I can have Bland up here, and Bland is the man to fix things for him if he should get into trouble with the authorities. Very easy. Six miles on a beeline to the railroad, I can reach Bixbee Station in half an hour, riding hard. Then I can wire the whole story to Bland and get him up here on a train. And Bland can get Dangerfield out of trouble. He knows everything about it, and he has wires into the governor. The only thing that has kept him from getting a pardon for the Kid before this is that young Dangerfield has been at large. The law can't pardon a man until he's in the law's power. There you are! And the minute the Kid is in danger, I simply send for Bland . . . and there you are again. You see, it's no danger at all. Now, you trot off to bed unless you want to tell me more about your talk with the Kid, eh?"

But something else had come into the mind of the girl. She bade him a hurried good night and was gone. She took only long enough to put on a hat, and then she slipped down the stairs and out to the stable, past the sleepy boy at the door, and to the stall of her favorite bay gelding. Ten minutes later she was in the saddle and galloping down the road to Bixbee Station. Whether or not The Phantom were taken, she had determined to have Steven Bland up from Jorgenville to take the affairs of the Kid in hand if there were really power in a telegram to bring him.

It was a little later than this hour that Jim Borden went into his bedroom, lighted the lamp, and became aware the next instant of the figure of a man installed calmly in a big chair by the window. The broad brim of his sombrero masked the upper part of his face in shadow, but enough was shown to identify the lean, dark face of Charlie Queen. The effect of this visitation upon the rancher was not alarm or even surprise.

"Well," he said quietly, "what's new?"

Charlie Queen replied with equal monotony of voice: "They've taken Jeffrey."

"No! If they can take him, they can take The Phantom!"

"Pretty near."

"Who done it?"

"The Kid. Him you had the mix with."

The face of the rancher darkened. "I've had a feeling in my bones ever since he came to light that he'd be a thorn. Charlie, what can we do?"

"Listen," said Charlie Queen, "when you asked me to go to Justis and act as his foreman and as chief hunter for The Phantom, when you asked me to play chief spy on Justis and go-between for you and The Phantom, I took the job, and I've played it pretty well, eh?"

"You have, Charlie. And I've paid you well."

"I don't deny that. But now, Borden, you've got to lend a hand. I've started The Phantom on Justis, as you asked me to. I've seen The Phantom push Justis almost

211

to the wall. Another couple of months and he'd have been bankrupt. But here I've struck a wall."

"Can't you handle the Kid?"

"It's a big chance," said Charlie Queen. "And I'd rather play safe. He gave me a close squeeze tonight. Jeffrey near spilled the beans. I had to shoot the fool through the window, and then I tried a crack at the Kid, but I missed him. He has luck on his side."

The rancher shuddered at this calm mention of the attempted double murder.

"Besides," said Charlie, "he's mixing in on my own little game."

"You and the girl? You still think you have a chance with her, Charlie?"

"If I could get rid of the Kid. She was getting sort of used to me. She talked to me a good deal before he come. But now I don't get a word out of her. All she can listen to is him. Blast his eyes!"

"I see," and the rancher nodded. "And where do I come in?"

"How d'you stand with the sheriff?"

"Pretty well. You know that."

"Could you get him to start up a posse?"

"Of course. Inside a day I could have him primed for work."

"All right. Then I'll give you the tip. First, would it hurt your feelings to get a stab in at the Kid?"

"Hurt my feelings? The young dog has made a laughingstock of me!"

"All right, then. I'll tell you who the Kid is. He's *the* Kid!"

"What d'you mean by that?"

"He's the Kid of Jorgenville!"

"Never heard of him or the town."

"If you'd ever been south on the range, you would have. I've been south, and I've heard the stories. He used to keep two doctors busy patching up the holes he shot in gents down that way. Always kept upwind from the law, till he had a bit of bad luck. Anyway, he got jailed at last, busted out, swiped a saddle and bridle, and jumped north, living off the land, so to speak."

"Ah," and Jim Borden chuckled, "so that's the hang of it, Charlie. Is that all? I'll have him nabbed and jailed before twenty-four hours are up."

"Easy, now," said Charlie, "it don't work so straight as that. If you jail him, he won't stay long. They've got nothing much on him . . . nothing that a friend of his named Bland can't get a pardon for from the governor. You'll put him behind the bars for a week, that's all. Then he'll be out and free again."

"Then what d'you want, Charlie?"

"Borden, how much would you like to get rid of the Kid?"

"You know me, Charlie. Men that stand up to me pay for it in the end, if I can make them. And I've always made them so far."

"Well, suppose you was to hand-pick the men that go along with the sheriff in that posse? Suppose you was to start a lot of talk with 'em first . . . or get one of your men to do it. Tell 'em that the Kid is a bad egg. Trump up a lot of faked stories. Imagine a couple of murders that he ain't committed. Get the boys red hot. And

213

after the arrest, while the posse is taking him toward town, have it fixed for the boys to jump the sheriff and tie him up and then just string the Kid up to a tree."

"Charlie," cried Borden, perspiration starting on his forehead, "I hope I never have you lined up against me!"

"I hope so, too," said Charlie coolly. "And if you turn this trick, you'll have me on your side to the end of my life. Will you do it?"

"After all," muttered Borden, "what's the risk? I give the sheriff the word. Then I pass another word to a fellow I know who'll get the posse together. I'll never appear. That posse will be red hot for action by the time they reach the Kid. And who'll connect me with the lynching when it's found out afterward that the Kid never done anything really bad?"

"Nobody'll connect you," and Charlie Queen grinned. "You're a pretty smooth one yourself, general. Want to know any more details?"

"No. I know enough. And Charlie, don't come here again. If folks were ever to suspect . . ."

"Hush," murmured Charlie Queen. "Nobody'll suspect. When I want to step soft, I can go and come as easy as The Phantom himself!"

So saying he rose from his chair, leaned a moment out of the window, and then clambered through it. A second later Borden heard the soft crunch of his feet as they struck the ground below but, when he himself stepped to the window and looked out, there was no one in sight. Certainly Charlie Queen was as good as his word.

When, the next morning, Charlie sat at the breakfast table with Marianne, Justis, and the Kid, they were astonished by his volubility. Particularly was he friendly with the Kid. In half an hour he had sketched half a dozen ways in which he would help the Kid work. "Under your orders," he always ended, "because you've proved yourself a better man than I am, Kid!"

To which young Dangerfield always responded uneasily: "Not a better man, but a luckier one, perhaps, Charlie."

The wiles of Charlie Queen were perfectly successful. Not a single shadow of suspicion marred the contentment of the Kid. Indeed, he felt that the work of capturing The Phantom was already almost accomplished if he could have such a man as Queen at his shoulder to aid in the battle.

That day he did not ride on the trails through the Black Hills. That evening he went to bed early after supper to make ready for a start with the first gray of dawn. Charlie Queen had promised to accompany him on this day's ride. He only delayed after supper to look thoroughly to his guns and, when he was assured that both revolvers were in perfect working order, he lay down upon his bed, dog-tired, and was almost instantly asleep.

Disturbed dreams followed him, for that day there had been a cloud over Marianne. She had seemed weary. She had not gone into the garden. He had noted that on several occasions she was keeping an anxious eye upon him. And so, in his dreams, her face appeared dimly time and again, shouting to him a warning that had no words. So vivid did one of these nightmares seem to him that he started up, wide awake, in time to see the hall door softly swing wide, and against the dim light beyond he made out a thronging host of the heads and shoulders of men.

He was wide enough awake to know that those numbers and that silence boded no good. One leap carried him to the wall on the far side of the room, and he whirled with his two revolvers in his hands. But though the weapons were directed toward them, the low-running volleys of shadowy figures still came on and even laughed in their rush. Were they madmen, then?

He pressed both triggers, aiming to kill, for the odds were great. There was only the hollow snapping of the hammers. Both guns had been emptied of cartridges. His astonishment unnerved him so that he could not struggle even with his bare hands. In a moment they were upon him. A score of hands gripped him. He was tied and shoved against the wall while someone lighted his lamp. Then he could make out their faces — a dozen range riders pressed in for this service, and among them his eyes caught the sheriff's badge of office gleaming faintly in the light.

There were others coming now — Hal Justis, Marianne, white of face, and then Charlie Queen, running. The Kid heard almost nothing that was said. He vaguely knew that Justis was pleading for him excitedly. He vaguely heard the growl of Charlie Queen cursing such night thieves as this sheriff and his men. What he saw more clearly was the damp shadow of the prison closing about him and shutting out the face of Marianne. She had pressed to him through the mob of men.

"There's still a ghost of a chance," she said, "to keep you here. And even if you go, you won't be kept long. Last night I wired to Steven Bland!"

Then she stepped back, smiling, but there was no hope in the Kid. That Bland, who had started him on this career, might now save him from it did not enter his brain. He followed his captors, a riot of satisfied voices, down into the lower hall, and here Hal Justis made a last attempt to delay the blow. The hour was growing late, the ride before them was long and dark, and there were beds in the house for all. Why not stay there till dawn? But the wily old sheriff shook his head.

"If you want to take a badger," he said, "first get him out of his hole. The ride ain't so long, and they's a moon up to light the way for us. We'll start on now."

His men exchanged glances and signified that they were in accord with the sheriff's sentiments. For the emissary of Borden had been at work, and they did not intend that ride should be completed with the Kid still among them. There were plenty of trees in the Black Hills with branches strong enough to sustain his weight on the end of a rope.

They stamped out through the door — they pushed the Kid onto the back of gray Tippety but, as they were taking their saddles themselves, they caught the rapid patter of distant horses galloping and finally made out two riders coming over the hill, showing black against the moon for a second, and then dipping into the dim shadows of the hollow.

"Somebody aimed for us," said the sheriff, "by the way they gallop. Wait here!"

The Kid did not hear. He was looking his last, he felt, on the sky, breathing his last breath of the fragrance of the evergreens. Then, into his dream rushed the voice of Steven Bland, and the face of Steven Bland appeared before him.

"Here!" shouted the sheriff. "What's all this? Stand off from that man, stranger!"

"My friend, Sheriff Gleason, will talk to you about this man," said Bland. He turned on the Kid: "Son," he said, "I was a fool, but I've been punished for my folly. We'll have you out of this in one minute."

Sheriff Gleason was talking straight from the shoulder to the other officer of the law. "They's a good many counties, friend," he said, "that have little things ag'in' the Kid. But my county comes first. He busted jail there, and we got the first call. So here's where I make the arrest and take him off your hands, if you're willing."

"We'll land him in jail first," said the other, "and then you can do your talkin' partner."

"Wait a minute," said Sheriff Gleason. "Here's the governor's pardon for Kantwell Irving Dangerfield, alias the Kid, as soon as he's apprehended by officers of the law. Does that let you out?"

The other snatched the paper and unfolded it, growling. He studied it a moment and then handed it back. "That let's me out," he said in a surly tone. "Take him! I never have no luck." He gathered his sullen posse about him.

As for the others, it was a gay party that passed back into the house of Justis. There Marianne told of her ride to Bixbee Station and the sending of the telegram which had brought Bland and the sheriff in the nick of time — how barely in the nick of time only Jim Borden and his agents in the posse could tell.

"But," said Bland, when he had drawn apart with Justis a little later, "what's the lay of the land between your girl, yonder, and the Kid?"

"Why," said Justis, "if you look close and make out how foolish they both look, it ought to be easy for you to see just how that land lies."

Steven Bland followed the suggestion and grinned broadly.

"And you're not averse?" he said.

"Partner," said Hal Justis, "there's only one thing I regret, and that is that you didn't come a week later, because by that time the Kid would have landed The Phantom for me. As it is, I'm afraid Marianne will have something to say about him following that trail. She's starting to say it now in fact."

CHAPTER ELEVEN

Laying the Phantom

Indeed, how the Kid ever regained his room that night without first depositing with Marianne a promise that he would give up this and all other man trails was more than he himself knew. But he came at last, happy and tired, back to the place where he had been captured so short a time before. And there, hardly knowing why he did it, he sat on the edge of his bed and reloaded his revolvers.

Who had in the first place managed to steal into his room and empty the chambers of cartridges, he could not guess, but he shrewdly suspected that consummately disappearing agent, The Phantom. As he shoved the guns back into their holsters, he found on the table a rather convincing proof that The Phantom had indeed been there and even later than his own seizure. Strange as it appeared to be, the daring fellow had braved all the dangers of the two sheriffs and the posse, had slipped into the house, and there on the table appeared the familiar clumsy scrawl, as though traced by a child or by a man using his left hand.

If you ride alone, you'll find me tonight at the place where you shot Jeffrey.

Beneath it was the well-known signature — a roughly made cross.

If he rode alone? If he placed himself in that desperate jeopardy when all need for risks such as this had passed from his life? Yet, as he stared down at the paper, the temptation grew in him momentarily. He harked back to the words of Bland many a time in the past: "You'll keep on till you kill your man, and you'll keep on till you're hungry for a killing. That's why I want you to give up your guns."

He shook his head. It would be madness to accept that invitation. If he did not ride alone, The Phantom would not appear. And if he rode alone, what would keep The Phantom from posting his band about the place and laying an ambush? Only one hope to prevent that. The marauder must have left the house only recently and, if the Kid on Tippety rode full speed to the site mentioned, he must arrive there, unless The Phantom used a method of transport far swifter than horseflesh, before the outlaw could possibly have summoned his men to his assistance. Then all scruple was swept from the mind of the Kid. He must go there at once. He must face this strange murderer and plunderer. Other men had been as tenpins, set up one moment to be knocked down by him the next. The Phantom was doubtless far different. To drop him would need the swiftest speed of hand, the most steadiness of eye and nerve.

221

With that temptation flaunting before him, he slipped down the stairs, wandered to the rear of the stable, saddled and mounted Tippety, and rode out on the moonlight trail. The Black Hills were silvery bright under the moon. Not a breath of wind stirred the deep shadows under the trees. It was a setting to freeze the blood, an ideal setting for The Phantom. It almost seemed that he had waited until he should find a time and a place best suited to unnerve his youngest and his most formidable foe.

The Kid shook off the fancies that began to assail him. He used only one precaution and that was to skirt about to the left and approach the trysting place from an unaccustomed angle. If there were an attempt at ambush, they would not be apt to watch this trail at least.

He climbed the last steep to the edge of the open plateau, with its meager dotting of trees here and there. He dismounted from Tippety, and from behind a tree he examined the ground around him. There was the place where Jeffrey had fallen — yonder, the bushes into which the wounded man had dragged himself. But where was The Phantom?

As though the other had heard the unspoken question, at this moment his figure appeared from behind a tree, a man of middle height, walking very slowly and solemnly, with his hat thrown off and only that ghastly white mask with the black cross covering his face. He came to the very center of the open arena and then halted, facing the Kid. The latter knew that he was seen and was awaited.

222

To tell the truth, his heart failed him. There was something so unhumanly assured in the bearing of this desperado that the Kid actually quivered for a moment with the thought that, after all, he might not be flesh and blood. He banished the superstition with a violent effort and stepped out into the moonshine. The moment he appeared The Phantom raised his hand as though to effect a truce. The Kid paused in easy speaking distance, straining his eyes but seeing nothing.

The Phantom spoke in a deep voice. "Young man," he said, "you have drawn this on yourself. I am not a butcherer of children but, when you shot Jeffrey, I could stand no more. We shall count to ten together. On the last count we fire."

Before the chill, which the voice struck through the Kid, had departed, the voice was counting. At three, the Kid joined him tremulously. At six his nerve was steadied. At eight he was himself again. Nine . . . ten . . .

He whipped out his revolver with such speed as he had never used before, but his movement was like the slow heave of a laborer compared to the lightning flash of The Phantom's hand. His gun was scarcely clear of the holster when the weapon of The Phantom spoke, and the Kid received a staggering blow in the left shoulder, turning him a quarter around. That blow, however, saved him from the second shot which immediately followed. And before the third shot came the Kid, aiming carefully despite the stabbing pain of his wound, fired into the breast of The Phantom.

There was no doubt about the reality of the latter's existence now. The revolver fell from his extended right hand, exploding for the third time as it struck the earth. The Phantom himself turned, staggered, and fell on his face.

The Kid stumbled forward to him, dazed by the sudden victory. His own wound was not serious. He himself could bind it and stop the flow. There had been no shattering of bones. With his right hand, he turned the victim, wrenched the mask from the face, and found beneath him the face of Charlie Queen. He had played his double game with everyone — with Jim Borden, with Hal Justis, with his own men, with the world at large. He was doubly a traitor in every respect.

"You got me," Charlie said. "Not you, but your cursed luck. The gat hung and pulled to the right. That's the only reason you're alive! From the beginning I seen what was coming. And . . ." A gush of crimson choked him. The Kid thought he had died, but in a moment he murmured: "Tell Marianne I'd've gone straight if she . . ."

There was a quiver of the body, and The Phantom was dead, his open eyes looking brightly up to the moon.

Outlaws All

Max Brand wrote a total of five short novels about Bull Hunter, that gentle giant of a man who sees so deeply into the human soul. "Bullets with Sense" was the first, appearing in Street & Smith's *Western Story Magazine* in the issue dated 7/9/21. This was later combined with the second, "Bull Hunter Feels His Oats" in *Western Story Magazine* (8/13/21), to form the book-length novel, BULL HUNTER (Chelsea House, 1924), published under the byline David Manning (even though the stories appeared under the Max Brand byline in the magazine). In 1981 Dodd, Mead & Company reprinted BULL HUNTER, this time under the Max Brand byline. In the first two short novels, Bull Hunter is intent on tracking down the notorious gunfighter, Pete Reeve, only for the two to end up becoming partners. "Outlaws All," the third short novel to feature Bull Hunter, was published in *Western Story Magazine* in the issue dated 9/10/21 and has not until now ever appeared in its entirety in bookform.

CHAPTER
ONE

To Satisfy Speculation

There were three points of strategic interest, each ignorant of the one behind because the rolling of the hills shortened every viewpoint, and the sense of smell was made useless by a strong, steady wind out of the east. First there was a big, red bull who in the pride of his strength had wandered far from his herd. Second was a gray figure skulking from bush to rock, and third was a medley of mounted men trailing a pack of huge wolfhounds up the wind. All were in a due line from east to west and, while the hounds knew vaguely of that distant gray figure, that ghostly thing itself could not use the trigger-balanced sense of smell and was aware only of the lordly bull.

The latter wandered idly. He had already taken his fill of the grass of the late spring, grass that had sleeked his ribs and layered him with fat. Now he strolled from tidbit to tidbit of the longest, darkest grass and, having licked up a tuft of it, he went on again. He was like a child on the seashore, wandering from shell to shell, each shell in the distance seeming larger than the one behind, and with the ominous roar of the sea to make it

227

forgetful of direction. Certainly the bull had forgotten the rest of the herd.

The sun was reassuringly warm. The wind came to him over the broad sweep of the hills thick with delicious ground-smells of growing things. The only threat visible under the whole of the noble arch of the sky was one black speck balancing far up against the sun. That was the buzzard, watching and waiting, the eternal skeleton at the feast of the wild things of the mountains, the symbol of death. But the lazy bull never looked so high. His eye was for the grass, save when he paused, now and then, and flashed his tail at the flies or swung his head ponderously and licked his flanks where they were swarming.

All of this the gray stalker had observed, now from a bush, now from a rock, as he glided shadow-like, his body close to the ground. He was that fleetest of all the things that run on four feet in the Western mountains — fleetest and most enduring. The deer which might run away from him in the opening spurt he would run to death in a few scant minutes. A greyhound might possibly — though it is doubtful — outsprint him, or a wolfhound in fine trim might outdistance him in the short run but, in ten minutes of ardent going, he would break the heart of the fleetest dog that ever stepped. He had more than speed under foot. Of all the wild creatures that kill beneath the sky, he was the wisest. The solemn old grizzly, lord of cattle-killers, compared to him, was blunt of wit, and the cleverest fox that ever ran was simply an impish child compared to the almost human brain of this mountain runner.

In a word, he was that king of the wolves, the great, gray lobo. The state would pay fifty dollars for his scalp, and the ranchmen would double, treble, quadruple the price. Indeed, there was no price they would not pay for his head, for the lobo prefers hot meat. He kills before he dines and, after he dines, he leaves his kill. For this particular animal the despairing ranchers had littered the country with traps and scoured the mountains and the plains with wolfhound packs and fast horses. But they never had come within shooting distance. He seemed to know the exact range and capabilities of a rifle in expert hands. When the sun sank and the treacherous light of the evening began, more than one hunter had seen the skulker running impudently close across the hills, a great, pale-gray, smoothly gliding form. For that reason they called him The Ghost.

A very palpable ghost, one would say, following the footprints well nigh as large as a man's hand to the rock behind which he had sunk to take another and a deliberate view of the bull. The lobo is the hugest of wolves perhaps, and The Ghost was a giant of his kind. He also differed from the ordinary wolf in many other ways. He had, to be sure, the lobo's gray pelt. He had the bushy tail and the long-snouted head, a broad head more bearish than dog-like in full face but sinisterly pointed in profile. It was by looking at The Ghost in full face that one was aware of his distinctive features most accurately. He had the black lines like brows above his light brown eyes, lines that gave him a whimsical, inquisitive look typical of his dreaded kind, but an expert would have noted that the head was excessively broad, the forehead most unusually high, and the eyes large beyond precedent. His pelt, too, was less than wolfishly rough. It promised to be pleasant to the touch and, where the wind parted the outer coat, one saw a silken inner lining — this in addition to the peculiarities of the head.

But what was it that was so different? Why was it that a man could look closely at The Ghost without the chill that strikes into one's blood when one sees a true wolf, even behind the bars of a menagerie cage? All the differences, all the peculiarities, could be covered with a single phrase — there was something of the dog about The Ghost.

He sat down behind the rock and, opening his mouth, grinned at the bull. That grin was all wolf. But now, as some distant sound came down the wind, and he pricked one ear and canted his head to listen — that was certainly the bay of a dog. When he stood up again, as the bull turned his back, it seemed plain that his shoulders were heavier than the shoulders of most wolves, his skin less loose, and his hind quarters more strongly developed. Moreover, his snout was blunter and broader and, take him all in all, it could be said that he had the size and strength of a wild wolf and the finish that comes from a thousand years of breeding dogs for their fine points. Beyond a doubt there was dog blood in him, though in what proportion it was impossible to tell.

As the bull sauntered away with a swishing of his tail, The Ghost slid from behind the rock. All wolf now. No dog since the beginning of time could have glided so shadow-like, his body trailing the grass, his shoulders low, and forepaws slipping out, one by one, with incredible softness. The twitching lips exposed the murderously long fangs — yes, he was all wolf now, and a strong man, a hunter, gun in hand, would have felt his skin prickle at the sight of him.

Beyond doubt he was trailing the bull, but that was more than strange. The stoutest lobo, unless he is pressed with hunger, immensely prefers veal, young veal at that, and he has a distinct dislike for the hide of a bull — and for the dangerous horns well nigh needle-sharp. Perhaps The Ghost was merely watching and trailing for amusement. He would do that for hours. He loved to spy. He could lie behind a rock for hours and hours at a time and watch the chipmunks, busy and clever and chattering. He could rest an untold time and observe the pranks and mischief of the blue jay in the trees. He delighted in the bright little tree squirrels and knew the least of their ways — as he also knew the exact height which he could leap to snap one of them off a branch. That, however, was for amusement's sake. He disdained such humble fare. It was more than possible that the terrible gray wolf was stalking the red bull so softly simply because he was a close student of nature.

If that illusion were present, it was suddenly dispelled. The bull had raised his head to look into the teeth of the wind and, the moment his head went up, The Ghost was at him, a gray blur shooting noiselessly along the ground. He swept in a semi-circle, edging

231

towards the side from which the red bull had turned his head and, cutting in at an angle, he snapped as he shot by. It was like the slash of two heavy, keen sabers. The bull, with a bellow, started to turn. Before the bellow was half uttered, before he had hobbled half way around, the silent savage had checked himself and leaped back in the other direction, slashing the other hind leg. Completely hamstrung, the bull's quarters slumped heavily to the ground. He raised his forequarters, roaring with pain, pawing, tossing his head and those terrible horns. But there was no hope for him now. The lobo could sink his teeth with impunity into the flank of his victim and wait for him to bleed to death. Oddly enough, that was not the plan of The Ghost.

He slipped around until he stood face to face with the bull. It brought a fresh paroxysm of pain and terror and rage from the red giant. Even the lofty form of The Ghost, compared to the high-humped bulk of the red bull, was a slight thing. It seemed impossible that the one had felled the other. But The Ghost, having done his terrible work with such neatness, now seemed to relapse once more into the innocent, close student of nature. He licked the blood from his lips and, with the most meticulous care, he cleansed a few random drops from the apron of white fur across his breast. One might gather the impression that he was disgusted by such a slovenly slaughter since now he lay down, a little to one side, and rested his head on his huge, outstretched paws. One ear flagged back a little, as though he would keep aware of the sounds which were traveling down the wind. The other ear pricked sharply toward his victim, and the big, intelligent brown eyes regarded the struggles of the red bull with a sort of scientific interest.

The bull, with such heaving and writhing, had worked himself around until he directly faced his antagonist. He had a mighty heart, had that red bull. His scarred front bore witness of many a battle with his peers from which he had emerged victorious, lord of his ranges. Now he shook his wide-spreading horns and bellowed defiance. Woe to the strongest lobo that ever lived, if it dared a face-to-face encounter with those horns. He knew the exact side flourish which would drive the stout points through hide and bones and flesh and pin the murderer to the earth. But further violence seemed infinitely far from the mind of The Ghost. He lay stretched out at ease, watching, waiting, with his big, gentle, brown eyes dwelling steadily on his victim.

That immobility on his side lasted for several minutes. Perhaps the bull began actually to doubt that this quiet creature could have been his assailant. At any rate he raised his head high and turned it to look downwind. Far off, topping a hill, he saw a rout of mounted hunters and the hounds coming.

The Ghost saw them as well. He noted what he saw with a ferocious flagging of his ears and a quick lift of his upper lip. But he noted, also, that the bull's head was turned and held high. The time for which he had waited so patiently had come. There was no gathering of feet beneath him, no collecting of the muscles, however deftly done. From the same position which he

233

had occupied so long and so quietly, he simply shot out through the air, a very low leap, driving all his body so close to the ground that the toes of his hind feet tickled the grass all the way. Fair and true, with the speed of a rock shot from the hand, he whipped under the lifted head of the red bull and, in passing, he snapped again. The force of his leap and the tear of his teeth jerked him around so that he spun through the air on the other side of his mark and turned a somersault before he hit the ground.

There was only a stifled and choked sound from the bull. The blood was gushing with the beat of the arteries from his throat where the double row of fangs had slashed deep and torn him. He made one last effort to rise and then dropped his nose to the ground and waited for death with eyes fierce and unconquered to the last.

As for The Ghost, he had landed with his head turned away from the bull, and he paid no further heed to his victim. He had performed the task he had set for himself. He had done the impossible. He had actually killed a full-grown bull by a frontal attack. Now he gave his attention to the active group that swept over the hills beyond, while he licked the blood from his lips for a second time.

CHAPTER
TWO

The Chase

They were close, dangerously close. The Ghost knew to the last scruple every degree of that danger. Knives and guns and dogs were coming, and above all that trebly horrible scent of man which was the one thing in the world he truly feared. Gather under one head all the meaning that was in the scents of the mountain lion with his claws and his hooked teeth, the grizzly bear with downright power of paw and bone-crushing jaws and deep wisdom, and the rattler with glide and strike and poison — add all these items together and put with them a certain mysterious horror, and one may gain some conception of what man meant to The Ghost.

But though they were close, he was in no hurry to flee. He lingered and, while he made that apron of white fur immaculate again, he continued to observe the onrushing hunt with keen little up-glances that missed no detail. The Ghost might have been termed a connoisseur of fear, one who loved danger because it tickled some deep-rooted imp of the perverse in him. Now he waited, rolling this tidbit of the terrible literally over his tongue.

On the whole he decided that it was the best-equipped chase that had ever lunged across mountains or plains behind him. There were a full dozen riders on fine horses. Before them ran a solid pack of wolfhounds, big, savage-jawed creatures who were now running well within their strength, as if they knew that only in a long chase would they have a chance of setting teeth in The Ghost. The vanguard was a round score of greyhounds, running with their snaky heads jerking in and out and their lank bodies flashing in the sun. Half delicate, half clumsily-sprawling creatures they looked as they bounded frantically forward. There had been a time when The Ghost had scorned them, feeling that he could break a dozen of them between his jaws one after another as they came up, but he had learned from experience that a greyhound can fight desperately, long enough to let the main body of wolfhounds catch up.

Something flashed in the distance — sun on a rifle barrel — and there was a wicked humming overhead that made The Ghost wince flat to the ground with down-shrinking of the ears. The sound went through him like a knife, vibrating electrically. Afterwards the report of the rifle cracked on his ears like two sledge hammers swung face to face — a sharp sound with a ring of metal at the tail of it. This was the last command. Now he must be off!

But still The Ghost lingered. He detested these flights. He was used to walking the ranges like a king. To have to scamper here and there and use his wits and his legs in turn was disgraceful. Yet today there might be a game in the running — and, above all things in the world, The Ghost loved a game. That was the dog in him. A wolf would have hated every sound and sight in that pack. But The Ghost did not. Vague instincts worked in him. A distant, dreamy feeling awoke and told him that some day in a forgotten past he had run in such a pack. Some day in the unknown future he might run in such a pack once more. That, again, was the dog in him. He had never felt it so keenly as on this day. Indeed, the reason he hated and dreaded men as he did was because, at the root of his nature, there was something that would have made it possible for him to love them. The dog's voice of the centuries full of unreasoning trust and faith was in The Ghost, obscured by his wild life and his wild wolf blood.

Now the excitement was growing in him. The greyhounds were shooting up the last slope beneath him. It was time, full time for running. He parted his teeth and gave them a terrible wolf-grin and then wheeled and fled over the grass towards the heart of the hills. He chose that course because every irregularity of the ground would be an advantage to him. He knew that country as a student knows the memorized page of a book. He knew the short cuts and ups and downs, where one saves strength and time by going straight up the steepest slope, and where it is better to take the long way around if one wishes to conserve the wind.

The greyhounds were perilously close, but The Ghost began slowly. In his puppy days he had been apt to break his heart and his wind in the first wild, hysterical, straight-away sprint. Now he knew a fast beginning cramps the muscles and blears the mind and leaves one broken, whether for fighting or for more running at the end of five miles. He went with that baffling wolf-lope which is unlike any gait in the world. A dog pounds his way along. A wolf seems to glide along and, when watched closely, he seems to be trying to get all four feet ahead of him at once. There is an easy, overlapping play of legs that shoots the body ahead.

Yet he went with amazing speed. To the hunters from behind he seemed merely a gray streak shooting across the green of the grass. From the side he seemed to be galloping lazily almost. And the greyhounds walked up on him hand over hand. He let them come, with one ear flagged back to give warning if some unusually fleet rascal had spurted from the pack to nail him. They were almost at his heels as he spurted over the nearest hilltop and entered the broken country. It was toothed with boulders and slashed across with low rock ridges.

The Ghost took the very roughest way because the greyhounds were now so close that he knew they would follow him blindly, for they were running blind-eyed, slavering with the lust to kill, furious with the scent of the game which a greyhound catches only when he is very close up. So straight through the heart of the very roughest of that rough stretch The Ghost led them. The result was that the sprinting pace broke the hearts of most of them. By the time they reached the far side and the smoother going again, two-thirds of the hounds were falling back or running with labored gaits, their heads jerking up and down, a sure sign that they were nearly spent. They might get their wind and come back for the kill, but at present they were done out.

There remained, however, a thick-grouped set of half a dozen in all, chosen dogs weeded from the rest. The Ghost tried them out by a breathless burst of running for half a mile and then canted his head a little and observed them. The result was that the average speed of the remaining group was sensibly diminished and, going up the slope beyond, The Ghost increased his gait even further. Beyond this hill the roughest sort of country began, where the men and the horses would have to make wide detours to follow the chase and where even the dogs would have a bad time following him. The chase, he felt, was as good as ended as soon as he got across the narrow valley beyond and entered the thick timber.

So he shot over the top of the hill at full speed, breathing deep to make his lungs clean for the last strong spurt of racing — and below him, streaming into the upper end of the valley, he saw five horsemen and a round dozen choice wolfhounds. He was cut off from the rough country and certain safety!

CHAPTER
THREE

Man Tricks

He slackened his gait. The wind had fallen so that he could hear the gasping of the spent greyhounds far behind him, but the wind held strong enough to bring the telltale scent of the man-kept dog, and to bring the crowning horror of the man scent itself out and up from the valley. As though his eyes alone did not tell him enough!

It was a man trick — typically a man trick — and he grinned with rage as he looked down at them. He knew at once what they had done. Guessing that he intended to detour through the heavy going to kill off the greyhounds before he cut in at the rough country where he would be comparatively impossible to follow, the leader of the hunt had detached part of his men and dogs to cut straight across for this valley and block it when the lobo turned. Now they were waiting there for him — rested, fresh, full of running, and ready to turn him south across the rolling hills where they would have every advantage and where, by teamwork of the trained packs, they might finally wear him down. Yes, it was a man trick from the first glance of it. No brute beast on earth would have thought of it. He himself had

240

not dreamed of it until he saw it done. How had they read his mind and his intentions?

It was the terrible mind of man which he could not outrun, the mind which planted traps and made the very ground he walked over full of danger, the mind which he sometimes felt to encompass him even in empty night, watching him with hidden eyes. The Ghost shook his loose-wrinkled pelt and snarled as he ran. A man trick! They were capable of anything. Had he not stalked their camp fires and drawn near at infinite price of peril, merely to look into their faces? What a thrill of pleasure and terror to look into those faces which commanded even when they were silent and to feel the mystery behind the eyes, those terrible eyes which had made him quake and cower in the darkness and which had drawn him with an insane desire to crawl out into the light. Many a time The Ghost had dreamed thereafter of going against his will, drawn by that mystery, into sight of human eyes, and into pointblank range of the death-dealing guns.

All of these emotions, blended by a consuming rage, were in the heart of The Ghost as he loped across the brow of the hill. A shout tingled up from the base of the valley. The hounds were cutting straight down the bottom of it to head him off even from the rolling country — to surround him. His lips wrinkled back from the fangs. He would show them one burst of real running. He would teach them some respect for speed.

Down the slope he went like a flash. The fastest greyhound ever whelped could never have measured against that gray streak. A rattling volley, the angry bee humming overhead, and the kissing of bullets against the grass showed that the huntsmen were vainly striving to head him off or drop him by a chance distance shot. As well shoot at the wind.

He was down the hill and into the rolling country. The greyhounds were hopelessly out of it now. But they had served their purpose well. They had taken the edge from his appetite for running, and now that he was partly winded the wolfhounds, running loosely and well, were at his very heels. He surveyed them with lightning side glimpses. Like the greyhounds, these were chosen fellows. Old experience had taught them how to run, how to fight, how to follow in a divided pack, how, when it came to the last battle, to use a hundred tricks that deceive and kill, how to jump and snap, and how to know a death-grip, once it is taken, and then to hang on till the wolf goes limp. They knew all this, and The Ghost knew they knew it. But this was no time for reminiscing. The pack followed hotly, and now they were so fresh that he greatly doubted his ability to shake them off in a straight-away run. It might be necessary to resort to a stratagem and feed mankind some of its own food. The thought tickled him. To fight humans with their own weapons!

Lightning fast but smooth-gaited as running water, he went up the next slope. It was steep, and there was easier going on the other side, but he knew that the main body of the hounds was close enough to follow him more or less blindly. He heard the men whistling as he raced — doubtless that was to encourage the dogs to try for the kill then and there. The Ghost grinned again.

There was reason behind this climb of the hill. On the other side of it, he well knew, there was a sandy-bottomed gulch thick with shrubbery. They would expect him to go straight across it or, if he did not appear on the other side, they would guess that he had gone down the gulch. But that was not his plan. As soon as he was out of sight in the thicket, he would double back at a sharp angle and go down the gulch, doubling on the whole hunt. At the worst the dogs would simply pick up his trail. There would be nothing lost. At the best, he could gain five minutes, which meant complete safety — or perhaps he would lose the whole hunt on the spot. So on he went like the wind.

The hounds dropped swiftly behind him, and in a moment more he had dipped over the brow of the hill and shot down into the thicketed gully. It was rank with the smell of sage and that would probably drown his scent to the hurrying hounds. At least it might delay them. So he took care to choose his way, never brushing for an instant even the tip of his tail against the foliage for fear that it would print his scent for the followers. Straight back down the gulch he rushed, though the loose sand hindered his going. But he rejoiced when he heard the hunt go crashing into the thicket well above him, and then the calling of the dogs faded a little in the opposite direction.

Still he kept up a brisk pace, although the game was, to all intents and purposes, practically done. He had successfully doubled on them, doubled in the very face of men. The savage brain of The Ghost rejoiced.

He remained in the shrubbery for some time until, sure of his place, he slid out into the basin of that main valley where they had cut him off. The whole pack had gone by. The shrill voices of the greyhounds sounded far off upwind. The Ghost was once more victorious.

But what was this? What was this deep voice not so far away, with the deep ring to it, and the heavy fiber? He whirled into the teeth of the wind, snarling with incredulous rage. And there they came! Unbelievably one man had outguessed him again. There was the rider in the very act of spurring his horse in the new direction, while his "Halloo" sent two rangy hounds away on the trail. They came like two bullets, great dark fellows, their long legs driving their bodies forward in straight lines. They were breathed and rested, too, by the rest that had been theirs while The Ghost was laboring through the sand and the shrubbery. Now they were on his heels as close as ever.

Furiously he took to flight again. There was no question of trickery or doubling now. He must show them a clean pair of heels or be run down and detained until the deadly rifle came up and did its work. The Ghost ran as he had never run before. The hallooing of the solitary hunter had picked up the pack on the other side of the hill. He heard the noise of the main body far off, rolling down the wind, but they were nothing at that distance. The whole danger had centered now on these two dogs and on the single horseman. But, by evil chance, the dogs were the best blooded, the best breathed, the biggest and most formidable of the whole pack, and the hunter behind them was mounted on the finest horse of the lot. An incredibly fine shot also, for he rode with his rifle in his hand and pumped in a snap shot time and again, shots that came perilously close at times and always, in spite of himself, the angry-bee humming made The Ghost wince towards the ground and falter for an instant in his running. Each of these falterings brought the hounds yards and yards nearer to him.

But the battle was by no means over. For the third consecutive time The Ghost was forced to sprint, and before ten minutes he was spent. Had there been only wild blood in him, he would have wheeled, then, and fought at bay. But there was more than wild blood in him. There was that mysterious "gameness" that a dog has, which enables it to toil on and labor on when strength of body is gone and only strength of nerve and willpower remains. On this electric reserve The Ghost called, his tail and his head flagging down a little, and the breathing coming burningly into his lungs with great gasps.

The wind was carrying scent and sound of the dogs to him now, and on the wind before long he heard their gasping as they followed. Plainly they were not in much better condition. Twice they spurted, and twice he answered the spurts and drew away. A third time they put forth their full strength, and a third time The Ghost answered. This time one of them came close enough for a leap, but his teeth closed a fraction of an inch from the tail of the wolf.

It was a dying effort, The Ghost sensed. The dogs still labored staunchly behind him, and the dizzy miles spun underfoot while they followed. They were still running with more and more effort, and The Ghost was beginning to come back to his wind and to his natural strength, tired by the frenzy of the long effort but still with much left. A few minutes more and the dogs were growing exhausted, while he was commencing to recuperate. He could have spurted again, but the wolfhounds were both nearly spent. They were fast dropping back to a dogged gait which they would maintain till they fell. But such bulldogging would never overtake The Ghost, no matter what it might do to other wolves.

He saw another thing now, as he turned his head. The long chase had distanced the man. He bobbed into view only momentarily, now and then on a hilltop, and dipped out of sight into the next gulch. His horse must be spent likewise. As for the rest of the chase, it was gone beyond sight, almost beyond hearing, laboring vaguely on in the hope that it might come up to view the kill.

There were two dogs running at his heels, two dogs that would not have dared to chase him a hundred yards had it not been for the support of the master. To be sure they were big fellows. One of them would have matched a common wolf. Two would have killed a big lobo with ease. But The Ghost was different, and he knew the difference. A dog fought by training and brain. A wolf fought by instinct. The Ghost brought all three elements into his fighting. How long would it take him to finish these dogs? What if the deadly rifle came in range while the battle was on? Once stung by one of those wickedly humming bullets even the strength of The Ghost would be numbed. Or what if, in the battle, he was so injured that the horseman could overtake him?

In spite of all objections, the mad desire to turn and fight began to make the brain of The Ghost reel. He had been shamed long enough. His decision came over him almost without his own volition. He waited till he had topped the next hill. Looking back, there was no horseman in sight. Then he wheeled and leaped back at the wolfhounds.

CHAPTER
FOUR

Unexpected Aid

They would fight by the book he knew. The Ghost knew the book, also. He leaped as though he were striving to get between them and, as he had expected, they at once sprang apart so as to take him one from each side and grip at his flanks. Knowing this, they were no sooner separated than The Ghost checked himself mid-plunge, shot sidewise with a sort of sweeping dance step, and rushed the wise-headed dog on the right.

Two dogs on their feet — two dogs like these — he knew he could not mate. His plan was shock tactics until one of them sprawled. His first charge went amiss. The big hound crouched and met the weight compactly, though the impetus of The Ghost crushed him flat. The Ghost, mid-spring, saw that he would have no success here and changed his mind while he was in the air. He had hardly struck when he wheeled and shot across the back of the first dog at the second. The latter was taken by surprise, for this first maneuver had needed only a fraction of a part of the time that it takes a horse a stamp his foot. He was only half turned as The Ghost's massive shoulder, set for that purpose, struck him and, before he could sink in his teeth, the hound was toppled on his back and the under part of him was ripped wide by the teeth of the wolf.

It was like the striking of two blows, and The Ghost leaped and met the spring of the first dog with a clash of teeth. Then he danced away, swift as a phantom. His purpose was a simple one. If he fought and fled at the same time, the wounded dog would drop behind — to die later perhaps. But now he discovered he could not draw one of the pair away from the other. They had been too well trained to separate. Moreover, they had already tasted the metal of this foe. Where was the man? And how much time was left?

Far off he saw the horseman coming, spurring desperately but far away indeed. The two dogs stood side by side, the injured one with lowered head but still strong as ever, for the loss of blood would not affect it for some moments unless it tried to run.

The Ghost circled them like a playing colt. The second dog followed him deftly to take the charge, but the injured one was not so agile. The Ghost found an infinitesimal opening and leaped. His teeth gashed the flank. He continued his leap high above the heads of both and landed on the far side. As he twisted to face them, the sound dog charged, infuriated by this dodging work. The Ghost met him joyously and gave him his shoulder cunningly low and to the side. He took a rip on the side of his jaw uncomplaining. The dog sprawled. Instantly a foreleg crunched in the teeth of The Ghost, and the wolf shot away to choose his next point of attack. They were both no better than dead now and, standing back to back, crouching together, one with a foreleg drawn up and one bleeding terribly from the body, they seemed to know it. The Ghost tried circling again and, as they swung to meet him, he glimpsed the rider shooting over a nearer ridge of hills. There was short time for work. He determined on a more or less blind risk and charged straight in, his head low as he always kept it for close quarters, for that gave the shaggy hide of his back and shoulders to the teeth of the enemy and gave him at least a hope of an opening at the point of points — the under throat.

In that instance, at least, it worked like a charm. One set of teeth closed on one shoulder and one on the other. Bad cuts those, perhaps. He cared not. He had twisted his head with snake-like agility, and his great fangs were buried in the throat of the dog with the broken leg. That terrible grip made the other release his own grip instantly. In a moment he was flat on his back. A wolf would have released his grip there and tried to spring away. The Ghost held it until he had worried his forefangs into life blood. Then he whirled with red-dripping muzzle from that quivering body and snapped at his remaining opponent.

The other had shifted for the throat of The Ghost, but it was a side grip. He had not the wolfish cunning of The Ghost which taught him the easiest way at the seat of life, but at least his grip made The Ghost helpless for biting. He realized it instantly and, at the expense of a badly torn neck, wrenched himself away and flung off at a distance for the last charge. It was only a formality. The final bolt of the dog had been fired. The terrible wound was taking its toll now, and his legs were bending under his weight. Before he charged, The Ghost saw the horse on the nearest hill.

He was amazed, first of all, to see that the horse was not in motion. Then he caught the glint of the sun on metal and understood. The rifle was at the shoulder of the marksman. Terror swept over The Ghost, the fear of man. He gave up the second killing, so temptingly near at hand, and wheeled to fly but, as he turned broadside, something stung him through the right thigh and tipped him on to that side as he tried to spring away.

Only that swerving to the side had kept the bullet from plowing through his brain. It seemed strange that so slight a thing should unnerve him, but there was no question about it. Slight though the pain had been, his right hind leg was useless. He found it out as he whirled to his feet, nearly falling again as he made his first stride. Again the gun barked, but this time the bullet sang evilly close yet harmless.

Behind him the deep music of the hunt was blowing up the wind as he dropped over the hill, running heavily on the three legs — a far, far sound. He would have given it no heed a little time before. But now it meant much indeed. One greyhound, the least of the pack, could finish him now. With bristling hair the great wolf bent to his work, panic-stricken. One dog killed, one dying — surely that was a handsome price for the life of The Ghost, but the big wolf had no mind for dying. He wanted at least some narrow place where he could stand at bay and make his dying battle as the king of wolves should do.

It was a marvel that he should run as he was running now, but he knew that it was a short effort that lay within the possibilities of his strength. The blood was flowing steadily from the wounded leg and, now that the numbness was gone, he felt a steady ache of pain.

Behind the hill there was the dull echo of a gun — that was when the sick-hearted huntsman killed his hopelessly wounded dog. Back there a voice was shouting — that was the hunter as he called up the rest of the hunt, and his halloo was sending the hounds hot on the blood trail. At that scent of blood a new note came into the voices of the yelling hounds, and the tired wolf heard it and knew the meaning. His own bay had rung with some such note on many a like trail.

Into yonder hills he felt that his strength would carry him, though now the chase was perilously near. In those hills he might find some hole in the ground where he could back. Then let the dogs come at him one by one or two by two, and he would teach them how a death fight should be made! Or perhaps when he gained some such shelter, a man would come and stand at a distance and kill him with one of those bee-humming bullets. But in that case it was no shame to die. Nothing in the mountains, The Ghost knew, dared face man. Nothing in the mountains dared hunt him except the mountain lion now and then — but the mountain lion was both a coward and a fool.

The hunt roared over the hills as he labored up the far slope. Would he last beyond the next crest? He doubted it much, but he toiled unwearyingly. The dogs were silent now. Instant expectation of the kill had choked their hot throats. It was the men who bayed on the trail. The chase had been long and hard, and there had been blood to mark it. Now their yelling came to The Ghost with a bestial note in it, and it made the wolf tremble.

He gained the hilltop with the gasping of the hounds close on the wind behind him. Past the rise the first thing that he saw was the house of a man, a shack huddled against the side of the hill. He shrank back, snarling. But then he saw only the narrow opening of the doorway. There was a place where he would have shelter for his back, and there he could turn at bay. In his panic he bore on again with his broken-gaited lope and plunged through the door.

Too late he saw the man inside close to the door. He braced his three feet, but the force of his gallop and his weight carried the blood-stained monster across the little room and crashing against the farther wall. There was a corner. The Ghost shrank into it and, with his forefeet braced and his red mouth gaping while panting racked his sides, he waited for the finish, unafraid. The man beside the door had risen, and he was other than the men whom The Ghost had seen when he crawled to lonely camp fires in the mountains. He was larger. It seemed that he would never stop rising as he stood up from the box on which he had been sitting. And The Ghost saw a marvel — in the hand of the big man was a glint of metal which was a sure sign of the wrath of man and that glint of metal which meant bullets so long as he was within range. The Ghost blinked, and then he saw that, though the symbol of wrath was in the hands of the man, there was no anger in his face. The eyes were as calm as midnight — the still, open midnight of the mountain which The Ghost might never see again.

Perhaps it was the size of the man. Perhaps it was this inexplicable calm. At any rate The Ghost cowered a little lower to the floor. The hunt crashed and roared over the crest and would be on them in a matter of seconds, but The Ghost did not hear it. All he was conscious of was that large, quiet face unmoved by wrath and the steady watchful eyes. Something swelled in the heart of The Ghost. He did not recognize the emotion. It was a pain that had nothing to do with the body. And with it there was a lifting of the spirit. Strange hopes of he knew not what came to him. A strange security settled over him, though he could see the sharp-headed hounds bursting down the far slope to get at him.

When the hand of the man was raised, The Ghost did not wince, for the instinct told him that the blow was not for him. After all, that instinct was not so strange. What was the wild wolf, a million years before, which first felt the power of the eye of a man and, flying from its enemies, crouched at the feet of one of them and whined for help? Such a sound, at least, formed deep in the body of The Ghost. It came, swelling his throat to bursting; not the harsh, terrible growl of a wolf but the whine of a dog!

The big man started with an exclamation, shoved the revolver into his holster, and slammed and barred the door in the face of the onrushing pack. The Ghost heard their bodies crash against the barrier and heard their anxious claws scrape the wood. A more venturesome wolfhound found the window open, and his long dark body hurtled inside. The Ghost made his grinning teeth ready but, before the big dog could spring, a great arm shot out, a great hand fastened on the back of the dog's neck. He was whirled up as though he had been a puppy, and the giant hurled him back through the window, driving before him the body of a close follower. Then the big man leaned there, blocking the way to the others with his own broad shoulders. Only one dog leaped, and it was met in mid-air by a tremendous fist that caught it in the breast and sent it catapulting away, to lie groveling and twisting on the ground.

So much for the dogs. But what of the men? What of the hunter whose dogs he had killed? The Ghost heard their voices stream over the crest of the hill. He dropped his huge head on his paws and pricked his ears to listen.

CHAPTER
FIVE

The Parley

Stern voices of command hushed in part the wild clamoring of the pack. The Ghost heard them scattering, heard them sniffing the wall of the cabin behind him. He heeded them not at all. There was still power in his jaws to crush more than one throat if the worst came to the worst. It was the men who counted now and, as he heard their voices, he crouched still lower, shuddering. One thing he knew distinctly. The door which would have been an impassable barrier to animals was nothing at all to the humans. And the scent of man blew sharp, overpowering, about him. Nothing could keep them away, save the power of their own kind, and that power, it seemed, lay in the huge man who now blocked the open window.

Presently others approached. The Ghost caught outlines of other men beyond the window. Above all there was the rider who had followed so long and so closely, the man who had out-guessed him, the man whose bullet had plowed the stinging furrow in his flesh, the man whose two dogs he had killed. He was a gaunt fellow, active of foot and hand and eye. Now that eye flamed. He had seen the two finest dogs in the mountains, dogs of his own rearing and his own fierce training, killed before his eyes. He wanted a return kill.

He went straight to the big man. "Stranger," he said, "our pack is smelling around this shack on the trail of a wounded wolf. Is they a hole under the cabin he could've got into?"

"I guess not," said the man of the cabin.

Here the other glanced past the man at the window and cried: "Boys, the wolf is inside! Stand away, partner, while I blow his head off!" He drew his revolver.

The big man did not stir from the window. "Look here," he said. "Why has the wolf got to die?"

This gaunt man gasped in astonishment, then his astonishment turned to anger. "You aim to get the scalp of that beast yourself, eh?"

"I don't want his scalp," said the other mildly. "But I don't want somebody else to get it either."

Fighting rage suffused the face of the hunter. "Say," he began, "if you think you can . . ."

Here he was interrupted by a companion who caught his arm and dragged him away, while others of the hunters pressed on to resume the strange argument with the man of the cabin.

"Look here, Steve," whispered the pacifier, "keep your tongue under the bit, will you? Know who the big boy is?"

"No, and I don't care," declared Steve.

"You will in a minute. That's Bull Hunter."

"He's big enough to be a bull . . . but the bigger they are the harder they fall."

"You fool, that's the man who dropped Jack Hood
. . . and that's the man who rode Diablo."

"No!"

"There's the hoss now!"

He pointed to a giant black stallion, close to
seventeen hands tall, with muscles like a Hercules of
horses, and tapered like a sprinter. He was going
uneasily to and fro in a little corral near the house. A
too-inquisitive wolfhound slipped through the fence to
talk to the stallion and was greeted with a snort and a
tigerish rush that sent him scampering to safety, with
his tail between his legs.

"Yes," admitted Steve, convinced and uneasy. "I've
heard about Diablo, and I guess it's him, all right. But
this Bull Hunter. What right has he got to keep me
from that wolf?"

"Listen to him talk, and you'll see. Stupid-talking
gent, ain't he? I dunno much about him, just heard
rumors. They say he's pretty soft on Mary Hood. That's
Jack Hood's daughter, the pretty one. But after he shot
her father, of course he had to run for it. Between you
and me they can't keep a gent as big as Hunter from
going back to the girl he loves one of these days and,
when he does, they'll be a pile of trouble. I guess he's
postponing it."

The giant at the window in the meantime had been
listening intently to the spokesman of the hunters, and
he listened with his brow puckered and with blank,
dazed eyes, as though it were hard for him to gather the
meaning of the simple words.

"Maybe you dunno what you got in there," he said to Hunter. "Maybe you dunno what that is. Ever hear of The Ghost?"

"I'm new to these parts," said Bull Hunter gently. "But I've heard that The Ghost is a big lobo."

"He is . . . the worst cattle-killer in the mountains, the trickiest, biggest wolf that ever trotted out to raise ruction day or night. And that's The Ghost squatting yonder in the corner."

Bull Hunter shook his head slowly. "If he's a wolf, how come he's run into my house?"

It seemed to stump the spokesman for a moment. Then he said: "The Ghost was shot through the leg. The hounds was close up, and he simply was run to death and ducked into your house. But they ain't any doubt 'bout him. Wolf? Why, look! It's written all over him."

Bull Hunter turned and regarded his strange guest with that thoughtful, half-dazed wrinkling of his brows. The Ghost regarded the man critically. He knew that the voices of the hunters were sharp, aggressive, painful, and threatening to hear. He knew that the voice of Hunter was gentle and pleasant to the ear — a voice that sent a tingle up and down his spine. Now the battery of those two pairs of eyes was turned upon him, and he dropped his head under the shock and watched them with a dangerous lifting of his lip above the fangs and a roll of his bloodshot eyes. The cuts from the fight with the dogs had tousled him with blood, and he made a terrifying figure, big enough for two wolves.

"Look at that!" exclaimed the huntsman. "You say he ain't a wolf?"

He pointed as he spoke, and The Ghost shuddered. He was being cornered. The next time that hand went out it might bear the glint of metal which meant an explosion and then death. The Ghost looked up into the face of Bull Hunter, his sides heaved, and the new sound, the dog-whine came from his throat. It had a strange effect on the giant. He made a long step toward The Ghost and then changed his mind and wheeled on the man outside the window.

"Ever hear a whine like that out of a wolf?" he asked.

The huntsman himself was barely beginning to recover from his astonishment, but he rallied quickly.

"Wolf or dog," he said, "and no man has to look at him twice to see what he is . . . but, wolf or dog, it don't make no difference. Every man on the range knows him. Every man knows what he's done. He's killed Steve Hendrick's two best dogs. And he slaughtered the big Jordan bull. That's one day's work for him, and it's about enough . . . but it's only an average day's work, I tell you. Man, the damage he's done runs up into the thousands of dollars every season. Stand aside and let me finish him!"

Bull Hunter stepped aside — and instantly moved back into his former place, blocking the way of the hunter's raised gun. When it was seen that he was determined on resistance, the rest of the hunters drew near with black looks. They had done a hard day's work. They were in no mood to be thwarted at the end of it by any human obstacle, certainly not by a single

man. Into those gloomy faces the big man stared with
eyes which had gradually cleared of doubts. At last he
was on firm ground and sure of his position and the
reasons for it. He talked firmly, fearlessly, never
shunning a single dark glance.

"Gents," he said, "the way I been raised up is to look
on everything that comes to my house and asks for a
shelter as a guest, and a guest while he's under my roof
can't be hurt by other folks without they put me out of
the way first. If a murderer and a thief came to my
house and asked me to keep him, I'd do it. The minute
he was outside the door again I might try to kill him
but, while he was inside, I'd treat him like a brother. If
I'd do that for a skunk of a man, d'you think I can turn
out a dumb beast that's come and whined at my feet?"

His voice rose a note or two and swelled out largely
at them.

"Gents, I can't do it! It ain't in me somehow. I've got
a little money. I'll pay the price of his scalp a good
many times over. But while he's inside my house, you
keep hands off. I guess that's final!"

He spoke firmly rather than threateningly and,
though there were uneasy movements towards guns in
the party he faced, there was no outright drawing of a
weapon. At the best it is hard to kill a man because of
a brute beast. Besides, there was something so novel in
the words of the single-minded giant that they paused
to consider what he said — and afterthought destroys
the possibilities of violent action. There was no question
that the big man meant what he said. As a last resource
he would fight to the death to keep them from the

261

bleeding wild beast which crouched in the corner of his shack. A man who would fight in such a cause was sure to fight terribly.

Bill Jordan, the oldest man who had ridden in the chase, came out of the rear of the group and, approaching the window, spoke for the first time. He was a withered old rancher with more money than he knew how to spend and with a reputation for keenness that was widely respected in the mountains. He was rolling a cigarette while he spoke. His whole manner was free from provocation or hint of viciousness. The sting of what he said lay entirely in the words themselves and not at all in the tone in which they were uttered.

"You're Bull Hunter . . . Charlie Hunter, I guess?"

"That's my name," said the mild-voiced giant.

"I'm Bill Jordan, tolerable well known in these parts."

"Glad to know you, Mister Jordan."

"Thanks. I owned that bull that was killed today. I've owned a good many other head that The Ghost has butchered . . . and it's got to be stopped. Is that plain?"

"It sounds reasonable," said Bull almost plaintively. "But you see my position?"

"Certainly," and Jordan nodded. Having finished rolling his smoke, he lighted it, never taking his wrinkled, thoughtful eyes from the face of the big man during this process. "Now," he went on, taking up a new phase of his idea, "you live up here with a man I've never seen, but I've heard him described as a smallish gent with gray hair and a nervous way with his hands. His name is Pete Reeve."

"Pete Reeve is my partner," said the big man with a sort of childish pride.

"Pete Reeve is a tolerable good sort of man to have for a partner," admitted the rancher, "but, if he ain't a man's partner, he ain't near so good to have around, I've heard folks say."

"Who?" asked the giant with a ring of danger in his voice, "who told you that?"

"You said you had enough money to pay for The Ghost's scalp several times over?"

"Yep."

"And where'd you get that money? Out of trapping? That's your business, isn't it?"

Another man might have been irritated by this close volley of questions, but the giant remained perfectly calm.

"Yep. I make a good deal of money out of trapping." He seemed to consider the questions of the rancher as implying compliments for his skill. "Maybe you've heard about the pile of skins I bring into town every once in a while?"

His smile of expectancy gradually faded. The wrinkling eyelids of the rancher bunched above eyes that were probing ceaselessly at the mind of the giant.

"And you get all your money that way? Out of the traps?"

"No, some of it is what Pete leaves around. Pete always has plenty of money. Come easy, go easy with Pete." The big man went on artlessly, unaware of the gathering fire in the glance of Bill Jordan. "He always leaves money around, and what's his is mine. So I can pay for the damage The Ghost has done."

"And how does Pete Reeve make his money?" asked Jordan softly.

"I dunno," replied Bull Hunter after a moment of thought. "I never ask much where he gets his money. Pete don't encourage questions none."

Jordan was stroking his chin. He seemed to be changing his mind about Hunter. "Partner," he said at length, smiling faintly, "you're either the deepest one I ever seen, or else you're a . . ." He checked himself, then he went on gravely. "We'll drop this matter about The Ghost for a while. Sooner or later the wolf will sneak out, and then one of us will drop him at sight. But he'll probably slaughter your horse out yonder before he's through with you. That isn't my business. It's strictly yours. In the meantime, when Pete Reeve comes back, you can tell him that some of us in these parts are a lot more curious about the way he makes his money than you are. We're so curious that we're apt to start inquiring after where he gets it. And when we start inquiring, we may come with guns. Don't forget. We've heard stories . . . no matter about what. But we're interested."

Bull made no reply. He stood expectantly, waiting as if for the other to go on.

"You just tell Pete," said Bill Jordan presently, as gravely as before. "Maybe he'll figure out what we mean when we say that the air around here don't agree with some gents, and they find out that they'd be a lot healthier if they moved. You just tell that to Pete and leave the rest of it to him to figure out. Come on, boys!"

He turned to the other members of the chase. They were by no means willing to give up so easily the quarry which they had run to the ground, but the sight of the burly shoulders of Hunter and the words of Jordan at length persuaded them. They finally departed with many a surly look over their shoulders at the little cabin which sheltered The Ghost from their dogs and their guns.

CHAPTER
SIX

Great Moments

With troubled eyes Bull Hunter watched them go. It may be inferred that the mind of the big man was not particularly active. His thoughts moved slowly toward any given end, and his conclusions came one by one. Under the circumstances his own course of action seemed to Hunter the only possible one. How he could have given up man or beast which had taken shelter under his roof was beyond him. When the last of the horsemen dropped over the ridge, he turned to his strange guest. As for the other problem, Pete Reeve would know how to decipher the puzzle, and Pete Reeve would tell him what they must do.

He found that The Ghost had not moved from his corner. His head was still on his paws, and he crouched in a slowly growing pool. Plainly the animal was bleeding to death.

Bull Hunter ripped a piece of old sheeting into strips for bandages and approached the great king of wolves with his hand outstretched, talking softly. But The Ghost heaved up his head and greeted his host with a terrible snarl. No dog ever whelped could have emitted that throat-tearing sound. It came with a great heave

266

and indrawing of the ribs. The whole power of the big brute seemed to go into that warning. Bull Hunter, instinctively thrilling with horror, nevertheless made another step forward. It brought The Ghost to his feet, the injured right hind leg drawn up clear of the floor but ample power remaining in the other three limbs. So standing, he lowered his head a little and waited for the charge.

He knew well enough that he had his death wounds unless something were done to them soon, and he knew also that to heal those wounds was beyond his power. But between the approach of the soft-voiced giant and the healing of his hurts he made no connection. He had seen men, at a distance, catch horses and dogs, and always they had used these methods of soft-voiced approach with one hand outstretched in sign of amity. Humanity, to The Ghost, meant nothing but a succession of wiles, dangerous stratagems.

The big man had halted at the second snarl, and now he stood looking quietly down into the face of the lobo. The Ghost trembled with fear. It had been thrilling enough, in the old days, to crawl to the edge of light circling around a camp fire and wait until the eyes of one of the men went towards him, unseeing but seeming to see. Then with the shadows to shelter him, he had always felt as if the glance of a man imprisoned him, tied him, paralyzed his strength. But to lie here in full daylight, barred from escape by the encircling walls, was far more terrible. An ecstasy of hysterical fear rose in him, only to be beaten back. For he knew that he was now facing a foe compared to whom the most mighty of grizzlies, the most swift and cunning of mountain lions, was nothing at all. He needed all the power of his body, all the strength of a cool, smooth-working brain. If he could have studied the face of the man, he felt that he might gain more strength. But he dared not look into the human eyes. They unnerved him. They turned his blood to water. They debased him and made him want to sink to the floor. They were an invisible weight under which he dared not move.

Worst of all, there was a continual temptation growing in him to give up the battle and surrender to this man as to the inevitable. The Ghost recognized the madness of that impulse with bristling hair and another throat-racking growl. Of course it was the dog instinct in him, and he fought valiantly against it. A strange desire came to him to let that extended hand touch him and then to close his eyes and wait for what should happen with a vague surety that it would only be pleasant.

He must fight that away. He must find a means of escape. But the door was still closed, and the only way out was through the window. In his one hind leg there was still power, he felt, to carry him through the window with a leap, but the man blocked the way. Therefore the man must be destroyed first. He looked at Bull Hunter, carefully avoiding the face and eyes. He discovered at once that, omitting the face, there was nothing terrible about a human being. Outside of the eyes there was nothing strange or strong. Those hands were weapons — he knew that — but he felt also that his fangs would sever the loose tendons and slice through the bones of the wrist. He looked still higher. There was the throat. Obviously the hide was not tough. A cub of six months could have torn its way to the life-seat in that throat with a single bite. And what would the bone-cutting, bone-smashing fangs of The Ghost do to it? The mouth of The Ghost slavered at the thought, and he lowered his head a little more to make ready for the spring.

At that moment the man stepped to one side and raised a broad cloth, such as The Ghost knew men wrap themselves in when they sleep at night. Had he not more than once slipped to the side of a solitary sleeper by the embers of a dying camp fire and pointed his cold nose close to the face of the unconscious man? For it had been a singular temptation to come and see this face dead of expression. When the eyes were closed, so far as The Ghost was concerned, the whole body of the man was disarmed. Now the man was out of the path, and however easy it seemed to kill him, The Ghost was wise enough to know that he had better get away without a fight if he could.

At that his move was like the uncoiling of a packed steel spring. Despite the hampering lack of that strong fourth leg, he went at the window with a rush like the flight of an arrow. Just as his nose was in smelling distance, so to speak, of the sunshine beyond the window, a shadow interposed — that cloth in which men sleep was flung over his head. Was it a weapon as well as a shelter, this protective hide which men took off and put on again at will? He had no time to think twice. The blanket folded about his head, stifling and blinding him, and two mighty arms picked him out of the air and crashed him down to the floor, sending a tooth of agony quivering through every wound in his slashed and battered body. He bore the pain in silence and commenced to fight. Yet, though the great teeth slashed and tore at the blanket, he could not bite his way to the light. He was confused, bewildered, and presently in the midst of his hysteria. One forepaw was caught, and a stout cord passed around it in a slipknot.

To The Ghost his forepaws were what hands are to a man. With them he dug. With them he held down a bone. With them on occasion he fought, the stout nails tearing almost like the cutting claws of a cat. With those paws he felt his way over dubious ground. With those paws, tapping with exquisite nicety, he had more than once sprung a trap. The Ghost fought like a demon to get that paw free — to no avail. The rope, serpent-like, twisted suddenly around the other forefoot, and then the second hind leg was brought up and gathered in the toils of the rope. The Ghost lay helplessly bound.

Knowing his defeat, he recognized it. A true wild wolf would have broken his heart struggling with shame and fear and rage, but the strain of the dog in The Ghost told him that the time for active resistance had passed. Best to lie still, perfectly still. Perhaps in that way he could make the man think that he was dead? No, the thundering of his heart, shaking his whole body from nose to paws, would show that he lived. But still it was best to remain passive. Best to endure without a whine whatever was coming, no matter what tortures the man devised for his end. In his heart, while he lay there, he admitted his folly in ever dreaming for an instant that this man would be an easy foe to defeat. In his heart he admitted the mastery of those big hands.

Something touched his wounded leg. That was to be it, then? Was it not natural that when the man tortured him to death, as he had seen men torture other wolves, his brothers, he should begin by tormenting that already wounded place, sensitive beyond words? The Ghost locked his teeth and stiffened a little, ready to endure. Vaguely he was grateful for the blanket about his head which kept him in ignorance of the next torturing movement.

He was right. Torture of the most exquisite description ensued. A demon in the torturer instructed him how to extract the utmost pain. First he thrust through the wound another tooth of prodigious length. Then he filled the wound with a liquid which was cold at first and suddenly turned to concentrated fire. The body of The Ghost quivered, but he lay still and endured. Here the wolf rose in him and taught him the way to die with dignity, yet it was a mighty anguish. It passed away slowly. Other agonies were being added. Something was being passed around his leg, crushing the wound together. The pressure did not relax, but presently the pain diminished. It decreased swiftly. The blood began slowly to circulate where the leg had been numb before. The wound grew warm. The cunning brain of the wild creature told it suddenly that the process of healing was beginning.

Then a mystery rolled across its brain. What was in the mind of the man? How, by his torture, had he

271

started that process of healing? Not only how, but why? Why did he do it? The blanket was lifted from his head.

It not only let in the fresh air and the light, but it also made him aware of the voice of the man. Then he knew that the voice had been speaking all the time. The terrible pain had made him unaware of it in the conscious mind, but unconsciously the voice had been working on him, building a basis of endurance and assurance in him. Now he was keenly aware of it. He had more strength and calm to be aware of it. For behold! The anguish of that injured leg was entirely gone.

He rolled a bloodshot eye and looked into the face of the tormentor and healer. Yes, that face was not grinning with the pleasure of the torturer. And now the great hand went out above him — he shrank under it as though the very shadow of the hand were a weight. It descended slowly, slowly. A wild impulse to swerve his head and snap came to him. He knew suddenly that no matter how swiftly the man moved his hand, he, The Ghost, could move his head more quickly, and with his teeth he could mangle that hand beyond recognition. But a second thought came. Suppose he snapped once? Suppose he mangled one member of the man? The rest of him would still be whole, and he, The Ghost, lay helpless.

He closed his eyes, shuddering, and waited for the hand to touch him. That hand fell. In the treating of the first wound he had been unaware of the touch of the hand. Pain had blurred all smaller sensations. But now, for the first time in his life, he was aware of the touch of the fingers of a man. Oh, strange sensation! A little tingle of electric happiness went down his back, trailing the slow passage of those fingers. And the voice went on at his ear. Strange voice. There was in it the quality of the touch of the fingertips. The same soothing. The same assurance of safety. A cloud of content blurred the mind of The Ghost.

Suddenly his brain cleared. The torment had begun again, and this time with a long slashing wound on his shoulder. Surely this time he should bite, even in self protection. The pain grew exquisite. He snapped his head about, and both double rows of teeth closed over the hand of the man, and the eyes of the wolf grew terribly green with hate and anger. But the hand was not torn away, slashed by the teeth as it was withdrawn. There was no break in the smoothness of the voice. In turning his head his eyes had been shocked, surprised, by the quiet eyes of the man. That shock now kept The Ghost from grinding his jaws together and ruining the good right hand of Bull Hunter forever. The man knew that only by a hair's breadth had he escaped catastrophe. His left hand still stroked the back of the wild beast. His right hand still lay on the wound. His eyes still held the eyes of the brute. The neck muscles of The Ghost slowly loosened, his teeth relaxed, his head fell back into its former position, and he waited. Bull Hunter looked at the double row of little white indentations across the back of his hand. From one pinhead puncture a tiny, tiny trickle was oozing. That escape had been close indeed, for if the wolf had tasted . . . Even big-hearted Bull Hunter trembled. For he knew that only a man can forgive bloodshed. To the wild ones the sight of it, the taste of it, is the signal for the death-battle.

He went on with his work with a strange peace in his heart and a sort of childish happiness. For, indeed, only a child would have been capable of that pure and calm exaltation of the spirits which came to Bull Hunter in his great moments. This was one of them. A wild beast had submitted to the power of hand and voice and eye. He felt that he was doing with kindness what all the speed and teeth and guns in the party of the chase had been unable to accomplish. As for The Ghost, he was infinitely amazed at himself; a little afraid too, because he had not closed those teeth of his when the occasion presented itself.

CHAPTER
SEVEN

A Real Friend

He had decided to wait. That first pain to the wound in his leg had resulted in no loss but a great comfort in the end. Perhaps it would be as well to experiment in the case of the second wound also.

It was the same torture — first a new opening of the wound and then the application of the cold liquid like water which presently turned into intense fire. Twice The Ghost came within an ace of turning his head to bite. Twice he fought back the impulse and waited, for now the pain never grew so great that he was unaware of the voice, and from time to time that slow hand went down his back, and the fingertips left the little electric trails of pleasure behind them. His patience was threefold rewarded before the end. The pain ceased even more quickly than that of the hind leg; there was the flush of comfort; and the pleasant sense of healing began.

The work went on. For every slash on head and body that process was repeated. When it was over, The Ghost was weak from the many pains, but he was warm with comfort. Still he waited, with his head stretched on the hard floor — waited for what might be coming to him from this man of many mysteries.

Other things happened, now, in swift succession. First, metal clanked, and then a weight of it encircled his neck. The collaring was something new. The smell of the iron, with the man-scent on it, made him tremble a little, but after all it was a small thing compared to much he had gone through this day of days. The next marvel was the severing of the rope which bound his feet. The cords had been drawn so tight that the feet were numb for lack of blood and, while the blood began to circulate again, tingling, The Ghost wondered.

Outside, the wind was rising. It would blow a gale this night, and a chill gale at that. A dry, sharp, cold wind, The Ghost knew at once — a terrible night for wounds! How could he keep warm if he had to lie here moveless in the cold wood? But the work of the man was by no means done.

Presently The Ghost heard a sharp rattle of metal. He looked askance. A thing of metal stood in the corner of the room. He eyed the engine quietly, waiting. Perhaps it would waken to life before long. No, it was obviously man-made, rank with the scent of man, as were all things in this cabin. Not only the scent of the big man, but of another. The Ghost bared his teeth at the very thought.

The big man was gone through the door and, left alone in the cabin, The Ghost became uneasy. The scent of the second man was doubly strong now. From the outside of the cabin came the clear odors where the hounds of the pack had walked and sniffed at the ground. He was more and more troubled. At length he hitched himself into a crouching position, leaning his hindquarters somewhat against the wall of the shack so that the weight was taken completely from his wounded rear leg. This accomplished, he waited for what should happen, more reassured now that he was in a position of some defense. The iron thing around his neck, he discovered, was hitched to a place in the wall with a flexible rope, of iron also. He tried it with his teeth at once and discovered that not only was the taste unpleasant to a degree, but the hardness of the iron made his jaws ache from the pressure.

At this point the big man came again through the door, shut out the wind, and deposited on the floor some dry wood sweet with the smell of resin. Then he took paper, crackling more than dry leaves under the foot of a heavy bull, and put it in the stove, and presently a match hissed on the trousers of Hunter and spurted into flame. The Ghost winced towards the floor at that sight. Here was the most dreaded of all things — the playmate and helpmate of man. Here was the inanimate life which he had seen become terrible in the forest, red and huge and roaring with a voice louder than the roar of a hundred grizzlies. His pointed ears worked back and forth, and the hair prickled down his back as he saw it. Then the paper was lighted and flared up.

He backed himself as far as possible against the wall. He began to understand the meaning of the chain. Perhaps the man had tied him there helplessly. Now he was setting fire to the shack and would leave it to burn with The Ghost.

Wood was piled on the fire. Presently the iron covers were replaced, and a roaring began up the chimney. That threatening voice filled the wolf with uneasiness, but the big man seemed full of cheer. As he walked to and fro through the cabin, he spoke from time to time to The Ghost, and always his voice was as gentle as ever.

Suddenly the smell of food struck the nostrils of The Ghost, and he grew weak with hunger. Slaver filled his mouth. He gulped it down and squinted at the face of Bull Hunter. Behold! Red meat, newly killed, was under the hands of the man, was being divided, and now a generous portion was placed before The Ghost. He looked straight over it at the man. Was the big creature a fool to think that he, The Ghost, who a thousand times had sniffed in contempt at man-handled meat with its promises of poison would now accept food which he had seen the hands of a man actually left and put down? Bull Hunter shoved the red meat nearer with his foot. The Ghost withdrew from it.

"All right," said Bull chuckling. "You're a suspicious devil, old boy, but you'll get used to these things after a while."

He sat down on his heels and looked the big wolf in the face. That sudden lowering of his head to the level of The Ghost's own eyes disturbed the latter. It overpowered him with man presence. Yet the thrill of that nearness was not altogether unpleasant. The man was offering him the meat in his very hand! The wonder of it almost made The Ghost forget to be suspicious. How did it happen that meat was being given? Was not this the thing for which every animal fought even to the death? Yet here it was being made a present. No battle to fight, no work to do.

A true wolf would never have touched that meat until he was on the verge of starving, and even then he might have chosen to starve rather than to eat. But the dog strain spoke strongly in The Ghost now in one of those rash impulses which overcame him occasionally. That impulse was to play with death, taste death in the very presence of him who might have poisoned the meat. Cautiously, with his eyes on the face of the big man, he stretched out his head and with a sudden snap he sheered away a corner of the meat as though with a knife. Then he crouched back with his spoils, snarling terribly. But there was no blow, no anger, no attempt to wrench that stolen meat from his jaws. No, the meat went sweetly down into his stomach in one great gulp. No poison about that mouthful at least. Perhaps another might be ventured at and stolen in safety.

But would this fool leave his meat still within range? Yes, it was unmoved. It was even shoved closer to him. The wolf looked up in vast wonder and beheld the man laughing. At that a great doubt and a great shame welled up in him. Never before had he seen a man laugh. Never before had he seen that senseless, strange contortion of the face and heard that ringing sound. First he snarled, then he crouched.

Now the laughter rang with redoubled force. At this the trouble waxed great in The Ghost. He wanted to hide his head. He wanted to ask questions. In his big, intelligent eyes a pain of question arose. He stood up on his three legs and suddenly — barked in the face of the man!

It put a sharp period to the laughter. The big man recoiled a step. No wolf since the beginning of time had uttered a sound just like this.

"By jingo," he muttered, "you've got a wolf's head and a wolf's body and a wolf's teeth, but you got the heart of a dog and the brain of a dog and the voice of a dog . . . and . . . and you are a dog, old fellow."

This, doubtless, was the serious explanation of the laughter which had been mocking him the moment before. The Ghost listened attentively, with his head canted at a judicious angle on one side, and his face, with the black, arched brows, was more human and wistful than ever.

"Steady, boy, there's no harm done," said Bull Hunter. "I won't laugh at you again if it riles you up like this . . . but you're sure a queer one."

He sat down on a box and considered his captive. The wise lobo looked back at him, finding it easier to see into his face without terror now. He was beginning to discover that it is almost impossible to look into the face of a man with anger, but it is comparatively easy to meet his eyes if one is merely bent on discovering what he wills in the hidden depths of his brain. While this man was apparently thinking of harmless things, why not steal another mouthful of the meat? He did so with a lightning snap, and still there was no punishment forthcoming. The big man merely nodded.

"Take you all in all, captain," he said, "you got the making of a fine dog in you . . . all wool and a yard wide dog, at that. And if you and me can hit it off together . . ."

He broke off to go to the corner of the room and returned with a tin of water which he placed beside the big animal. The Ghost sniffed it tentatively. Here was the man smell stiflingly strong, but there was no other scent worthy of calling up suspicions. He tasted the water. It was sweet. He drank eagerly, for he was burning with thirst from the run and the fever of the wounds and, as he drank, he watched the face of the man. Was it not one of the rules of keen hunting to attack a creature while in that most helpless of all positions — head bent to drink? But, instead of trying to steal on him, the big man sat nodding his head and smiling and talking softly.

"That goes to the right spot, I'll tell a man. That takes the heat out of your head, old boy, eh?"

How vaguely and pleasantly reassuring that voice was. Now that the wounds were all in comfort, and food had strengthened him, the warmth from the stove was beginning to steal about him and lull the ache of his weariness. Looking up to the kind face of the man from whom all these blessings had sprung, The Ghost intermittently lapped the water and growled terribly — and presently the long, bushy tail began to move slowly back and forth across the floor.

The Ghost himself was unaware of what that tail was doing. He only knew that he was happy, and that his

281

happiness made him do things. But Bull Hunter had clapped his hands in delight.

"Dog?" he said to himself. "Yes, sir, and dog clean through to his tail!"

CHAPTER
EIGHT

When Truth
Comes Out

A flesh wound in a wild animal, so long as the wound is clean, heals with marvelous rapidity. Before many days the wolf was putting his weight on the injured leg once more. There was still a bandage about it, but the other, slighter wounds had been left open for some time. Except for the right hind leg, The Ghost was quite recovered.

They had been days strange beyond precedent to him. Every hour his keen nose, his unfailing eyes, his ready ear had been drinking in knowledge. His life had been spent as a wolf. Now the dog nature, released, rushed into maturity overnight, almost literally. Among other things, the scent of that second man, which had been so fresh in the cabin on his first arrival, was now blurred away to obscurity. It remained keen only around the bunk on the far side of the room and about certain bits of clothing. The Ghost hated that smell because it was unknown, also because it was the smell of a man.

His life with Bull Hunter was not teaching him to understand the species. The big man was to him merely the great exception. He had felt the power of Bull Hunter's hand. He had experienced the wisdom and the cleverness of the big man's mind. But this learning had taught him that man was truly formidable, and his close-hand knowledge made him dread all the others. Here was the exception, this man of the calm voice and the wise eye. Here was the man who knew how to turn pain into comfort. But had not the wound been, in the first place, dealt by the hand of a man?

It was for this reason many nights later that the big animal wakened half way between dark and dawn and crouched lower to the floor. The night was warm. The door was open and through it blew the scent of horse and man coming over the hill. The Ghost slid a step towards the bunk of the master, but the master slept. He cautiously tried the strength of his chain. It was as powerful as ever. There was nothing for it but to crouch there and wait and endure.

The waiting did not last long. There were noises — creaking of leather, snort of a horse behind the shack, and then man and horse odors both approached. The horse odor came from something which the man carried. The man odor was that which had been in the cabin ever since The Ghost came there. He slid back against the wall so that, in case of need, he could use the full length of his chain for the purpose of making a leap.

The stranger came softly, making a faint singing sound beneath his breath. The Ghost had often heard

Bull Hunter make a similar sound, but the similarity did not make this the less offensive. Yet he waited without a growl.

Presently a sulfur match spurted into a faint blur of blue light, and then a lantern shone. It discovered a little man with hair streaked with gray and a withering, keen-eyed face. He hung the lantern on a nail and, as he did so, The Ghost made his leap. He had calculated well, aiming to drive his long head just above the man's shoulder and give the full range of his fangs to the soft flesh of the throat.

By one inch he came short of his mark. The chain jerked taut as he shot through the air, his murderous fangs clashed under the chin of the little man. As he fell towards the floor, he made a frantic effort to make up for the first failure by settling his teeth in the man's leg. That would bring him toppling down and, once down, The Ghost would get at his throat. But the little man had skipped back with a tingling yell, and the Colt winked in his hand with the speed of his draw. The thundering call of Bull Hunter saved the life of The Ghost by the split part of a second.

"But it's a wolf!" shouted the stranger.

"It is . . . no! . . . a dog, Pete. Let me explain."

"It's a wolf, and of all the ornery, no account critters in the world a wolf is the meanest. That one is going to die *pronto*. D'you think you can turn this shack into a menagerie?"

"Pete, don't you see he's chained? Otherwise you'd be a dead one yourself instead of talking about killing."

The little man rubbed his throat ruefully, still feeling in imagination the tearing grip of those fangs.

"Besides," Bull went on, getting up from his bunk, "he's not a wolf."

"Look out!" shouted Pete Reeve, whipping out his gun again.

His gigantic companion was going toward him quite regardless of the fact that in so doing he was placing himself in range of the teeth of The Ghost. The Ghost, indeed, had flung himself in the path of the advancing master and tried to drive him back with one of his most terrible growls.

"Watch out, Bull!" cried Pete Reeve again. "The beast is going to give you his teeth. Jump out of line with my gun, and I'll blow his brains out."

"You put up your gun," commanded Bull Hunter. "I'd rather have you shoot one of my legs off than shoot The Ghost."

"The Ghost!" breathed Pete Reeve, changing color. "That murdering devil? Is that The Ghost?"

"That's him," said Bull.

"He's crouching for his jump right now, Bull!"

"I dunno what's got into him," muttered Bull.

He leaned over, Pete Reeve quaking when he saw his companion bring his face a foot from the snarling head of the wolf.

"What's wrong, partner?" said Bull to the big animal.

For answer The Ghost whirled and, facing Pete Reeve, he threw himself back against the legs of Bull Hunter. Bull Hunter began to laugh.

"Don't you see it?" he cried happily. "The Ghost don't know you. And he don't like you. He's trying to keep me from getting near a dangerous gent like you, Pete."

"He don't like me, hey?" grumbled Pete Reeve, gradually adjusting himself to the strange state of affairs which he had found in his shack. "Well, no more do I like him. But . . . what's it mean, Bull? What you done to him?"

"Treated him like a dog," said Bull quietly, "and that's just turned him from a wolf into a dog. Look at that. No wolf, no real, full-blooded wolf, could ever be tamed. They're wild all the way through. But this Ghost is half dog, Pete. The wolf shows on the outside. He's all dog on the inside."

"Half dog? *Half snake!*" said Pete Reeve, partly in disgust and partly with relief. He sat down on a box and examined the snarling giant more closely. "My, but he's got a devil's disposition, Bull. And that's The Ghost? . . . but you're right, Bull. I know wolves back and forth and sidewise, and there never was a real one that ever run quite as big or as heavy in the shoulders as that. And there never was one near as broad across the eyes. Nor with a coat near as silky as that. Besides, he's clean skinned. Not the wolf rankness about him."

Bull nodded and looked admiringly at his companion. "You sure see things, Pete," he said. "I never noticed none of those things."

"I see the outside," said Pete shortly, "but I got an idea you see a lot more on the inside than I'll ever be able to see. But . . . The Ghost! How come?"

287

Bull sat down on his bunk. He could not move to another place nearer his friend, for The Ghost squatted before him and checked every attempt of his to advance with a wicked glint of the eyes and a growl. He looked big as a bear in that lantern light and thrice as dangerous. Sitting on the bunk, Bull told the story hastily. While he talked, he stroked the great head of The Ghost from time to time and, each time the fingers touched him, the head was lowered a little, and the eyes of the big wolf softened. When the tale was ended, Pete Reeve swore softly with admiration.

"It's you that have the nerve, Bull," he declared. "The rest of us aren't a thing beside you! Why . . . maybe you'll get some good out of the brute . . . and him The Ghost!"

That name seemed to be the big stumbling block for Pete's astonishment.

"Another thing," went on Bull. "There was a rancher with the hunters. Name was Jordan."

"I know him," said Pete, sharpening with interest. "I know him pretty well. What about him?"

"You say that," said Bull, "as if you didn't like him much."

"I don't. But fire away. What did he have to say?"

"He left a message for you. You see, I offered to buy off The Ghost for the price of the dogs he'd killed during the chase. Killed two, you see. And Jordan seemed sort of surprised to find out I had that much money."

"And did you pay for the dogs?"

288

"Nope. They didn't want money. They went off grumbling. They wanted The Ghost's scalp, they said, not the price of it."

"I don't blame 'em. But get back to Jordan. I'll bet he wasn't talking for any good!"

"Well, he seemed to wonder how I happened to've made that much money out of traps. So I told him that part of the money was yours. You generally had plenty and didn't mind if I spent it like it was my own."

"No more do I, lad," said Pete Reeve with a sudden warmth. "But go on."

"He seemed surprised to find out that you made so much money. Wanted to know how you made it."

"And you told him it was by prospecting . . . finding good claims and selling 'em quick? You told him that?" asked Pete Reeve eagerly.

Bull Hunter flushed and hesitated. "Partner," he said slowly, "I've heard you talk about prospecting and mines, but I've never seen you go out with a hammer and a pick and powder and a drill in your pack. I've never seen you bring home no specimens. I've never seen you with a gent who was going to buy one of your claims. I've never seen you with a single raw nugget. So how could I tell him that you make a living out of mining?"

"Ain't my word good enough for you?" asked Pete Reeve coldly, but the frown which he summoned very patently covered a weakness which he felt to be in his position. He did not wait for the answer to this direct question but ran on: "What did you tell him, Bull?"

"I . . . I told him I didn't know."

Pete Reeve swore. Then he rose and walked quickly back and forth through the cabin with a light, soundless step. Suddenly he whirled on Bull Hunter.

"They's times, Bull, when I think you ain't got any sense!"

The big man nodded. "I'm not very bright," he said humbly.

At that Pete Reeve's keen eyes softened. "I don't mean it that way. Forgive me, Bull. But why didn't you tell Jordan my story, or make up one of your own just as good?"

"Pete, I ain't got a very good imagination. Besides . . ." He paused, miserably. "Pete, Jordan is plumb wrought up about you. He told me to tell you a lot of queer things."

"Tell them!"

"Something about a lot of people around here being interested in you and your ways and watching you close. Also, he wanted me to tell you that some folks had found the air around here plumb bad for them and had moved away to other parts."

Pete Reeve came to his feet and stamped. "Did he say that?"

"Don't get riled up. What's he driving at?"

"Does he think he can run me out? They don't make the kind of men in these parts that can run me. They ain't a dozen together that could make me budge a step."

"I know that, Pete, but what's the use of getting so mad about it then?"

"Because he's a fool. Jordan! Bah, I could eat ten like him. I . . ." He stopped short.

"I sure don't see anything wrong with the air here in the mountains," said Bull innocently.

The little man scowled at him. "They's times," he said, "when I think that you're laughing at me up your sleeve. But I know you ain't." He began to walk the floor once more. At length he faced Bull again in his sudden way. "Bull, what do you think I do when I'm off and away from the cabin for these long spells?"

He spoke in that fierce tone of the man whose conscience is ill at ease, but who defies another to tax him with his sins.

"I dunno, Pete," said the big man. "Once I sort of guessed."

"What?"

"It was back there the first time I left you," said Bull Hunter. "That friend of yours had come along. You were out on the verandah of the hotel talking together. I heard him ask you to cut loose from me and go back with him. And you said . . . that you were going to stay with me . . . and stay straight!"

He spoke sadly and sighed when the little man cried in fury: "You were eavesdropping on me, eh?"

"I'm sorry," said Bull. "The way it happened I couldn't help hearing. That's why I slipped away from you, so you could lead your own life if you wanted to. But you and me being partners, you followed me, of course, and here we are."

There was something so disarming, so simple about this, that Pete Reeve passed from anger to guilty

291

sorrow. "What have you been thinking about these trips I've made and the stories I've told you about them? That they was all lies?"

"I haven't thought," said Bull quietly. "I've worried a pile about 'em, but I haven't dared think."

"Well," cried Pete Reeve, "they were lies that I've told you. Want to know the straight of what I am? Want to know it?"

He thrust the words at Bull with his meager, extended arm.

"It's your business," said Bull faintly. "Not mine!" Then he shrugged his shoulders and sat straighter. "But, we being partners, everything that's your business is my business, too. Go ahead and tell me, Pete."

"I can tell you, short and sweet. I've lived the way The Ghost, there, has lived . . . by taking the things that belong to other men!"

Bull stood up slowly, an enormous, imposing figure in the shadows.

"I've been a man-killer, Bull," continued the shrill-voiced little man in a frenzy of grief and self-accusation such as comes to everyone now and then, "just the way The Ghost has been a cattle-killer. And I've robbed and stolen and fought other men for money I didn't have no right to. That's the truth about me and, if it was ever known, they could hang me ten times for what I've done. There's the truth. And now get out and leave me. Go your way, and I'll go mine!"

He had expected an outburst of emotion. The calm of the big man stunned him.

"Why, Pete, if it's that way, it looks to me like you had more need of me than ever."

Pete Reeve gasped and choked. "You mean that, Bull?" he whispered. "You mean that?"

"You and me being partners," said Bull slowly, "of course I mean it."

CHAPTER
NINE

Jordan's Scheme

Bill Jordan was an impatient man by nature and by training. He had warned the entire countryside to be on the watch for Pete Reeve, and he had arranged to call up a posse at a moment's notice. But, after he had alarmed the entire widespread community, word came that Pete Reeve was no longer going on the strange journeys but had settled down to the peaceful life of a trapper in company with big Charlie Hunter. Men began to say that Bill Jordan had gone off half-cocked on this topic of Pete Reeve's lawlessness. But Bill Jordan was certain that he was right. He decided that either his warning had frightened Reeve into a temporary quiet, or else the little man had made so much money in his recent raids that he had determined to settle down for the time being at least. All of Bill's preparedness went for nothing.

This was intensely irritating. It put him in the position of a false prophet, a role for which he had no liking. He determined finally that if Pete Reeve would not fall into the way of temptation he, Bill Jordan, would send the temptation to wait on Pete Reeve. After all, it was a simple plan, worked out on the theory that

animals which cannot be shot in broad daylight may
often be trapped by night. Bill Jordan had arranged for
the trap, and now he set about finding bait for it.

Here accident played into his hand for, on a trip to
Willowville, interesting tidings were told to him by the
sheriff. No less a person than Bud Fuller, suspected of
many crimes and distinctly not wanted in most parts of
the mountains, had felt the urge towards a peaceful life
and had approached the sheriff, offering to give bond
for peaceful and law-abiding conduct if the sheriff, on
the other hand, would guarantee his support. For Bud
Fuller had defied the law and law-abiding citizens so
long that he now needed protection. This the sheriff
hesitated to extend to him.

To Bill Jordan the news was manna from heaven. It
gave him new life. He instantly unfolded his plan to the
sheriff. The sheriff listened first with wonder and then
with a grin of interest. For the plan of Bill Jordan was
that Bud Fuller should show his intention of becoming
a peaceful citizen by first acting as a decoy to take in
another one of the lawless. In a word, Bud Fuller
should be the bait for the trap which was to close over
the head of Pete Reeve. The sheriff doubted the
possibility of using Bud for a bait.

"He's a fox, and Bud Fuller is a fox," said the sheriff,
"and it'll take a cleverer man than either of us, Bill, to
use them together."

"Poison fights poison," insisted Bill Jordan. "You
send for Bud Fuller and leave the rest to me."

Bud Fuller, accordingly, was sent for. He was a
middle-aged fellow with a worn and solemn face. His

295

smile was a painful thing to see, and it twisted ironically to the side of his face. That smile appeared when Bill Jordan, in the presence of the sheriff, made his offer. The smile even persisted when the sheriff in his turn, as soon as Jordan was silent, announced that if the scheme were put through he would see that people were kept from troubling Bud Fuller, and he could manage this by the simple and efficient expedient of making Bud a deputy sheriff.

"Listen, gents," said Bud Fuller when both had finished their speeches, "do either of you know Pete Reeve . . . well?"

"I know he has a long record, just what that record is I can't say," said the sheriff.

"Nor nobody else can say," declared Fuller. "Nobody else knows just what Pete Reeve has done. Speaking personal, I don't want to know. But I've run into enough stuff about him to know that he's one of the hardest gunmen that ever packed a Colt." He turned on the sheriff. "You remember Denman?"

"Sure."

"Was he bad?"

"One of the worst."

"And a fighter?"

"Fight a bull with his bare hands."

"D'you know who finished him?"

"No."

"Pete Reeve. And they's others. I could go on talking, but I won't. No, sir, give me an easy job while you're at it. No Pete Reeve in my game. Tell me to go out and pick up a handful of rattlers. Sure, that's easy. But Pete Reeve? Not in a thousand years!"

He said this with such fervor that both the sheriff and Bill Jordan were shaken in their purpose.

"Besides," said Bud Fuller, "how do you know that Pete Reeve ain't settled down? I tell you, he's been bad enough to be good now. It's these in-and-outers who never turn straight. But a gent that's really raised ructions will get his stomach full of it sooner or later. I ain't denying that I'm one that has. I say I want to go straight, and I mean it. Maybe Pete Reeve has figured it out the same way. He's lived long enough. And Pete has a brain. Besides he's got a sidekicker that may be straightening him out."

"You mean the big man who lives with him?" asked the rancher with sudden interest. Bull Hunter had lingered strangely in his memory. "That big, simple-minded fellow?"

"Simple-minded?" said Bud Fuller. "Partner, where d'you get your news about folks? If Bull Hunter is simple-minded, I'm a plumb fool. Simple-minded? That's because he talks soft and thinks slow. But when he gets his brain around a corner, he's always right. Simple-minded? I've heard of some that's thought that way about him. They've changed their minds later on, and they've all lost some weight doing the changing!" He chuckled at his memories. "I never even see him, mind you, but I know what's been done by Hunter. It was him that tackled Pete Reeve bare-handed. And then when Pete filled him full of lead, he kept right on coming and got Pete down and could've killed him with

297

his bare hands. But he wouldn't. That's what made 'em friends. He's saved Pete's life more'n once, and Pete has done the same by him. That pair is thick. And it was him that broke Diablo for riding. And he's the gent that dropped Jack Hood. Well, sirs, it's Bull Hunter that's trying to turn Reeve straight, and maybe he's doing it. He can do it, if anybody can."

Bill Jordan had been thinking hard and fast. Now he entered the argument decisively. He began to clip off his points on the tips of his fingers. "Look here, Fuller: you want to go straight. You're tired of law-breaking, as you say. But there are a pile of gents who won't believe that you've quit your old game. And there are a pile more who don't care whether you've quit or not. They're on your trail, and they want to get you. Is that straight?"

At the latter part of his speech Fuller winced and then thrust out his lower jaw, but it was the savagery of desperation rather than of courage. "I know! They want me bad, some of the boys."

"And who's going to keep them away?"

"The . . . the sheriff. It's his job."

"You know the sheriff can't be your bodyguard. It's public opinion that's got to protect you, Bud. You ought to see that. Just now public opinion ain't for you. People around here don't think much of you, if you want me to be frank. They think you're just down here as part of another of your games. What you've got to do is to prove that you're on the side of law and order. Once that's proved, everybody will be your friend. You can count on the gun of every law-abiding citizen. And they're the people who will make these parts too hot for anyone that's after you. Bud, ain't that something worth having?" He concluded swiftly: "Maybe you will run some risk with Pete Reeve. But you can take care of yourself with him or any other man, and . . ."

Here Bud broke in: "Don't make no mistake there. Sure, I can take care of myself with most any man, but Pete Reeve is different. I wouldn't have no chance ag'in him, and I know it."

"But think it over, Bud. How will he ever suspect you?"

"He's a fox, I tell you . . . a wise old fox . . . and he'd smell me out."

"Then make your choice, Bud. Either you follow my plan and help us catch Pete Reeve, or else you stay here . . . unguarded, helpless . . . and the first pair of your enemies who happen to get together, there'll be an end of Bud Fuller. But it's nothing to us. Make your choice!"

It was a brutal way of putting the situation, but Bud Fuller was sufficiently brutal himself to be appealed to by such methods. For a long time he sat with his head bowed and his forehead corrugated in thought. When he raised his head, his eye was dull and his face resigned.

"I'm going to take the chance and make the play for you," said Bud Fuller, "but the chances is ten to one that this job will finish me."

The sheriff and Bill Jordan apparently appreciated the importance of the decision. They rose in turn, solemnly, and shook hands with him. And then Jordan

299

entered into the final detail of the scheme. When it was finished, Bud made no delay. His horse stood saddled before the building. Five minutes later he was jogging out of town.

He headed straight for the little shack where Pete and Hunter lived and, camping that night on the way, he jogged into the vicinity of the shack a little past noon of the next day. It was a commonplace, sun-blistered little building, but the heart of Bud Fuller leaped in him as he saw it. For there was to be performed the first part of the most exciting, important, and dangerous adventure he had ever undertaken in a life crammed with action and fighting.

Bud let his pony jog on slowly and, dismounting before the door, he looked straight at the profile of little Pete Reeve. Something about the expression of the formidable gunfighter, and something about the tenseness of his position, made Bud Fuller stop beating his trousers with the quirt and stare. For Reeve sat tilting forward on a box, his face set, his right hand twitching towards his hip. By something about his eyes Fuller knew that some object was approaching steadily, an object which Pete Reeve viewed with terror. Fuller was bewildered.

Then a deep voice boomed from the shack: "Steady, boy."

Into the range of Bud's vision came the ominous head of an enormous wolf, carried close to the floor; the gray, terrible head of the lobo. Instinctively Fuller brought out his gun, wondering why Reeve had not shot already. Then he noted that the lobo carried a red cloth in his mouth.

"Down! Down with it!" said the heavy voice from the hidden part of the shack.

The huge head slowly sank still lower. At the feet of Pete Reeve the red handkerchief was deposited, and then the giant wolf, whose powerful shoulders also had come into view, winced away with a snarl of hate.

"That's enough!" cried Pete Reeve. "If I have to face that four-footed devil coming towards me again, I'll lose my nerve and go for my gun. No more, Bull."

"The minute you go for your gun he'll go for your throat," the deep, smooth voice said and chuckled.

"But," cried Reeve, "it's facing death, I tell you, Bull!"

"Not a bit. I can stop him in the middle of the air with a call. Try it, Pete."

"Not for a thousand dollars! If you're crazy, I'm not."

Here Fuller, wondering, approached the door and showed himself. He saw, at the far end of the shack, the great body of the wolf backed up between the knees of Hunter and snarling at the man before whose feet he had just deposited the handkerchief. No wonder the nerve of Pete was nearly gone. It was the face of a wise devil in the skin of a wolf.

"This beats me!" cried Fuller. "A tame lobo!"

"Tame devil, you mean," said Reeve, rising and mopping his brow. "And I'd trust him just as far." He turned to Fuller and extended his hand with a rather drawn smile. "How are you, Fuller? What are you doing in these parts?"

"Just happened along, nothing special in mind," said Fuller.

"Glad to see you. This is my pal, Charlie Hunter."

"I've heard a pile about you, Hunter," said the newcomer, approaching with a cheerily extended hand.

He was stopped by a terrific snarl from the wolf that made him jerk his hand back to his revolver.

"Devil is right!" gasped out Fuller, eyeing the bristling wolf-dog in horror.

"Just a minute," the big man said, grinning, "and I'll send him out. Go talk to Diablo, boy. Look yonder!"

He went to the window and pointed out. The Ghost followed and, having cast a snarling look over his shoulder to make sure that the other two men were at a safe distance behind him, he reared. Planting his forelegs on the window sill, he looked out. Raised in this fashion, he was well nigh as tall as a man. The big hand of Hunter stroked the head of The Ghost while he talked.

"Go out to Diablo. He's waiting for you. Getting so he misses you, partner!"

The Ghost turned his head, flashed a glance up into the face of his master, and then made for the door. He went slinking close to the wall, giving the two men ample chance to look at his huge white fangs as he went. At the door he was transformed into a gray streak that whipped out of sight.

"Now look here," called Pete. "This is worth watching!"

He led the way to the window and, looking out, Fuller saw the great lobo clear the fence of the corral with a mighty bound and land in the middle of the enclosure. Instinctively Fuller cried out in horror, for in that corral also stood a black stallion, a mighty animal fully seventeen hands tall, it seemed to Fuller, and exquisitely limbed for speed and endurance in running. He thought to see the next leap of the lobo carry him at the throat of the stallion, and again he reached for his gun, but the giant beside him laid on his arm a grip that paralyzed the muscles.

"Easy," he said. "They're friends."

Indeed the wolf-dog, instead of springing again, turned slowly towards the stallion who approached with pricking ears and lowered head. Before the startled eyes of Fuller the two big, beautiful animals, each a king of his kind, touched noses, and then The Ghost stretched himself at ease in the shade of Diablo.

CHAPTER
TEN

Setting the Trap

"Am I seeing things?" breathed Fuller, watching with fascinated eyes. "How come?"

"His work," said little Pete Reeve, nodding to Bull Hunter, not without pride. "Nobody but Bull Hunter could've done that with a wolf. Though why he spent the time on him I can't say."

"Wolf?" echoed Bull Hunter with a sudden anger which surprised Fuller, who had heard much about the equable temper of the big man. "Wolf? Who says he's a wolf? Look at that head! Is that a wolf's head . . . really? Is that fur a wolf's fur? And ain't he got all of a dog's ways? I tell you he's a real dog just cast in the shape of a wolf, that's all."

Pete Reeve winked at the newcomer as much as to say that this was a sore topic with his gigantic companion.

"It took Bull a whole month of steady work . . . five or six hours a day . . . to teach The Ghost that he wasn't to jump at Diablo every time he seen him."

"The Ghost?" cried Fuller. "Is that The Ghost?"

"Right!"

304

Reeve enjoyed the thrill of this announcement. And Fuller went, wondering, for another glance.

"That's him. The rascal snooped up to my fire one night. But how come he ain't been shot by one of the ranchers around these parts? Last I heard they all hated him like poison and then some."

"They've tried to get him," Reeve said, nodding, "but Bull here went down to the village and paid every claim he could find ag'in The Ghost. After that he promised to break the heads of the first crew that tried to pot The Ghost near the cabin. The Montgomery boys didn't think he meant it, and they come prowling up here. Luckily they missed The Ghost the first shot and, before they could get a second bead on him, Bull was at 'em." Reeve laughed at the exciting memory. "They was a ten-second argument. After that Bull picked up one of 'em under each arm and brought 'em in here, and we patched 'em up and sent 'em home again."

"And the Montgomery boys is big men," said Fuller thoughtfully, eyeing the giant with new interest.

"They are," said Pete quietly.

To escape from this embarrassing talk Bull found some excuse which brought him outside the cabin.

"Don't like to be talked about," said Pete, chuckling. "Bashful as a girl, the big fellow is. He's all gold, Fuller."

"But how'd he ever do it?"

"Patience," said Reeve. "That's the only way I can explain it. And then he's so kind and honest that even a hoss and a wolf can't help seeing that he won't ever do

305

'em any harm. Look at him out there now. He can't keep away from 'em, and they can't keep away from him."

Fuller glanced through the window towards the corral and saw the giant in the act of leaping on the back of the great stallion. Diablo waited until his master was safely in place and then began an exhibition of mock bucking. It was near enough to the real article to make the pulse of Fuller jump. High into the air the giant horse sprang; on his back even the bulk of Bull Hunter seemed small as that of the average man. Down shot the black monster, but he landed on flexing legs which broke the jar as though they were four marvelous springs. Here and there across the corral Diablo fought, or seemed to fight, now dancing sidewise, now pitching up on his rear legs, a tremendous figure as he reared, now vaulting again, but always swinging from one motion to another easily, smoothly, as a waltzer to music, so that the big rider merely swayed in his seat.

"He's a rotten rider," commented Pete Reeve, "but Diablo knows how to make his back like a rocking chair. Never seen such a hoss!"

"Nor me!" breathed Fuller. "But what's happening to the wolf?"

The Ghost had stood back and watched the beginning of the gambol with a lolling tongue and eyes full of quiet interest, following each move and wagging his tail a little when the pair came closer to him. But now, as Diablo increased the pace of his exertions, The Ghost became more and more uneasy, and finally he sprang before Diablo and crouched with a threatening, throat-tearing snarl.

"He's jealous because Bull pays so much attention to Diablo," decided Pete Reeve. "And maybe he's a little bit worried because the way Diablo is acting up Bull may get hurt. Watches Bull like a baby all the time. If a stranger comes near, The Ghost wants to go for his throat. Look now."

At a word from the master Diablo stood motionless. The Ghost stood up on his hind legs and planted his paws on the leg of Hunter, looking eagerly into his face as though he feared some harm might come to him. Fuller cursed softly in wonder.

"Like a pair of lambs, ain't they, that hoss and dog?" queried Pete Reeve. "But they're only lambs for Bull Hunter. I tried to ride Diablo once." He rubbed his shoulder thoughtfully. "Luckily I hit a soft place. There they go again. Pretty soon Bull will get off and start teaching 'em things. He's got The Ghost so's he'll jump up and ride on Diablo's back. Works with 'em by the hour. Ain't got no use for me at all."

He chuckled a little ruefully as he turned away. Then his face straightened as he met the eye of Fuller quizzically turned upon him.

"Now, Bud, what's up? I know you ain't just happened by here. You never just happen by any place. What's the game?"

Fuller was delighted to have the subject broached so frankly. "The biggest, easiest game you ever was led to," he said ingratiatingly. Then he saw that Reeve was nodding with understanding rather than enthusiasm.

"I knew it was something like that. Ain't you heard the news, Bud?"

"What news?"

"I've gone straight."

"No!" cried Bud, admirably affecting surprise.

"It's true. But . . . Bull is enough to turn any man straight. Funny thing if he couldn't do it. Gent that makes a wolf into a law-abiding dog ought to be able to teach a growed-up man some sense."

"You didn't act like you was particular fond of the law-abiding dog," said Bud, artfully refraining from making a direct attack on the little man's conscience.

"Didn't I? You mean when he was bringing me that handkerchief? Well, I admit I ain't. But it's Bull's idea that The Ghost has got to learn to know me. And I've got to go through an hour of torment every day. Yesterday Bull made me pat his head." Pete wiped his brow, which glistened with perspiration at the memory. "Had to pat the head of that man-killing devil with him crouching and snarling and begging Bull to give him a chance to go at my throat. Well, this day's work with The Ghost is over. Hadn't been for you coming, Bull would've kept me at it another half hour." He smiled gratefully at Fuller. "To go back to your proposition, Bud, I ain't interested. Mighty good of you to come to me, but Sandy Lawson is in these parts, and Sandy could act sidekicker to you as well as any man."

"Him? Sandy Lawson? I'm man enough to do anything Sandy can do. I don't take many partners and, when I do, I want a man!"

Reeve would have been more than human had he not melted a little before this compliment. He smiled and shook his head.

"You see," explained Bud, "it's got to do with cracking a safe. I'm not a bit of good with the soup . . . and you're a wonder at that game. I need you bad, Pete."

Pete grew more sober than ever. "What's in the back of your head, Bud?" he asked sharply at length. "You know me, and I know you. But we've never pulled a job together before. Why bother me? I take it for a compliment, but why not go back to one of your old partners?"

The making or the breaking of his game was before Bud, and he rose to the occasion with a master stroke. He got up from the chair and turned coldly on Pete.

"If I ain't good enough for you," he said sternly, "I guess that's about all the talking we need do. I can get along without you, I guess."

"Wait a minute," said Reeve. "Don't get hot in a minute. I'm off any safe-busting, or any other business. But I don't want you to go away misunderstanding me."

"I ain't misunderstanding you, I hope," said Bud. "But listen to me, Pete. Gorgie is dead. He was my old pal. And Lammer is in the jug. So I'm left alone. That's why I've come to you."

"I knew Gorgie was dead," admitted Pete thoughtfully. "But I hadn't heard about Lammer. Too bad, Bud. Why don't you take that as a signal and break away from the game?"

"I'm going to after this deal," said Bud. "But this one was too big for me to pass up."

"How big?"

"Only eighty thousand dollars," said Bud, drawling the words. Pete gasped.

"Eighty thousand dollars," went on Bud, avoiding the face of Pete and musing, as though already planning how he would spend his share of the money, "and it's in a tin box you could split with a can opener. Easy! Eighty thousand for picking it up."

"And how far?"

"Get there before midnight if you start at dark, or a little before."

Pete sighed and shook his head. The temptation was vast. He had not saved up a great deal of money in spite of his life of adventure. Come easy, go easy had been his motto for too many years.

"You ain't talking to me, Bud," he decided. "Sorry, but you ain't talking to me. Drop it!"

And again Bud showed his intelligence by failing to press his request.

"Matter of fact," he said a little later, "I think I can manage the job all by myself instead of only forty thousand. It's a rickety old safe. And I have all the time I want. Blockhead hired me to guard his safe! He's away from his ranch, and they ain't nobody but me there. Can you beat that?"

"I can't raise that," said Pete dryly. "He hires you to guard his coin, and then you grab it from him? No, I sure can't lay one over that."

"Don't get me wrong," protested Bud. "This gent is about the orneriest that you ever seen. Don't see nothing but the worst side of everybody. Don't really trust me, but he figures they's no way into the safe except through the combination."

Bud chuckled at the idea.

"What's his name?" asked Pete.

"You ain't been long in these parts," said Bud cautiously. "Probably you wouldn't know him."

"Try me."

"Bill Jordan is his name."

Bud knew that there had been one clash between Jordan and Reeve already. He had saved this shot for the final effect, and he was not disappointed. Pete Reeve came out of his chair as though an invisible hand had jerked him up.

"Jordan?" he said through his teeth. "That skunk?"

"You know him?"

"Know him! It was him that threatened to run me out of the country!" Pete Reeve bit his lip nervously, drew out his revolver and looked to its action, shoved it hastily back into the holster, and then looked with a strange mixture of dismay and eagerness at Bud. "I'd give ten thousand if I hadn't seen you today, Bud," he said.

"Why?" said Bud innocently.

The reply was an oath. Pete Reeve hurriedly left the shack, but Bud smiled his lopsided smile and nodded in content. He knew that he had hooked his fish and, now that the hook was in, it might be well to let the fish run for a while instead of attempting to land him at once.

And patience was rewarded. Within ten minutes Pete Reeve had come back into the shack.

"Are you sure about the coin?" he said abruptly.

"Dead sure."

"Then I'm with you."

"Shake!"

"It's for tonight?"

"Tonight."

"And then I'm through."

"Me, too," said Bud, with more meaning than Pete Reeve could guess.

CHAPTER
ELEVEN

The Rescue

It was not difficult to make their excuses to Bull Hunter. Bud told the big man during the afternoon that he preferred, as a rule, to make his journeys by night during the hot weather. As for the absence of Pete Reeve, he was merely riding a step or two along the way with his old friend, for Bud was leaving that region and would not be back for many a moon.

The grave face of Bull Hunter did not change by one iota during this explanation. He heard it from Bud, in fact, with his head turned partly away, stroking the big head of the lobo but, just as he himself was nodding to the explanation, The Ghost lurched a little forward. Bull became thoughtful. It was the invariable habit of the big animal to twitch forward in this uneasy fashion when someone winked at him. A dozen times he had done it when his master had squinted inadvertently. But who could have winked now? Bud Fuller, of course, winking at Pete Reeve, as much as to say: "You and I know the real truth about this night journey."

Bull, still with head bowed lest they should see in his raised face his emotion, knew sadly what was coming. The long inactivity of Pete had at last proved too much for him, and now he was about to start another wild career. Yet Bull was wise enough to make no protest, give no advice, offer no plea. Pete had practically promised to give up the old life and, when a man broke a promise, it is foolish to remind him of it. Friendships that have lasted half a lifetime are destroyed by just such strokes. So Bull said nothing but waited gloomily for the dark and their departure.

They left, however, while the twilight was still bright, waving carelessly to Bull. He watched them drop over the hill, and absently he stroked the head of The Ghost, who had whined with pleasure the minute the two men disappeared. The Ghost's conception of happiness lay, apparently, in the absence of all men other than the master. And this, indeed, was the truth. The presence of other men was a ceaseless mental strain for The Ghost. He was continually uneasy under their eyes, their criticism, their mocking laughter which, whenever he heard it, seemed to be directed at him. One reason that he loved Bull Hunter was doubtless that the big man seldom laughed. Only with the greatest difficulty had the cardinal truth been imprinted in his mind that he must never, under any circumstances, harm little Pete Reeve. Why, The Ghost could not tell. Why the master, in his great and calm wisdom, should tolerate this little creature was beyond the comprehension of The Ghost. He would as soon have run in company with a coyote. But there were many mysteries about the master, and it was well to make few efforts to find out the wherefore of his orders. As for Diablo, the black horse was a companion, sensible, quiet, well ordered, inoffensive.

So on this evening The Ghost whined with pleasure when he saw that they were to be left alone. He picked the red rag of a handkerchief off the floor — that hateful rag which he had so often been forced to carry to little Pete Reeve — and took it into hiding in a far corner. Some day he promised himself the pleasure of tearing that rag into small bits. As he dropped it in hiding, the master appeared behind him, stooped, and picked up the rag. After this he began walking up and down the shack, and The Ghost followed at his side, whipping back and forth close to the wall and always keeping the face of the master in view. The big man was in thought; his decision was a sudden leaving of the shack, bearing a saddle over his arm.

The wolf-dog followed, rejoicing. The saddle meant a long ride on Diablo, and those rides were always a joy to The Ghost. They gave him a vague taste of his old life. The moment Bull swung into the saddle and sped across the hills, The Ghost started at his gliding gallop, with which not even the gait of Diablo could compare. That frictionless lope kept him up with the stallion and carried him easily far ahead, but he had learned from the frequent calls of his master during other rides that he was never to pass out of sight or out of hearing. That, apparently, was against the law. So he merely wove a loosely twisting trail back and forth about the straight line of the stallion's course. As The Ghost ran, he was reading the story of the night, his accurate dog-nose noting every sign.

Here was the rank scent of fox. Here the trails of fox and rabbit blended. Here the rabbit began to run, and

315

here the fox darted after it — only to be hopelessly outdistanced. Again The Ghost snarled with anger. He had crossed the odor of bobcat, and all the feline race was hateful to him. Yet they were nasty little creatures to kill. The way to do it was to take them firmly by the back of the neck and crunch — once. But the way to securing that hold was generally paved with a fury of biting and scratching. There were other stories woven invisibly across the ground, and there were stories in the air also, dim legends floating down the warm wind. The Ghost read them with a leisurely enjoyment.

Presently, on the horizon straight before them, he saw two riders against the sky and, shooting to the left, his nose caught the scent of the little man's horse. They were following Pete Reeve, then, and his companion! If that were the case, he would overtake them at once. He loosed himself into a few seconds of wild running, only to be caught by the soft, controlled alarm whistle of the master. He turned and found that Bull Hunter was sending his horse down the slope, taking advantage of a clump of trees which he artfully kept between him and the two distant riders of the night.

The Ghost paused with his head on one side to think. The manner of a stalking man are the manners of a stalking beast, and it was apparent to The Ghost at once that Bull Hunter was chasing the two rather than trying to catch up with them. It ceased to be a stupid ride. It gained an interest, even an excitement.

Now The Ghost glided off into the night and, on the top of the next ridge, he flattened upon the ground. Sure enough, the two horsemen were in the midst of

the next gully, traveling leisurely. The Ghost looked
back and saw the master coming swiftly.

"Good boy!" said Bull kindly when he came up.
"Find 'em again."

The Ghost darted ahead in obedience to the forward
wave of the arm. Obviously the thing for him to do was
act as a half way point, keeping sight of the two
horsemen himself and remaining in view of the master
who was then in touch with the two at second hand, so
to speak. Had not The Ghost seen the coyotes hunt in
packs in this manner, one clever scout bringing on the
rest of the pack?

He loved the game and played it perfectly. While he
easily kept the horsemen from catching a glimpse of
him, it was easy also for Bull Hunter to keep in view the
gray body of the wolf, like a ghost indeed through the
starlight and in the clear mountain air. At length The
Ghost halted and waited for the master again, and Bull
came up in time to see the two indistinct figures pause
before a house and dismount.

Every doubt left him when he saw that the windows
in the big house were blank, unlighted. They had come
to rob. Bull slid from the saddle and leaned against
Diablo in an agony of suspense. But what could he do?
He would never be forgiven if he interrupted his
partner at work. And yet in some manner he must
intervene. A low growl from The Ghost made him
aware that the wolf-dog was running back and forth,
heading slowly up wind, his nose held high to catch
some blowing scent, and the sound of the growl
distinctly meant "man." Bull peered in that direction,

and finally he saw, drawing swiftly out of the night, a group of around a dozen riders. He called The Ghost back with a soft whistle and, with the wolf-dog beside him an interested onlooker, he watched the proceeding of the newcomers. Strange proceedings indeed, for they left their horses with one man near a group of cottonwoods and began to spread on foot in a loose circle around the house. More than a dozen. There were fifteen or twenty of these silent hunters, and there could be only one thing they hunted — Pete Reeve.

How could he reach him? To try to charge through the line was the worst sort of folly. He might indeed break through, but that would only mean that he would be cooped up with his partner. He could act better as a rear guard and strike at the critical moment by surprise. Below the hill he could see the cordon spread. Odd that they should have arrived so pat after the two disappeared inside the house. Was it not possible that this Fuller had played the part of traitor? He had hated the man's twisted smile and, instantly, he was sure. But, while his blood grew hot, he was still thinking. There must be a warning given to Pete. Perhaps by discharging his revolver? No, that was a clumsy method. Then the idea came to him. He took out an envelope and, with a stub of a pencil, he wrote blindly in the dark a few words. This he wrapped in the red handkerchief of Pete Reeve and placed it in the mouth of The Ghost. The big animal snarled with anger, but Bull hushed him.

"Quick!" he said and, as The Ghost started off towards the house, Bull struck him on the flank sharply.

It turned The Ghost into a running streak but, in spite of his speed, he was using cunning also. He had seen the glint of metal in the hands of that spreading cordon, and he was of no mind to come in sight of one of those stealthy hunters. Bull, grinning with pleasure, watched The Ghost fade into a gully and disappear. The gray streak appeared again directly before the house and was blotted out in the dark of the interior.

It was not difficult for The Ghost to find Pete Reeve. The scent was as plain to him as pointing arrows to a man. It led through the open door and up the stairs then down the upper hall. The Ghost twisted into a dark room on the third floor.

A single lantern light showed Bud Fuller at the window and Pete working busily before the safe. It was the exclamation of Fuller that called Reeve's attention to the big wolf-dog. He turned as The Ghost crouched, for Bud Fuller had made that inevitable movement toward his gun which, to The Ghost, meant battle instantly. But the movement was not completed, and The Ghost rose from the floor and slipped to Reeve. At his feet he deposited the red handkerchief.

"Well," muttered Pete, "the fool dog has got in the habit of chasing me with that red rag."

He picked it up gingerly from under the snarling nose of The Ghost, who began to back slowly toward the door. No sooner had Pete's hand touched the handkerchief than he felt the stiff paper beneath. He took it out, and at once the sprawling, heavy, almost illegible handwriting of Bull stared him in the face.

319

House surrounded. Fuller crooked. Break for high hill in front of house. I'm there.

That was all. Pete, crunching the paper slowly in his hand, turned on his companion. He said nothing. He was too dazed to show even a great wonder, but Bud Fuller knew instantly that his hand had been shown in some mysterious way, and he went for his gun like a flash. In the stupefaction of the moment the hand of Pete Reeve was chained. That would have been his last battle had there not been help from without, and that help came.

The telltale move of Fuller's hand had caught the eye of the wolf from the door, and instantly he leaped. Already the gun was clear of the holster when he shot into range of Bud's vision, and with a startled cry the latter turned and threw up his shoulder to save his throat from the fangs. His throat was saved, but the fangs of The Ghost crushed his shoulder, and the next instant the weight of the big animal, lurching around, whirled Bud and flung him against the wall. His head struck the sill of the window, and he slipped an inert pile to the floor.

The Ghost released his grip and leaped back into the middle of the room, ready for a second attack. But Pete Reeve was already at the door. To kill Bud meant a pistol shot, and a shot would be warning to the men outside. Silence was his most valuable ally now.

As he ran down the stairs, The Ghost rushed past him with paws that scratched on the floor below and then disappeared outside the house. Pete followed more

320

slowly and, venturing cautiously out onto the verandah, he scanned the ground about the house. The cordon of the watchers had taken shelter here and there behind small mounds of earth, and not a one was in view, not even a glint of metal from their guns. There was nothing for it but to spring from the verandah onto the saddle and send home his spurs in vague hope that he might take them by surprise before they could center an effectual fire upon him. As he slipped toward his mount a faint voice cried from the upper part of the house: "Help! Help!"

It was Bud regaining his senses, and his shout was what saved Pete Reeve. For it started the cordon on the run for the house, expecting to find their quarry already engaged in battle with Bud. To their amazement a figure leaped from the verandah onto a horse. There were three men of the cordon directly before the house. Before they could halt in the middle of their run and turn their guns on the fugitive, he was through their lines, riding low over the pommel of his saddle. They sent a scattered volley, which failed to bring him down, and then dropped to their knees for steady rifle work but, as they did so, a gun spoke from the hill before the house, and bullets crashed into the wall behind them. They took to shelter before they tried another shot and, by the time they were in shelter, they could hear the beat of Reeve's galloping horse, but the man himself was a shadow bobbing against the skyline over the hill.

Bull Hunter was swinging into place on Diablo as his comrade shot past him. Twenty of the black stallion's long strides carried him to the side of Pete. He saw

Pete's head turned toward him, but not a word was spoken. As soon as they were beyond the next ridge of hills, they turned north, away from the shack where they had lived so many months. They could never go back to it again, and they swung north at a steady gallop. The sound of the pursuit crashed away in the opposite direction.

The moon came up late that night. It found the two horsemen toiling up the slope of the higher mountains, the same mountains towards which the wolf had directed his run when the hounds chased him. And, when the moon was bright, Pete Reeve stopped his horse. Bull followed his example. The Ghost sat down before them, looking steadily up into the face of his master.

It was characteristic of Pete Reeve that he neither complained to Bull for following him nor directly thanked him for that rescue. But he said with a sort of wonder: "What beats me, Bull, is that you save the life of a wolf because you love the critter, and then he turns around and saves the life of a gent that he hates. Can you beat that?"

"No," said Bull, "I can't beat that."

They started on but, when they reached the summit, Pete checked his tired horse again and sat the saddle looking over the darkly forested mountain ridges tumbling down before them.

"Between you and me, Bull," he said, "I always figured that the pair of us would be hard to beat. Then I figured that the three of us, counting in Diablo, is hard to mate, but the four of us, counting in that laughing devil there, can snap our fingers at the world, even if the world makes outlaws of us all."

Bull Hunter smiled faintly and looked at The Ghost, and The Ghost, his tongue lolling, was now laughing at the moon.

IN MEDIAS RES

About the Author

Max Brand™ is the best-known pen name of Frederick Faust, creator of Dr. Kildare, Destry, and many other fictional characters popular with readers and viewers worldwide. Faust wrote for a variety of audiences in many genres. His enormous output, totaling approximately thirty million words or the equivalent of 530 ordinary books, covered nearly every field: crime, fantasy, historical romance, espionage, Westerns, science fiction, adventure, animal stories, love, war, and fashionable society, big business and big medicine. Eighty motion pictures have been based on his work along with many radio and television programs. For good measure he also published four volumes of poetry. Perhaps no other author has reached more people in more different ways.

Born in Seattle in 1892, orphaned early, Faust grew up in the rural San Joaquin Valley of California. At Berkeley he became a student rebel and one-man literary movement, contributing prodigiously to all campus publications. Denied a degree because of unconventional conduct, he embarked on a series of adventures culminating in New York City where, after a period of near starvation, he received simultaneous recognition as a serious poet and successful popular-prose writer. Later, he traveled widely, making his home in New York, then in Florence, and finally in Los Angeles.

Once the United States entered the Second World War, Faust abandoned his lucrative writing career and his work as a screen-writer to serve as a war correspondent with the infantry in Italy, despite his fifty-one years and a bad heart. He was killed during a night attack on a hilltop village held by the German army. New books based on magazine serials or unpublished manuscripts or restored versions continue to appear so that, alive or dead, he has averaged a new book every four months for seventy-five years. In the United States alone nine publishers now issue his work. Beyond this, some work by him is newly reprinted every week of every year in one or another format somewhere in the world. Yet, only recently have the full dimensions of this extraordinarily versatile and prolific writer come to be recognized and his stature as a protean literary figure in the 20th Century acknowledged. His popularity continues to grow throughout the world.

ISIS publish a wide range of books in large print, from fiction to biography. Any suggestions for books you would like to see in large print or audio are always welcome. Please send to the Editorial Department at:

ISIS Publishing Limited
7 Centremead
Osney Mead
Oxford OX2 0ES

A full list of titles is available free of charge from:

Ulverscroft Large Print Books Limited

(UK)
The Green
Bradgate Road, Anstey
Leicester LE7 7FU
Tel: (0116) 236 4325

(Australia)
P.O. Box 314
St Leonards
NSW 1590
Tel: (02) 9436 2622

(USA)
P.O. Box 1230
West Seneca
N.Y. 14224-1230
Tel: (716) 674 4270

(Canada)
P.O. Box 80038
Burlington
Ontario L7L 6B1
Tel: (905) 637 8734

(New Zealand)
P.O. Box 456
Feilding
Tel: (06) 323 6828

Details of **ISIS** complete and unabridged audio books are also available from these offices. Alternatively, contact your local library for details of their collection of **ISIS** large print and unabridged audio books.